What peopl

Some Books /

A rollicking tale by Howard Chesley, about a book scout who loses his prize signed copy of *The Old Man and the Sea* and goes on an Ahab-like journey to get it back, burrowing deep into the bookseller subculture of L.A. like a spelunker into a dark cave. A great first novel by a skillful storyteller supreme!
Lucian Truscott IV, *Salon* Magazine

Story telling like T.C. Boyle, characters worthy of Robert Stone. Howard Marc Chesley draws you into a world of seemingly ordinary people who are seething and boiling on the inside as they struggle in a world of yard sales, internet trading and parenthood. Creating compelling drama from everyday events, he turns the life of an internet bookseller into a thriller. I couldn't stop reading.
David Webb Peoples, Writer of *Blade Runner* and *Unforgiven*

Howard Chesley has written a provocative *Bicycle Thief* -like odyssey through an LA underworld you never dreamed existed. Compulsive reading. What a debut!
William Stadiem, writer, columnist

Deep yearning, perseverance and love of family underlie the sparkling prose, the dark humor and compounding ironies of this startling first novel. It's wonderfully appropriate that it all happens in Los Angeles, the fool's paradise that brought you the trope "It will make you laugh. It will make you cry."
Richard Tuggle, writer of *Escape from Alcatraz*

As a long-time bookseller I'm impressed by the genuineness and detail of this breezy trip through the streets of LA in the eccentric company of book scouts, pickers and bibliophiles. As a lover of smart novels, I'm just knocked out by what a strong, deep and moving story that underlies the fun. Just a great read. **Esaias Baitel**, Eliabooks LLC booksellers

Some Books Aren't for Reading

A Novel

Some Books Aren't for Reading

A Novel

Howard Marc Chesley

ROUNDFIRE
BOOKS

Winchester, UK
Washington, USA

First published by Roundfire Books, 2019
Roundfire Books is an imprint of John Hunt Publishing Ltd., No. 3 East St., Alresford,
Hampshire SO24 9EE, UK
office1@jhpbooks.net
www.johnhuntpublishing.com
www.roundfire-books.com

For distributor details and how to order please visit the 'Ordering' section on our website.

Text copyright: Howard Marc Chesley 2018

ISBN: 978 1 78535 878 4
978 1 78535 879 1 (ebook)
Library of Congress Control Number: 2017962235

A CIP catalogue record for this book is available from the British Library.

Design: Stuart Davies

UK: Printed and bound by CPI Group (UK) Ltd, Croydon, CRO 4YY
US: Printed and bound by Thomson Shore, 7300 West Joy Road, Dexter, MI 48130

We operate a distinctive and ethical publishing philosophy in
all areas of our business, from our global network of authors to
production and worldwide distribution.

Chapter 1

Fucking John Grisham. Fucking Danielle Steele. Fucking Richard Patterson and fucking Clive Cussler. Worthless thick, shiny-jacketed, coarse-paper, airport novels sucking up precious space in a bin that could be filled with crisp volumes on Finnish architecture and Chinese history, fragrant leatherbacks with raised-band spines and gilt edges, or linen-covered quartos crammed with fine-paper prints of valuable Depression-era photographs. Books that will shine in a nicely offset stack of two or three on an original Mies coffee table. Books that I can buy at the Volunteer Veterans for a few dollars and sell for a hundred or more. Instead, I find yet another copy of *The Greatest Generation* by Tom Brokaw, with slight edge wear to the dust jacket and a Christmas inscription inside from Susan to Granddad. Experience has taught me that some books are for reading and some books are for selling.

A dozen different sellers on Amazon offer this yesteryear bestseller for a dollar. How can they sell a book for a dollar and survive? They're mills. They wrap the books in old newsprint, stuff them into cheap manila envelopes, mail them at bulk-rate a few hundred a day and glean an extra dollar of profit from the spread in the Amazon postage allowance. Or they're lonely housewives somewhere in Utah or South Dakota who value the act of selling a book to a stranger in a faraway state not in dollars earned but as a sad substitute for genuine social interaction.

I need to find and sell at least twenty mid-priced books every day including Sundays just to make rent, groceries and car insurance. I want to take Caleb to the San Diego Zoo. With souvenirs and overpriced hamburgers it's a hundred and fifty easy and I'm low on inventory. Nick warned me that Anaheim is sewn up by a belligerent local and that I should stay away, but I thought I would just take a drive down and check it out. I don't have to buy.

I lean over and dig deep in the big canvas bin. It's brown-smog hot in Anaheim. My polo shirt and I reek of sweat. What have we here? Beneath some orphaned volumes of a scarred and worthless Compton's Encyclopedia I see the heartening flash of a shiny white and red dust jacket. I pick up the book—*Value Based Investing* by Alvin W. Simpson, McGraw-Hill Publishers. Despite having been pummeled by a hundred other books thrown heedlessly into the bin, it remains in respectable shape. Books are exemplary in their resilience, as am I. There's a wrinkle on the dust jacket, but the pages are crisp. I have sold this title before. It's still in print with a jacket price of $49.95. It will bring about fifteen dollars on Amazon in designated "very good" used condition.

I open it up. Oops. What's that written on the fly page? An author's signature could add several dollars to the selling price. If it's just a gift inscription from some middle-exec to his golf pro, I'll have to take five dollars off. Am I feeling lucky? Maybe not today.

"Decent title," I hear behind me. I look up and see a thickset guy in his thirties with a crew cut, a T-shirt over a beer belly and tattoos on hambone arms. He focuses squinty, challenging eyes on me and my book. This volume is ranked 26,790 in popularity on the Amazon website, a semi-good number. There's an army of Amazon online shoppers out there ready to pounce on a good price for a clean copy.

"Not bad," I say warily as I look around.

I'm in an asphalt courtyard enclosed by a decaying chain-link fence and cinderblock walls. Around me is a small crowd, mostly Mexicans, Guatemalans and Salvadorans, sorting through big laundry-style bins of discarded clothing and old shoes. Some chat amiably in Spanish among big metal racks overflowing with obsolete computer parts, dead coffeemakers and aging fax machines. These hopeful entrepreneurs take what they believe they can sell on the streets of the barrio and stuff it into big cardboard boxes and carry the boxes out to beat-up vans and pickup trucks. The sub-detritus that remains gets thrown into dumpsters provided by the Volunteer Veterans and hauled away later on a flatbed truck.

"Where you from?" Buzzcut asks. His stance is tribal and territorial.

I think back to the California Mariners Yacht Club where I was once a member and kept a small J/24 sailboat for local club races. We could get tribal and territorial if an errant tourist wandered through our gate and onto our grounds looking to rent a boat by the hour for a harbor sail. But we managed to put forth a Corinthian facade.

At the CMYC one might be folding a sail or washing down a deck but it is *noblesse oblige* to exhibit forbearance to the interloper. "Ah... the marina can be confusing. I'm sorry but this is a private yacht club and we don't really rent boats here. Try over at Fisherman's Village. They have a dock there where you can rent a boat by the hour."

In landlocked Anaheim, I sense an absence of gentility. This guy's lips are tight as he awaits my response.

"Santa Monica," I reply, reaching for an ingenuous smile.

"Santa Monica." He spits the name of my benign city by the sea as if it were Sodom. "I haven't seen you here before."

"First time. Just to check it out." I am the sheep rancher walking into the cattleman's saloon.

"Nothing but shit pickings down here. Probably not worth the gas."

"Yeah. I'm definitely not finding much," I say, feigning bonhomie.

He wanders over to my pile of books and looks them over with an appraiser's eye. I have piled up a lot of heal-yourself, conquer-cancer-with-vegetables, New-Age crap—trade paperbacks in new or near-new condition. Some doomed optimist probably expired while hewing to one of these pathetic programs and then a relative dumped the books in a box and they wound up clumped in a bin at the Volunteer Veterans distribution center. Volunteer Veterans, already overstocked with merchandise for its shelves, relegated them as surplus to be unloaded in bulk to buyers like me. Books like these will sell quickly online at around seven to ten dollars, and I've got a few dozen stacked up already.

I also have an aging copy of *The Old Man and the Sea*. It's a hardcover with a mildly faded dust jacket that I put in the stack mostly for sentimental reasons. I read it when I was a boy and recall that its hero, Santiago, had gone many weeks without catching a fish before hooking into the big one. I remember it as a great tale of patience, persistence and reward. A copy is common as dirt so it's not worth anything to sell but I think I'll take it to read to Caleb.

There's one promising textbook, *Literature and Language*, a current edition in perfect condition with a sealed CD-ROM in its sleeve on the inside cover. I can sell it overnight for sixty bucks. I paid forty dollars for the bin and I've only looked at half the books, so theoretically I'm already ahead, a fact that does not seem to be lost on Buzzcut as he peruses.

"Haven't they got a Salvation Army auction in Santa Monica?" he asks. He knows they do.

"They've got a new manager who's skimming all the decent books." This is the truth, but I know it sounds like pure mendacity as it leaves my lips.

"Yeah. Well, it's not so terrific here either. That don't mean I'm gonna go tooling up the 405 and poach on somebody else's territory." He takes an aggressive step toward me.

I have the wisdom to be obsequious. I worked in advertising for sixteen years. I have a long history of baring my neck. Just tell him this is my first time here and I didn't realize that it was staked out and I don't want to cause a problem. Just act stupid and naive and back away. Except that today magma is bubbling and festering in my core. I struggle to suppress it.

"You're right," I say. "I missed you on the 405." I'm not even sure what that means, but it comes out fuck-you hostile. Buzzcut doesn't take it well. His red face turns redder.

Then erupting out of my mouth comes, "Of course I'm usually not trolling for shitkickers when I'm driving." Uh-oh. What am I doing? I haven't raised a fist since prep school. Maybe he's going to haul off and slug me. No. He simmers for a beat, and then turns on his heels and walks away. I could follow him. No. It's not even rage I feel. There's nothing to accomplish. I'll finish packing my books, leave, and never return to the Volunteer Veterans in Anaheim.

When I first arrived there were six bins of books sitting on the loading dock and no book buyers—local or imported. Except for the choking inland smog, everything seemed benign. The auctioneer, an out-of-rehab, ear-ringed, jive black ectomorph who looked like he had begun his life again at least a dozen times asked me if I was looking to bid.

"You got books to sell?" I ask, trying to sound seasoned and casual. It is at times like this that I wish that I had inherited more from my black grandfather than his upwardly mobile yearnings and a slight nappiness to my hair. For this moment at least, I would have preferred to have his dark brown skin and a hint of his smooth Louisiana drawl.

"How many you looking for, my man?" he shoots back. He probably takes me with my brownish tint for a swarthy, Sephardic Jew. Many do, especially my fellow African-Americans.

"Just a few."

"Forty a bin. I got four bins out here now and more comin'. How many you want?"

I had already scoped out one of the crammed containers. Mostly fiction and junk paperbacks, salted with a few promising textbooks and some trade non-fiction. They had only minor potential.

"How about twenty-five?" I say, hoping for thirty and willing to settle for thirty-five.

"These are good bins, my man. I can sell these bins all day for fifty." For emphasis he starts to turn away to a Mexican who is tugging at his sleeve about a large rack full of decrepit DVD players.

"Thirty would work better," I say, trying to keep his attention. He sneers.

"I got one price. You want it at forty or you don't?"

"Okay," I say. "Four bins." I'm desperate for product. He smells it.

"Go get a number," he says, pointing to a flimsy little makeshift ticket-booth/shed where a young woman with stylish glasses and a streak of purple in her hair sits imprisoned with a calculator and a cash box. She hands me a small, worn bidding paddle hand—inscribed in magic marker with lucky number "84." I hold up the number to the ectomorph who writes "84" on the form on his clipboard and I hand the woman in the booth eight twenties. She writes a crude receipt. I know I am overpaying, but I need the inventory. I pull my empty boxes out of the car and begin sorting.

From over my shoulder I hear, "Take what you got and go back to Santa Monica." I turn to see Buzzcut on his way out. I wait two beats but I don't seem to be in control of my lips.

"Asshole." I say, mostly to myself. Not too loud. Loud enough so that it catches the ears of a few of the Mexicans. Loud enough apparently for Buzzcut. He wheels around and narrows his eyes, but moves on with a sneer. I go back to sorting these unspectacular books.

Things were not always like this. Long ago, I am told, in former halcyon days of thrift store book auctions, these bins could easily be cornucopias that brought forth magic. That was before the Volunteer Veterans and the Salvation Army and the

Goodwill started skimming the really good titles off the top for their own online stores. There was once a golden time when managers in charge naively believed that the only worth of their book donations was as two-dollar fodder for parsimonious eggheads while the real money was in selling broken-down Sony TVs and castoff ten-speed bikes. It is said in the great body of booksellers' myth and apocrypha that once, in a Pasadena Salvation Army auction, on a misty June morning, a dozen first-edition Steinbecks in pristine original dust jackets, signed by the master Depression-era author himself, were sold in a sixty-dollar bin along with the Danielle Steeles and the National Geographics. Once, it is told and retold in clusters of nostalgic booksellers that stand waiting for library book sales to open, one could regularly expect to find these bins replete with large, heavy volumes on art and architecture, and shiny new textbooks discarded by wastrel community college students who dropped their survey courses after a week or two without opening their books. Before Lucent and JDS Uniphase, and Enron. Before the towers fell and before George W. Bush. When all was right with the world.

I stack my books carefully in the file boxes. I buy the boxes new and unassembled and get continual and surprising satisfaction from folding a flat piece of cardboard into a crisp, sturdy box in a few seconds. Some of my compatriots are happy to toss books willy-nilly into discarded wine cartons. That is not my choice. I pack them thoughtfully. One stack of large books occupies half the space, and two stacks of smaller books take the other half. Never should books be creased or bent to fit. The secret is in interleaving them perfectly, so that they all fit snugly. I am good at it. Nick, a friendly competitor and seer who has been at it for years, is a master. He can pack books like a stonemason can build a wall. Without a crack. The smallness and specificity of my task is soothing. As I pack today's haul I feel better and thoughts of Buzzcut evaporate.

I put the boxes into three piles of three. Any higher than three and the cardboard sags and crushes from the weight of the books. I unfold my little dolly and stack three of the boxes on it. I look around and find a friendly face—a squat, wide-faced woman who is triaging a bin of old shoes. I have no idea where one sells used shoes. Not on eBay or even Craigslist.

I know that because of my darkish skin she expects to be spoken to in Spanish. She smiles blankly when I ask, "Could you keep an eye on these for a minute?" So I use sign language and an idiot grin. She nods agreeably to the caveman gestures. I wheel my boxes out the gate to the parking lot where I will load them into the Volvo.

The Volvo sports an assortment of parking lot dings and scratches. I bought it new five years ago from the dealer, flush with my stock market successes at the time. I opted for the intercooled turbo engine and the leather heated seats—good for the frequent Sierra ski trips that I expected to take.

On the tony west side of Los Angeles, this prematurely obsolescent, slate-gray Swedish iron, with its worn tires, whiny power steering and cracked taillight lens marks me as a has-been. Of course in the parking lot of Volunteer Veterans in Anaheim, in the company of ancient vans and rusting pickups, I seem quite the country squire.

I wheel my neatly stacked bounty out to the parking lot. The Volvo is in a corner, far away from the busy area where the pickups and vans move in and out. As I approach I see that my wagon hunkers down in the back left, sitting on the wheel rim, the tire squashed airless and flat. I examine the tire, expecting to find a nail, and discover an eight-inch knife-cut on the sidewall.

I look around the lot. The few people present pointedly avoid my gaze. Near the entrance, about fifty yards away, I intersect Buzzcut's glance as he stands next to a new Dodge 4x4 pickup. He chuckles fraternally with the auctioneer guy and looks away from me dismissively.

Behind the tailgate I have a jack and a worn spare. It will take twenty minutes to change the tire as Buzzcut postures and guffaws to the locals. Because in my former life I had sprung for the gaudy and useless eighteen-inch alloy spoke wheels, the big tire will cost me a day's wage to replace, and put me closer to the limit on my newly acquired, pauper-class Fleet Bank MasterCard on which I will pay 28 percent. And thus I will sink further into debt. I walk toward Buzzcut. He pretends not to notice. I'm twenty feet from him and he looks up at me with a sneer.

"Did you slash my tire?" I don't know why I'm even asking. I don't anticipate a response that would satisfy.

"Say what, Captain?" he smirks.

I reflexively catapult headlong into unyielding righteousness and repeat, "Did you slash my fucking tire?!!"

Without responding he opens the door of the pickup, gets in and revs the big V8. I move to the front of the truck and he looks at me with a put-on look of incredulity. I hold my ground. I see his right arm move and I hear the beefy truck's transmission thunk into gear.

Defiance is not necessarily a bad posture. In the best of circumstances it demonstrates sincerity and courage. But in the rock-paper-scissors ordering of the Volunteer Veterans parking lot, it doesn't top his wise-guy disdain. So I alter my stance and feign diffidence. As Buzzcut stares me down from the driver's seat, I shrug as if to say, "None of this is worth my valuable attention." I turn away for effect and start to walk. It must be undoubtedly clear to any street-wise observer that I am just trying to save face.

Confident and with me out of his path, Buzzcut pulls out. That's when I go for the chunk of cinderblock that I've held in the corner of my vision. It's a couple of steps away on the asphalt, put there to hold the swinging gate open. As Buzzcut roars by I grab the block, loft it over my shoulder and let fly at the passenger-side window.

There is, within the instant of an act of violence, not a suspension of the notion of consequence as many might say, but rather an invitation to consequence. It is not only that one isn't aware that there may be a penalty for a transgression, but that one is so briefly, irrationally consumed with anger at one's self, rather than the other person, that one relishes and invites the consequence.

It is incontrovertibly satisfying to see safety glass shattering into a million pieces. I brim with adolescent awe. Suddenly, where there was once a window there are thousands of tiny pebbles of glass. Filling the newly created void is the slack-jawed face of Buzzcut. And then he's not there anymore. He's out of the car and coming fast at me. I look around to see if anybody's going to be brave and good enough to come between us. The auctioneer fades away. The Mexicans retreat. I reverse a couple of steps. Buzzcut's face is beet red. His giant forearms are cocked for action.

I put my hands in front of my face. He regards this as an invitation. I see something coming at me, perhaps a fist. It's over in an instant. Lights out.

Chapter 2

I wake up lying on the asphalt. A concerned Chicana stands over me. Time has escaped me. This is new.

"Did I...?" I begin to ask. I have never passed out before.

"*Tres minutos*," she replies, holding up three fingers. My mind slips and I dig for traction. My head throbs unspeakably. My cheek is sore and there is a raw bump on the back of my skull—no doubt where I hit the ground. I sit up and look around. Cinderblock wall. Chain-link fence. Rusted pickups. I know where I am. I look over and see an empty space where Buzzcut's Dodge was. Oh, yes.

It could be worse. Synapses will reconnect. I start to get up, but I am interrupted by shooting, numbing, excruciating pain radiating from my shoulder and chest. I return to the pavement. The woman looks at me puzzled.

I try to reach for my phone, but the pain in my shoulder is too much for my right arm and I am propped on my left.

"My phone. In my pocket," I cough out.

She hesitates, and then seems to comprehend. She reaches into my pocket, pulls out my phone, and puts it in my open hand. I dial Nick. As I tell him my story I already know what he'll say. Nick doesn't disappoint. "What are you doing in Anaheim? I told you not to go to Anaheim."

"I know you did, but could you please help me out?"

Nick and Doreen arrive as a couple about an hour after my call. Nick owns two Toyota trucks with camper shells. They drive the ratty, ten-year-old one with chalked and scratched gray paint and torn upholstery. When Nick is scouting books he doesn't want anybody to suppose there's a living in what he's doing and to expect more than pennies for their books. The rotting truck makes the case eloquently. The shiny big-tired, four-wheel-drive model at home has a near-new two thousand miles on it and is reserved for nights on the town. For sunny-day recreation he owns a pristine, totally optioned and chromed Harley-Davidson Duoglide.

When they arrive I am sitting in the passenger seat of my Volvo, very much the pariah of the parking lot. Once it had become clear that I would survive, the locals went out of their way not to notice my presence. My tire was still flat, and no doubt I could have paid someone ten bucks to put on the spare, but my ribs hurt far too much to drive home. When I made a list of possible rescuers, only Nick and Yellow Cab came to mind.

"You look turrible," Nick says as he approaches me. Nick left Queens thirty years ago, but Queens didn't leave him.

"Thanks for coming."

"I couldn't leave you here." He looks around warily. "You could get killed."

Doreen emerges from the car, looks at me and then Nick who studies the flat tire. "Tell me you got a spare, Ralphie," Nick says.

My real name is Mitchell. Mitchell Fourchette. I'm often openly addressed by my moniker "Ralph" or "Ralphie" by compatriots in the book biz because I have a habit of wearing Ralph Lauren polo shirts. They fit better and last longer than the other brands, even if the little embroidered polo pony on the front is an affectation. In my former life I would buy them at department stores for fifty bucks apiece. Now I buy them secondhand at thrift stores for about six.

I make a move to help Nick find the spare and wince in pain.

"Jeez," Nick shakes his head admonishingly.

"You told Ralphie not to go, didn't you, baby?" Doreen interjects. Nick ignores her, as is his custom and sets to work replacing my tire. Doreen offers me a bottle of Los Angeles tap water repackaged in a battered Evian container as Nick finishes the job smoothly, his honed street sense dictating that quick and quiet is the safest path out of Anaheim. He chauffeurs me back to his house in the Volvo as Doreen follows in the truck. As we drive, Nick complains to me about her tailgating.

I lie on the sofa at Nick's house, head throbbing, ribs aching, Doreen enters from the kitchen with a steaming mug and a handful of tablets and capsules.

"Valerian tea," she says as she offers the mug. She's wearing a seedy maroon bathrobe. Dull, stringy, brown hair hangs long over her shoulders. Her face is lathered with drugstore makeup.

"Do you have any Advil?" I ask. I am pretty sure I haven't broken anything. I now can flex my shoulder with only minor discomfort. It is my rib cage that really pains me.

"This is better," she says offering the capsules.

"It's not going to make me hallucinate or anything?"

"Everything is a hallucination. All we know is what the mind sees."

"He's not here for Zen, Doreen," says Nick. Nick is a small man, wiry, probably in his early sixties. His hair is Clairol-dyed in an unlikely Roy Orbison black sheen and combed neatly across a large bald area above his wavy forehead. His face is rodent-like and perpetually on edge, as if he is only too aware that to most of the world he is prey.

"It's Chinese herbs. It's better than Advil," she proffers.

I know Doreen had a previous proclivity for combining vodka and seconal. Nick told me recently that she spends two evenings a week in a court-mandated rehab program. But I am ready for anything. I take three capsules from her and down them with some hot, sweet-tasting tea, a small part of me hoping for something spectacular. I adjust my body on the sofa and a dagger of pain assaults my chest.

"Maybe you broke a rib," says Doreen. I nod. I expect what inevitably follows—a recitation of those supposedly obscure factoids that everyone knows, but to which we are nonetheless required to ritually pay homage.

"There's nothing you can do, anyway," she continues. "Same

treatment if it's bruised or broken. Don't do anything. If it's better in a week it's bruised. If it's better in six weeks it's broken. They used to tape them."

"Yeah. I know they don't tape ribs anymore." When will the last person die who still remembers that doctors once wrapped tape around broken ribs in a futile attempt to promote healing? Am I part of that generation? It seems they taped ribs when I was very young.

The diagnosis suits me fine. Having been drummed out of Blue Cross months ago for missing payments, I can do nicely without a trip to the emergency room.

I am mostly tuned in to the roar of big diesel trucks. Nick lives in a two-story converted garage behind a house in West Los Angeles. From the window of his back bathroom you can read the numbers on the license plates on the trucks barreling down the Santa Monica Freeway. You can hear them from anywhere in the house, even with the windows closed and the curtains drawn. You can smell them too, along with indigenous incense, mildew and cat pee.

Nick owns the front house and rents it for eighteen hundred a month to a twenty-something who edits music videos. Nick bought the place twenty-four years ago for ninety thousand dollars and converted the garage ten years ago. Being a landlord nets him about a thousand a month after he pays his mortgage, and even with the fumes and the noise, the house is worth an instant eight hundred thousand on its 40x120 lot. This rodent-like scrounge and one-time refrigerator repairman had figured out that Westside real estate trumped the tech stock high flyers of the NASDAQ, something neither Hotchkiss nor Yale managed to teach me.

"Did I tell you not to go to Anaheim?" he asks for the twentieth time.

"You told me, Nick."

He turns to Doreen. "I told him. I told him that those guys in

14

Anaheim are animals."

"They're animals down there." Doreen nods in sage agreement.

There can be no question that Nick and Doreen's familiarity with life on the nether rungs outstrips mine, and if they say that they are animals in Anaheim, then it must be so. It is reassuring to me that I am in the presence of their expertise and experience. Everything in my own life has been laid open to question, and Nick and Doreen have become my anchors as I am buffeted by the rips and currents of doubt.

It is a testament to the eternal power of that which works that Nick and Doreen found each other. Doreen is easily two inches taller than the diminutive Nick. Her parched skin hangs loosely on a thin, bony frame. Her teeth are umber from cigarettes and she has a red scar on her forehead where a careless dermatologist once crudely excised a sketchy keratosis. No doubt they were a marginally more attractive couple when they met eleven years ago. Perhaps Nick didn't have a need to dye his hair. Doreen probably had a warmer and suppler epidermis in gentler days before court-mandated rehab. But let's face it. Nick could have walked down the beach boardwalk in Santa Monica on any day in summer and seen beautiful young women with tight honey skin, pouty lips, firm bellies and flared hips. As a younger, but nonetheless scrawny and shriveled prole with a demeanor that might charitably be described as interior, it wouldn't take long for him to find out that these women were unavailable to him. But what was his process for so comfortably aspiring to tobacco-stained Doreen? And so not to appear as unsympathetic and sexist, let us consider the reverse. What was it that Doreen found in Nick that made her so content to be nestled into the crook of his bony arm on the sofa, watching cheap porn on a fuzzy projection TV? When and why did they lower their aspirations? If I could study Nick and Doreen, and clarify the mysteries of their mutual attraction, then perhaps I could unravel the disappointment and disaster that has become my life and free myself from the struggle that dogs me and subsumes me.

Why, for example, did I choose the chimerical JDS Uniphase, Lucent and Qualcomm when I could have chosen the reliable, stalwart and available Fidelity Asset Manager balanced fund conservatively managed by seasoned MBAs? I could have massaged my portfolio of premium large cap stocks with a 40 percent mix of short- and long-term bonds to cushion any possible decline in equities. Just as Nick would have been predictably rebuffed by the beach hardbodies for overreaching, I was rebuffed as a hapless *untermench* by the NASDAQ.

My eyelids laze to mid-pupil. I begin to drift. I am grateful that Nick and Doreen came to my rescue without hesitation, without the customary offering of reluctant, insincere alternatives preferred by former friends. ("Of course I'd be glad to come if you need me, but it'll take me forever to get to Anaheim from here. Don't you think you'd be better off if you called an ambulance or the Auto Club?") If Caleb were ten years older and eligible to have a driver's license, I know that he would have rushed to his dad's rescue.

I think of the look on Caleb's face when the family court mediator asked him to chat with her for a little while by himself and leave his parents in the waiting room. He responded to her false smile with a brave nod and followed her into her office. He had to know that even though his father and mother struggled to spare him responsibility by appearing light and jolly for this occasion, the stakes were monstrously high for him. I am sure that he spoke well of me on the other side of the door. I hope he told her how I make him cashew nut butter sandwiches on honey wheat bread with raisins and sunflower seeds after school and how he has his own little desk and chair in a corner of the living room of my small apartment on Idaho Avenue. California law requires mediation.

3170. (a) *If it appears on the face of a petition, application, or other pleading to obtain or modify a temporary or permanent custody or visitation order that custody, visitation, or both are contested, the court shall set the contested issues for mediation.*

The office smelled faintly of old magazines and dirty diapers. "I'll be out in the hall," I said to True. We were both there because neither of us trusted the other to deliver Caleb to the mediator without infusing him with last-minute bias. In fact, our white-hot enmity had less to do with the past circumstances that broke us apart and more to do with our anger at each other for what each perceived as an effort to deprive the other of the presence of our beloved child. Our feelings were strong, elemental and predictable. True held a month-old *Time* magazine in front of her face. I wouldn't have been surprised if the excited molecules of the shiny pages spontaneously combusted under the focused beam of her angry gaze. She didn't reply, didn't look up. Did the State of California really expect me to sit there in the waiting room and submit to her anger and contempt for the twenty minutes that Caleb was with the mediator?

The mediator, a superficially sincere young woman in a Macy's suit, had explained to us on a previous visit that she wanted to talk to Caleb alone, but that their policy is to never ask a child which parent the child would prefer to live with.

"Talking to Caleb will help me assist you in developing an effective parent plan," she said as she approximated eye contact. Effective parent plan? How about we cut him in half at his balance point? That would be effective.

Let me tell you about an effective parent plan. A year ago I moved out of our big house in Mar Vista and into a one-bedroom apartment in a nondescript triplex in Santa Monica. We can get into the circumstances later, but you can probably guess that they were very painful and subject to a Rashomonic panoply of interpretation.

Unlike nearby Santa Monica and Culver City, which are incorporated towns and have their own school systems, Mar

Vista is part of the bottom-of-the-barrel Los Angeles Unified School District. The dilapidated local school on 27th Street has the air of a concrete and chain-link prison. Local gang graffiti adorns the exterior walls. Inside it festers with oversized classes, tired, pessimistic teachers and nurture-starved children.

Santa Monica has very good schools. My $800-a-month, rent-controlled apartment in the posher northern part of the city is within the district boundaries of the jewel of the elementary school crown, Bayside School. It is recently painted, cheery and benign. Its classroom walls are proudly papered with student art and teacher decoupage. If any good was to come out of the wrenching dissolution of our family, it was that Caleb would be upgraded to kindergarten at Bayside School.

Even True couldn't deny the simple good sense of Caleb's attending Bayside in what she could only perceive to be my territory. We usually had limited, tense communications regarding his welfare and upbringing. They occurred exclusively by telephone. We traded custody by picking up Caleb at the end of the preschool day to spare him an encounter dripping with the residue of our enmity. Although we undoubtedly traumatized him by making him a pawn in our protracted battle, there was no doubt that each of us loved him to the depths of our souls and beyond. Each of us was absolutely convinced that we acted exclusively in Caleb's best interests.

In August, two weeks before Caleb was to begin school at Bayside by mutual agreement, True called me. I knew from the cool hello that her agenda would be fixed and unpleasant.

"I've been thinking." (I took this as warning.) "I don't know if it's good for Caleb to be in a place that's overrun with pampered rich brats." (Uh-oh.)

"They're five and six years old. It's not like they're all driving Porsches and eating off the grazing menu at Spago," I replied, knowing full well that sarcasm never works in my favor.

"I thought you were the great populist."

In fact, despite being a half-black and half-Italian Catholic, I had gone to Hotchkiss School, an Episcopalian boarding school in Lakeville, Connecticut. It was the sort of experience that would make one either a Republican or an anarchist.

True continued her attack.

"Would you rather drop him off in front of a lineup of Range Rovers driven by blonde ponytails with cell phone implants?" It might have sounded like good-natured ribbing, but trust me — it wasn't.

"I want him to be in a benign place with small classes where they don't sell crack from vending machines."

"Are there any children of color in the class at all?"

I blanch at "children of color." I think I'd even prefer the old-fashioned "darkies" as the patronizing term of choice.

"I haven't taken a poll," I responded. Of course, if a poll were to be taken, the likely result would be one or two out of thirty, probably with doctor or TV-producer parents.

Technically, of course, Caleb is a "child of color" himself, but all of the color had been bleached and strained out of his chromosomes, at least as far as I can see. I think True was a bit disappointed. I wonder if True would have shown such an initial interest in me if I hadn't told her the story of my black great-grandfather, Ambrose Fourchette, who worked in the cane fields in Louisiana, but made extra money lending to the black and Italian workers who were less thrifty than he was. Ambrose's entrepreneurial spirit allowed him to send his son Junius to Dillard University in New Orleans. When Junius wanted to pursue a law degree he found it necessary to travel north to Chicago where his intelligence and perspicacity earned him a fellowship at Northwestern.

Junius then moved to Newark where he opened an office and specialized in real estate law. He was a dapper figure who frequented jazz clubs and kept a cottage near the beach in Atlantic City. He married his secretary, Lina, a white woman whose Sicilian family (he already felt a closeness to Italians) boycotted their wedding and to whom she never spoke after the marriage. They had three children, two of whom were dark and one who had coffee skin. The latter was my father, Alexander. Alexander went to Rutgers where he earned a law degree. There he met and married a white woman, my mother, Sylvia, who is coincidentally also of Italian descent, so at least in some way he followed his father's footsteps. He invented a process for dry cleaning and opened a shop where he perfected and branded it and sold it to other dry cleaners. He and my mother moved to Scarsdale, where he bought a large white house with Monticello columns and this was where I was born. I had a difficult birth that ordained I would be an only child. I came out with a lightly tanned complexion and nappy, dark hair. Before our current cosmopolitan era my swarthy appearance might have been a handicap in the cracker-dominated upper strata of American society. I think of it now as the "new cosmopolitan" look. If I were driving a Bentley others might assume that I was an Arab prince or a globe-trotting broker of arcane financial instruments.

True continued to press. "I mean are we trying to raise one more little elitist snob?"

"True, can we not..." I implored, trying to stem the descent of the conversation.

"Really, Mitchell. I am serious."

Her credibility here was strong. True never calls me now except when she is serious. I knew that in this moment she confused her anger at me with what is best for Caleb.

"Bayside is a gentle and nurturing place." I engaged with her as if it made a difference. I am addicted to go-nowhere dialectic. "I think Caleb has enough to deal with under present circumstances without saddling him with big social challenges." I said this waiting for True's bottom line. It is rarely a long wait.

"I want him to go to Jefferson."

"We discussed this before."

"I know we did. But I've had a chance to think it over."

"What are you saying to me?"

"I'm saying I want him to go to Jefferson."

"You just can't stand the idea of his going to school closer to me. You think it diminishes you as a mother."

"I think being separated means I don't have to listen to another self-serving, narcissistic analysis of me."

Self-serving may be near the mark. But I would like to think that my narcissism was the chaff that was separated from me when my already pounded life and career were tossed into the wind. In this regard, I think I am a better person for what has happened to me. Nonetheless I tried to respond evenly to True.

"Fine. Now what?"

"I think he should go to Jefferson."

"And if I don't agree?"

"He is six years old, Mitchell! I am his mother! Mothers are the ones who take care of six-year-olds, not fathers! You can teach him to play baseball when he's eight! Get a life!"

She hung up, very much aware that by choosing the telephone for communication she retained the option of cutting me off after having delivered the last word. Experience has shown that she uses the cutoff option about one time in five. I suspected, however, that her threat was empty. Although we hadn't made a legal custody arrangement, we had been sharing Caleb on an almost equal basis since our separation. He stayed with her four nights a week, with me for three.

It was a hard compromise at the time. I argued through my attorney that because of True's responsibilities at the college, I would have more freedom to see to his needs and therefore should be granted sole physical custody. It was really a tactical position—a lowball first offer. I didn't want to deprive Caleb of his mother. I just wanted to make sure I was in the picture and not relegated to taking him to Disneyland and McDonald's on every other weekend. This position didn't go well with True. She had issues of trust when dealing with me and I will admit that they are, considering the past year's events, completely justified. No doubt she felt vulnerable, cornered and panicked. Although we had agreed before to work through a mutually agreed upon mediator, she precipitously hired a lawyer, a dowdy, obese, angry woman who radiated man-hater the first time I saw her.

It had to be clear to True that, if she went to court, no judge was going to send Caleb to Jefferson over Bayside. Even her harpy feminist lawyer had to know that. In family court the interests of the child always come first. I am a responsible, caring and doting father and Bayside is the perfect school. She had to lose, so there was no sense for her to push it. This was one storm I could weather. Or so I thought. Since then I have learned that the first rule of the law is that it will always blindside you.

That afternoon there was a polite knock on my door. The frozen doorbell button, a rent-control staple, had long been immobilized with thick layers of petrified paint. I opened the door to find a man in his twenties standing impolitely close to the threshold, dressed in a neatly ironed polo shirt and creased khakis. I first suspected he might be bearing long-awaited news of Jesus to any stranger who might be cloddish enough to answer the door, but then he spoke my name.

"Mr. Fourchette?"

I was torn. I didn't like that he knew my name. On the other hand, his wide smile suggested good news. I risked a response.

"Yes."

He raised his left hand which held some papers. As they came into view I could see that they were court papers. He offered them to me. Unthinkingly, I reached out to accept.

"You're served."

The papers turned to kryptonite in my hands as the server turned on his heels and left. I read them twice, put in a call to my lawyer, and then read them a dozen times more.

You must not molest, threaten, harass, batter, sexually threaten, telephone, send messages to, follow, stalk, destroy personal property or disturb the peace of True Fourchette.

I thought it was interesting that she chose to use her married name on the petition. She rarely used it otherwise, preferring to be known as True Whitbridge.

You must stay at least two hundred yards away from True Fourchette. You must stay at least two hundred yards away from 3299 Colonial Avenue.

Are we forgetting who put up half the down payment on that house? Are we forgetting who paid most of the mortgage for four years?

True Fourchette is given temporary physical custody and control of the following minor children of the parties: Caleb Jeffrey Fourchette, age 6.

How could this be? How could she get temporary custody without my speaking a word? Isn't this America?

Reasonable grounds for the issuance of this order exist and an emergency protective order is necessary to prevent the recurrence of domestic violence, child abuse, child abduction, elder or dependent adult abuse or stalking.

Reasonable grounds? What reasonable grounds could there be to keep me from Caleb?

This order will remain in effect for seven calendar or five court days, whichever is less.

The strategy revealed itself. Jefferson School began in four days. Of course! She was planning on enrolling Caleb at Jefferson during her brief window of unfettered custody. The phone rang. It was Myra, my divorce lawyer returning my call. She was third tier on her best day, but I liked her dress code (muumuus) and her relaxed, ex-hippie attitude. In retrospect I think I might have chosen more pragmatically.

"It's SOP family attorney bullshit," Myra said. "When there is an accusation of spousal abuse, the court will admit an *ex parte* seven-day restraining order without notifying the respondent."

"If they don't notify me, why do they call me the respondent? I can't respond."

"People take advantage of the statute and use it as a wedge. I guarantee you they won't even appear to get it extended. I can lodge a bar complaint against her attorney but it will go nowhere."

"Then I'll enroll him at Bayside when the order is lifted."

"She'll take you to court. And then you'll be petitioning to change his school instead of just enrolling him. There is potential trauma to the child. The court likes continuity and doesn't like changes."

"You mean this cheap shot is going to work?"

"It depends," she replied.

"On what?"

"On how hard you want to fight. We'd have to go to court. Are you in a position to do that financially? And think about what you are willing to put Caleb through. There will have to be a hearing and he'll probably have already settled into his new school."

"I can't believe this is happening."

"True is a mama bear and you are trying to take away her cub."

"I am not trying to take away her cub."

"I am just trying to explain how she feels. And what you can expect."

"And I'm supposed to walk away?"

"Of course not. Not if you care about your son. He needs you both."

You might be thinking that they don't hand out restraining orders willy-nilly without at least the complainant having offered a reason. Surely True must have told the judge some kind of story to get the restraining order. The truth is that there was an area of vulnerability in our interactions that might be misinterpreted and that True brashly exploited. I regretted the incident long before the ugly legal document was thrust at me. Now I doubly regretted it. In life there is no action without reaction. In the tightening net of time, I sensed an acceleration of consequence.

"And Mitchell..." Myra continued. I know the tone. I know the facts. I expected what was coming. "This is pretty much going to wipe out what's left in the retainer."

"You know I'm having problems, Myra."

"I do. But I'm going to have to ask you for a new retainer. I'm sorry."

"I don't know what to say."

"Can you make two thousand dollars? That will keep us going, anyway."

"I'll work on it, Myra."

Chapter 3

Let me try to clarify the issue of "the incident" and the resulting restraining order by giving you some background. When I departed from our home six months ago, I made an effort to leave cleanly, taking only the clothes from my closet, a boom box and a few books and CDs. Considering the circumstances, I thought anything else might look like looting. The first week out of the house I slept on a pullout sofa in my work mate Steve's Marina del Rey condo and I would like now to thank him for his kindness and loyalty. At the time almost all of the people I regarded as friends had abandoned me. Some didn't return calls. Others seemed pained when I caught them on the phone and they fast-forwarded the conversations with news of appointments to get to and children to take care of.

A few years earlier, when True and I bickered over what in retrospect seems a small matter, I slammed the door and stomped off into the night without a plan. Too stubborn to come home to apologize I took a room at the Four Seasons in Beverly Hills and had crab cakes at the Ivy. We reconciled tearfully the next day and made good, heavy, grasping love that night. This time there was no money for the Four Seasons, or for the Motel 6 on Santa Monica Boulevard. All my credit cards were maxed. No one but Steve would give me a bed.

The incident in question took place two weeks ago. I was at home shortly after returning from the post office for my daily book mailing. My second-floor apartment, part of a triplex from the fifties, has three smallish rooms and a bathroom. Also there is a garage facing an alley in the back that I use to store my books. The bedroom has a bed without a headboard and an Ikea dresser that emits a lingering acrid chemical smell.

The living room is sparse, but pleasant, with hardwood floors and a large window that lets in ample light. I keep it neat for

Caleb. There is a sofa bed fitted with railroad train motif sheets. Caleb is a fan of trains and together we have taken Amtrak south to San Diego and north to Santa Barbara, pressing our noses against the window as the scenery rolls by.

The television has a Sony PlayStation attached and a rack of videogames for Caleb. I'm not a fan of mixing pixels with playtime, but they give me an edge in the never-ending competition with True for Caleb's affections. At her house he has only a previous-generation Nintendo and a few outdated games.

It pains me that Caleb doesn't have a room of his own when he is with me, but I dedicated a closet off the living room for him. When I first showed him the apartment I opened the door to the closet and told him that this space belonged to him alone and that only his things would go in there. He seemed genuinely pleased, but soon asked when I was coming back to the house to live with him and mommy.

I have a tiny kitchen with a cheap, narrow stove, a noisy refrigerator, and a small area for a table. I keep my computer on that table and my printer on a milk crate underneath. This is where each day I receive book orders, send email and print postage labels. The orders arrive as email from Amazon with a pleasant and upbeat Pavlovian *ding*.

The night before the incident I had returned around eight from the late drop at the airport post office. I pulled a Budweiser from the refrigerator and went to the computer to check for new orders. I sat down at the flimsy kitchen chair and touched the spacebar key to wake the computer.

My email page came to life with four new messages in my book-selling account at terminalbooks@earthlinknet. There were only two orders, a twelve dollar book and a nine dollar book. Disappointing, but at least I wasn't totally skunked. There was a spam solicitation to buy natural herbs that I deleted. The last one was from mailerdemon@amazon.com. I clicked on it and it appeared full screen.

Your email is being returned to you because there was a problem with its delivery. The address which was undeliverable is listed in the section labeled: "— —The following addresses had permanent fatal errors — —."

At the bottom of the page were two file icons. It was not the first time customer email has been returned. I reflexively and fatefully clicked on one.

Ding/ding/ding/ding. Something had taken over my computer and was broadcasting infected spam emails from me to every person in my address book. All of my book customers. All of my contacts from my old job. All of the friends that used to belong to True and me that now were loyal to True. Based on the returned emails in my in-box from defunct addresses, I realized that I was sending them all personal solicitations to buy Viagra from Canada.

I tried to shut down my mail program, but the mouse and keyboard did nothing. Desperate, I poked the power button to reboot. When the screen lit up again, there was no Windows desktop, only the infamous Microsoft blue screen of death and the cryptic message:

PAGE_FAULT_IN_NONPAGED_AREA
Win32K.sys
000050(0XFFFFFFE4,0X00000000,0X8E2DB8EC,0X00000000)
Win32K.sys - Address 8E2DB8EC base at 8E200000, Date Stamp 4549aea2

I got on the phone with tech support. They nicked me for $75 as my warranty was expired. The next excruciating five hours (at least an hour of them on hold) with tech support aren't worth detailing. Mostly I was worried about losing unfulfilled orders and I was desperate to retrieve my data. I sat at the kitchen table, depending on the respective mercies of Sami, Gwen, Mike and Rajid, all sitting in Bangalore, all of them presumably with their own personal problems more important than my blue screen, and no doubt with a boss who docked them when they spent too much company time with one caller.

My kitchen table is the redoubtable Ikea Ingo, accompanied by three of Ikea's classic and simple Ivar dining chairs. The Ivar is fine for sitting with a microwaved meal and reading the *Los Angeles Times* spread out on the Ingo but it's a disaster as a working desk chair. After two hours planted in front of the computer on the Ivar, the lower back no longer works as a transparent and synergistic part of the body team. After I sat for five hours trying to subdue the intruder virus, my lower back attacked me with deep, recalcitrant spasms.

At three in the morning, my computer was mostly restored and I collapsed on my bed. Being flat on my stomach was the only tolerable position due to my rib pain. When I awoke at eight needing to pee, I was unable to lift myself out of the bed and needed to roll off the edge, placing my knees on the floor. From there I crawled to the dresser, grabbed on and hauled myself up, and then hobbled to the bathroom.

Standing in front of the toilet, attempting the yogic discipline of trying to empty my bladder without tensing my lower back and thus inciting another spasm, I began to ruminate wistfully on the Herman Miller Aeron chair that was still at True's (formerly Mitchell's and True's) Mar Vista house. After weeks of experimentation with its controls, I had zeroed in on the perfect combination of seat height, lumbar depth, lumbar height and tilt tension. That chair and I were as one. Eight hundred dollars seemed extravagant, even in the salad days of a comfortable salary and a booming stock market, but that chair stands out as one of my all-time best purchases.

The next morning I managed to get out of bed without the floor as an intermediary. I made it to the kitchen and scarfed ibuprofen while ruminating about the Aeron poised in front of the glass-topped desk in the upstairs office of the Mar Vista house. True never liked the chair. She said it looked like some kind of insect. She preferred to sit Quaker-style in a straight ladder-back chair. I hadn't been upstairs in that house for four months, but my presumption was that True had moved the Aeron from the desk, preferring to sit bolt upright in the ladder-back as she filled out more scurrilous court petitions against me.

I poured some cereal and milk into a bowl and tried to sit at the table, but my back screamed in protest and I ate standing up. My mind was fixating on the Aeron and its accommodating curves.

Perhaps True would be pleased to be rid of the piece of furniture she always claimed to detest. It would be of no real cost to her to ease my misery. My back and my entire well-being used to be a matter of concern for her. There was a time when she took pleasure in straddling me in the bed and giving me deep-muscle back massages after I played tennis. Sometimes they would end with both of us naked and breathless on the bed.

Not from anger, but out of naive optimism I reached for the phone. It was early and I would probably find her in. I dialed my former number with small bravado.

"Hello?" True answered without inflection. Was it a good day or a bad day for her? I couldn't tell.

Her silence seemed acrimonious. "It's Mitchell. I'm having a back problem and I was...uh.... wondering if you were using the Aeron."

I heard a click and then a dial tone. This could have been predicted.

All right. I would move on. What was on the agenda for the day? There were about ten boxes of books sitting in the garage waiting to be sorted and listed. That would take most of the morning and I could do a tour of thrift stores in the afternoon. But I couldn't sit in the Ivar doing computer work. That was out. Most of the thrift stores don't open until ten.

It wasn't as if True used the Aeron. And it's not that I don't understand her anger. But we had a child to raise together, and doing that as enemies was not only impractical but unlikely to produce a healthy environment for Caleb. Surely True could understand that. Perhaps she would come around to seeing that sharing the Aeron was the logical first step in a détente that was in Caleb's best interest.

Caleb had preschool from 8:30 to 12:00. True would have left to teach her ten o'clock class. She had informed me shortly after our breakup that she had changed the locks on the doors. But there were at least three or four defective window latches. Legally there had been no final disposition that said that I couldn't enter and leave the house as freely as True. Legally I would be entering my house to get my chair.

I felt my pulse rise as I turned the corner onto Colonial Avenue. I flashed on six years ago, sitting next to roundly pregnant True at the kitchen table with Amy Greenberg, the realtor from Coldwell Banker. What a wonderful name for a company with fiduciary responsibility — Coldwell Banker. Better even than Ivar or Ingo. Were there really a Coldwell and a Banker, or was it a made-up name that reeked of substance in order to inspire confidence? The names added waspy Wall Street heft even to diminutive, Brooklyn-accented, frizzy-haired Amy Greenberg. She looked at our loan worksheet with my $130,000 salary and True's $54,000, and our $300,000 bank account and she said that we were a cinch to qualify at a very good interest rate. We could almost buy it and pay cash. She could pretty much assure us that the owners would accept an offer of $440,000, ten thousand under asking. This house could be ours with a nod.

I know I should have requested a moment for us to confer. Instead I looked at True and she looked at me. "Let's do it," I said. *Let's jump out of the plane and look to see if we have a parachute on the way down. Let's run across the freeway and think about those sixteen-wheelers when we get to the other side. Let's take a handful of these funny little yellow pills and see if they make us feel good.*

"Let me write up an offer, then," said Amy, barely allowing a breath of pause between my words and her putting pen to paper.

As I turned the corner onto Colonial I was feeling an echo of that weak-in-the-knees feeling I had with Amy Greenberg. Substantial and conservative like the Mormon businessman who built it in 1933, the house had an expansive bottom story that spread itself over two small lots. This was the proud seigniorial dwelling on the street. Perched on top was a smaller second story that contained three little bedrooms and a single bath. It was our plan to add a second master bath later, when our yet-to-be born child might be an intrusion on our bathroom privacy. No doubt post-Depression Mormons would have looked on such thoughts as frivolous excess. There was a large picture window that looked out onto the street and through the window I could see hanging the large painting by an unknown Venice artist I was sure was a comer, but whose career never took off. The grass was browner than when I had left. The rosebushes were unkempt and the garden full of weeds. True never liked to work in the garden, and we had let the gardener go weeks before I left.

True's Camry wasn't in the driveway. I parked on the street. There were no neighbors around. Emboldened, I got out of the car and walked around to the back of the house. I tried the back door. One of the house's charms is that it has an old-fashioned service porch. There were shopping bags of recyclables sitting on the floor at the side of the back door. Along with the empty plastic milk and water bottles I noticed several Coca-Cola cans. When we were together, True and I had an agreement that we wouldn't feed Caleb sodas. We didn't want to be Nazis about it, just not buy them and have them in the house. This makes me uncomfortable.

I tried the door. It was locked. I went outside. Another Mormon retort to the tawdry reductionism of California construction was a full cellar with an outside entry. In the basement door stairwell I tried the doorknob. The window next to the stairwell is held by a flimsy catch between two dry-rotted shutter frames. It bent and then yielded when I pushed. I scanned for curious neighbors, and then climbed through, head first, dropping on my hands on the cement cellar floor. The dark space smelled like cool, damp earth and wet newspaper.

I climbed the cellar stairs and opened the interior door into the kitchen. The kitchen had old-fashioned, pale yellow tile countertops and dowdy, white-painted cabinets. Breakfast dishes were piled in the sink. Before the debacle that led to my departure, True and I had been shopping a kitchen remodel, and we were getting surprisingly comfortable with a price around eighty thousand dollars. We had convinced ourselves that granite counters and upscale appliances were an investment in the value of our house that would be more than paid back if we sold it to move to larger quarters. Now I can't help but think of them from the point of view of the hopeful pickers in their aging pickups that frequent the Volunteer Veterans auction early every morning. What would they think of a couple of young people who drop ten thousand precious dollars on a shiny new Viking range?

The living room was relatively kempt by True standards. I never loved her for her neatness. She made it no secret that she had to let the housekeeper go, and Sarah, the neighborhood teenager who helps take care of Caleb, makes more mess than she cleans up.

My eyes moved to the long, scarred and distressed pine table against the wall, the one that we bought in the pricey store on Montana Avenue, knowing full well that we were overpaying for a table that was antiqued and not antique. It still served as a platform for desk-framed photographs—a small shrine to Caleb: Caleb at two months bathing in the kitchen sink. True with baby Caleb in his snuggly in front of the house (picture taken by me). Caleb in Pampers taking some unsteady first steps on the Tabriz. Caleb at five with his maternal grandmother poolside at the Beverly Summit Hotel. Caleb blowing out the candles on his fifth birthday cake in our old apartment living room in Brentwood. Here is something new—Caleb and True in front of the Mad Hatter Teacups at Disneyland. A month ago Caleb had told me that his mother took him to Disneyland and that his favorite attraction was Goofy's Bounce House. Millions of dollars invested by Disney on the state-of-the-art House of Terror was wasted on my gentle, terror-averse six-year-old.

The picture of me standing next to Caleb astride a pony at the Santa Monica Sunday farmer's market had been expunged in a callous and heavy-handed program of deMitchellification. In her bitterness would she prefer Caleb to believe that our wonderful Sunday interlude with fresh croissants and a pony ride never happened?

I climbed the narrow staircase to the second floor with its three small bedrooms. One that was for True and me (now for True alone), one for Caleb and then a tiny room that serves as an office and the area where my treasured chair should reside.

The stairs creaked in a pleasantly familiar way. The ridges of the wrought iron banister under my palm tickled my sense memory. At the top landing a look into Caleb's room revealed his small bed—unmade. When Caleb is in my house he and I have a ritual of making his fold-out bed together every morning before I drop him at preschool, neatly tucking in the corners, putting the bed pillows on the chair next to the sofa and then folding the bed frame back into the sofa. We perform the reverse each night after dinner. I like to think that the constancy of the ritual is stabilizing for him.

Toys littered the floor—several I didn't recognize—notably a large, expensive Tonka dump truck and a child-sized plastic easel. I was surprised that Caleb never mentioned them to me. On the easel was a watercolor picture of what appeared to be this house. There was no mommy or daddy, only a house and a tree and a sun. Make of it what you will. Thank God the sun seemed bright and optimistic.

I looked from the hall into the office. I was right about the chair. It had been replaced at the desk by the ladder-back with the straw seat and the Aeron was tucked in a corner. Although the office and the Aeron were my destination, our old bedroom across the hall made a siren call I couldn't resist.

The bed is queen sized with a large antique mahogany headboard that was never properly mated to the steel frame. As a result, when True and I did our most seismic lovemaking, the frame would pound against the headboard that, in turn, would pound against the wall.

The bed was unmade, with the bedcovers pushed down to the foot. I intended to have a quick look-around. Jog the senses and leave. A quick glance to the nightstand revealed the traditional pile of a half-dozen or so crisp and new review copies that are regularly doled out to academics. And an irresistible distraction to a book scout.

Principles and Application (Evaluation in Education and Human Services) by Ronald K Hambleton. Small academic press. Hard-to-find. A lot of those books would sell "Like New" on Amazon for fifty or sixty dollars apiece. True, of course, would rather burn them all than see me get one.

I move on, mindful that True, unlike me, doesn't see this book as a sixty-dollar payday. She naively believes it to be a large arrangement of words offering information and opinion on the subject of education evaluation.

On the floor by the bed where I would expect to see her flannel nightgown were crumpled blue jeans and panties. I picked up the panties—not in a sexual way because I never found used underwear with its fecal aura to be the faintest turn-on, but rather with forensic intent. They were not her usual cotton, up to the navel and over the butt cheeks variety that I had accepted for our conjugal norm. They were shiny, lacy, slender and red with a high arch on the thigh, designed to impress rather than give comfort. They certainly didn't give comfort to me.

I searched for condoms under the bed. There were none that I could see among the dust bunnies, even when I removed the lamp from the bed stand and shined it underneath the mattress. I sneezed from the dust and replaced the lamp, making sure that it was positioned as I had found it.

I strained to shun the image of True under some energetic new lover in our conjugal bed. I didn't need a memo from the ACLU to remind me that as a separated woman she had the right to thrust her middle parts where and when and with whom she pleased. It was, however, something on which I tried hard not to dwell, despite my inability to do anything but. And when my mind inevitably wandered in that direction, I found I couldn't settle on a face to go with the dick.

Someone from the college? Maybe Cesar Pimentel—a wavy gray-haired, tennis-playing, fiftyish Argentinean fop. He's the always-on-the-make co-chair of the department with a pandering book about bilingual education. Cesar has made an alternate career of inveigling himself onto panels at education conferences, displaying his intellectual wares in a way that is the academic equivalent of stuffing a sock into the crotch of one's Levi's, with the primary intent of seducing lithesome female conference attendees. My hostility toward Cesar grew as I tried to banish from my mind the image of him brushing his veneered teeth in my bathroom.

Wait a second. Who was the taker of that picture of True and Caleb at the Wild Teacups at Disneyland? Was it a threesome or did she hand the camera to a passer-by? This was more than I could bear to have ping-ponging against the walls of my brain. Let her have sex with the entire faculty and student body—just don't have anyone surrogating fatherhood to Caleb. Please. For God's sake. That's all I ask. No other guy displacing me with an arm draped paternally over Caleb's diminutive shoulder as they share a tram in the Indiana Jones Adventure. Nobody buying him overpriced Pluto-dogs and Goofy-fries and helping him tear open his little foil packets of mustard and ketchup.

Then who was the unknown picture-taker? This thinking was clearly counterproductive, getting in the way of my mission.

I strained to create a more pleasing, alternate vision. True, alone with Caleb, hands her little Olympus camera to one of a pair of bubbly young girls visiting from Osaka, Japan. The girl, sporting a fresh-off-the-kiosk Buzz Lightyear T-shirt, takes the camera with a shy giggle. As True and Caleb pose in front of the teacups ride, she asks them to "*smirel.*" Having driven out my demons for the moment I left the bedroom.

The Aeron was my sole mission. Anything else was a trap. I entered the office. Except for the reversal of the natural hierarchy of chairs, everything seemed much as it had been. On the desk was another stack of books. I resisted the temptation to look up their selling price, leaving my smartphone holstered. Also there were some opened envelopes and a few manila file folders, what should be a resistible diversion. I am, however, only a human variety of a spurned spouse with all of the attendant foibles. There was a letter already open on the desk. The letterhead was from True's college—California State University, Northridge.

Dear True:

I just wanted to let you know personally that after looking into all of the possibilities for teaching evening extension classes there weren't any available openings for the upcoming quarter. Dean Ames spoke very well of you and normally we would be honored to have someone from the education department with your credentials and experience teach in the extension school. You are at the top of the list if anything should turn up.

Sincerely,

Richard Shelton
Dean of the Extension School

True was looking to bring in some extra money. Not a surprise under the circumstances. My reaction was uneasy and mixed. It somehow seemed fair to me that she was now getting a taste of the job market's hard knocks. I remembered well how, when I had trouble finding work after our separation, she ran out of sympathy quickly. On the other hand, if she got the job she would no doubt be bitter about having to teach evening hours in the extension school to make ends meet. Moreover, those who still held me in any esteem at all (if there were any of those left) would see True's working of two jobs as further evidence of my callous abandonment.

I pulled the Aeron away from the wall and delicately eased myself into it. We fit together like space modules docking—the perfection of the mating of two finely machined and polished surfaces. All of my painstaking adjustments to lumbar height and lumbar depth seemed to remain untouched. The arm height was exactly where I had left it, low enough not to be a hindrance while I worked at the desk, yet high enough to fall pleasingly under my forearm when I was in the contemplative, relaxed mode.

I luxuriated briefly in the embrace of my old friend. The Aeron, despite its use of the latest composite materials, is a bulky fifty pounds. My back was in a delicate state. One step at a time. It rolled nicely over the rug and onto the hardwood floor of the upstairs hall. Rather than carry it I decided to precede it on the stairs using the casters to ease it down. Like a cowhand's trusty horse, it seemed to sense my hobbled state and cooperated nicely as we eased our way to the bottom landing. All I had to do was roll it out the front door, down a few steps and then lift it into the Volvo. Of course I wouldn't be telling this story if that was all there was to it.

Apparently Elizabeth Selgrath who lives in the house diagonally across the street and who knows me and my Volvo, saw me in front of the house while she was closing an upstairs window. I should say that I had no reason in particular to expect any hostility from Elizabeth. She and her husband, Ronnie, were nodding neighbors and outside of our social circle. While I never suspected that the circumstances of my departure from our family would be a secret from the neighborhood, I didn't consider myself the same sort of pariah with the neighbors that I was among our friends. On the other hand, it stands to reason that those who know me less are apt to demonize me more. In Elizabeth's case the fact that I could never warm to her silly-looking Shih Tzu when she walked the dwarf-dog in front of our house no doubt contributed to her enmity. In any case, Elizabeth apparently considered herself duty-bound to call True's cell phone and report that I was sneaking around the house. True found my presence at the house that we legally, technically still own together such a cause for concern that she turned around on the Burbank Boulevard off ramp of the northbound 405 and raced south to Mar Vista, leaving her class to fend for itself. I was loading the Aeron into the back of the Volvo when True's Camry bounded across Colonial Avenue and into the driveway. She leapt out of the car and stomped toward me and the open tailgate of the Volvo.

"What the hell do you think you're doing?"

Torn between placating and defying, I chose both.

"My back is killing me and I'm taking my chair."

She responded by reaching for her phone. "I'm calling the police." I could see her fingers tap the nine and then twice on one.

"You don't need to do that."

"You are trespassing!"

"True!"

"Are you a complete and total sociopath?"

"I bought this chair! I need it!"

She spoke into the cell phone. "Can you send an officer to 3248 Colonial Avenue? My ex-husband just broke into my house."

"There is no need to…"

"He's still here…. No, he's in front now." She looked at me, holding the phone away from her mouth. "They want to know if you have a weapon."

"True…"

Our nosey neighbor, Elizabeth, had come out of her house and was standing on her doorstep, poised in that stance of official witness for True.

"Not that I can see but I am concerned for my safety. 3248 Colonial. Cross Street is Palms. Thank you." She clicked the off button, and then looked at me with icy coldness. "Take the chair out of the car."

"It's my chair."

"Nothing belongs to you!" she screamed. "Nothing! You owe me three hundred thousand dollars!"

"You don't want this chair, True. You don't use it. I didn't try to hurt you. Why do you want to hurt me?"

"You didn't hurt me?!!! You didn't hurt me?!!!"

"I said I didn't try to hurt you!" Did I really think that this was a time to parse her sentence? Discuss semantics? Logic had left her. It was probably about time to leave me. I wheeled around to defiantly close the lift gate of the Volvo over the Aeron.

True reached to stop me, putting her hand under the edge of the lift gate, holding it open. I pushed down. She pushed up. My adrenalin had completely subsumed any resistance my sore back might have given to the motion and she was no match for my strength or my greater leverage. The door whipped down, wrenching her arm in the process. She cried in pain. I stopped before the lift gate latched. She grabbed her arm, shocked and disoriented with the pain and surprise. I removed my hand from the lift gate.

"Are you all right?" I asked, nonplussed. In all the confrontations of our married life, I never grabbed her, hit her, pushed her or pulled her. This breech was unintentional.

True didn't say a word. She stood there with tears in her eyes. She had the bewildered air of a faithful dog freshly kicked by a drunken owner.

"I'm sorry. I didn't..."

"Get out!"

"True!"

"The cops are coming. I need to go to class. Take the fucking chair."

I closed the tailgate, got into the car and left her standing in the driveway. There was no reference to a police report on my restraining order, only to an alleged "physical assault," so I presume that she left for class before the cop ever appeared. As my adrenalin wore off in the next hour, my own pain returned, doubled.

Chapter 4

In the fall of 1995, True was in her third trimester with Caleb. We had pretty much decided on the name. True liked Colby, which was her great-grandfather's name, but I thought it was both cold and generically uptight. Colby sounded like a supermarket's house brand for frozen food. Caleb had heart. It was biblical. Caleb was an attendant of Moses noted for his powers of observation. (Granted, we had to look that one up in the baby name book.)

We attended classes together on Monday and Thursday evenings at the Baba Yaga Yoga Center, a storefront on Main Street in Santa Monica. Marcy Lu, a certified midwife (whatever that meant, I never demanded to see her certificate), schooled us in the Bradley Method. It was there that we learned that only if we (I can say "we" because with the Bradley Method, the husband is an almost equal partner) maintained a united front by refusing painkillers and Pitocin, would we be assured of a naturally born and naturally perfect child.

We created a birth plan that specified that there would be no shaving of pubic hair (alas), no enemas, no episiotomy. We would be soothed with James Taylor, Nina Simone and Vivaldi. We did not want a fetal monitor unless there were signs of distress and there would be no intravenous injection unless True became seriously dehydrated. I would cut the umbilical cord. I was a tad nervous about it. True regarded it as a minimal investment considering her contribution.

We chose Santa Monica hospital for its earth-toned and unclinical birthing rooms replete with CD players and Barcaloungers. All of the benefits of high-end Los Angeles techno-hospitaling were a few doors away if the unlikely need arose. We had foregone amnio, not wanting to take the one in a thousand chance of an errant needle tip affecting our treasure, but True's pregnancy had gone perfectly. Her weight gain was smack in the middle of the chart. She ate vegetables and protein, took her vitamins, and exercised gingerly. She had never smoked and had reduced wine to a few salutary sips with dinner. The ultrasounds had been perfect. Dr. Green glibly pointed out Caleb's budding penis on the monitor and, while pleased, I reassured True that next time we would have a girl. I deeply felt something like God's favor and that our next would surely be a girl because our life was about perfection.

As we approached the final weeks we considered ourselves to be something like the birthing equivalent of Whole Foods— thoughtful, healthful, enlightened, successful and diffidently upscale.

In the middle of the night on November 1st, I woke up to find the bed soaking wet. True was sitting silently on its edge. She had both hands over her belly.

"True?"

"My water broke."

"Okay," I said, stumped for a follow-up.

"I'm having really strong contractions. I'm going to take a shower so I can be clean for the hospital."

She was surprisingly calm and matter-of-fact. It was a challenge for me to be likewise.

"Should I call Dr. Green?" I said.

"Let's just wait a bit and see," she replied.

"I'll get dressed," I said and got out of bed, noting 3 AM on the alarm clock. I heard the shower and then I heard a scream from True. I ran into the bathroom to find her doubled over in pain.

"It's all right," she said, grimacing like a dying cowboy. "It's just a contraction."

How did she know it was just a contraction? We really didn't know anything for sure. This was all new.

"Breathe," I told her. "Short quick breaths."

I called Dr. Green's number, got the exchange, and excitedly told the operator that we were leaving for the hospital. She said that Dr. Green would call me back soon on my cell phone.

True was standing up now.

"I'm okay," she said. "Let's go."

She dressed herself mostly while sitting on the edge of the bed. I grabbed her packed suitcase with the flannel nightgown, slippers, her grandmother's patchwork quilt, CDs and copies of the *New Yorker* and the *American Educational Research Journal* inside and put it by the door. My cell phone rang and before Doctor Sharon Green could say anything past her name I interrupted.

"Her water broke about half an hour ago. The contractions are about five minutes apart and regular and they're lasting about a minute." I wanted to be useful and precise.

"She's right on schedule. I think it is very possible you guys might be having a baby today." Her coyness annoyed me. "Bring her on in and then the hospital will page me as soon as I'm needed."

Call me when you need me? I need you now. I need you here in the bedroom and in the car on the way over. I don't even want birthing-coach-extraordinaire Marcy Lu. I want you, Dr. Green.

"I think she may be really close," I pleaded.

"I'm a mile from the hospital. I can be over there in minutes."

Okay. No sweat. We can do this.

At the hospital an orderly greeted us at the entrance with a wheelchair. Check-in was fast, friendly and efficient. We quickly were enveloped in the reassuring sand-and-taupe palette of Birthing Room C and in the large and competent hands of obstetrical nurse Bernice Alvarado, an expansive brown-skinned woman in her forties. It was soon clear that with her Guatemalan large-family upbringing and her nursing school education, she knew everything about giving birth and we knew nothing. Marcy Lu had given us the impression that we would be wholly responsible for delivering the baby by ourselves.

Bernice eased True into a gown, made the bed comfortable and then helped her onto it. True had a contraction immediately and gasped in pain. I took her hand and reminded her "short breaths." Bernice had the grace not to treat us as ignorant parvenus as she noted the timing on the wall clock. "That's very good," she said. After the contraction ebbed she examined True.

"She's at seven centimeters. That's good."

"Have you called Dr. Green?" I queried.

"Dr. Green likes us to call at eight centimeters if mom is doing okay." She sensed my anxiety. "Don't worry. She'll get here. Doctors need to sleep so they can be good for their patients. And Dr. Green almost always comes herself."

"Almost always?" I was thinking. Bernice managed my anxiety by giving me a task. "You guys did all your Lamaze, right?"

I nodded. I actually liked that she was handling me. It demonstrated competence and experience.

"Then you're gonna help missus with her breathing, right? I have shaved ice and peppermints and everything you need. You want to do the natural childbirth, you gotta work at it. It's not gonna be a party."

The ob/gyn resident stopped in, introduced himself with zero eye contact as Dr. Zafardi, picked up True's chart and examined her. He confirmed Bernice's assessment of progress and said it would be a few hours before True started real labor. He left and said he would be close by.

Marcy Lu, if you are out there, I would like to tell you that the picture you painted for us of what our natural birth experience would be was at best a well-intentioned fraud. I am wiser now, and I do know that the responsibility for giving credence to unlikely promises lies with me, so I do not blame you. And if we disregard process, then we did just fine, for nobody can argue with the outcome. Caleb was pink, seven pounds, eleven ounces and effervescent with life. He passed his first exam with a boisterous "eight" Apgar score (with special commendations from the doctor for his outstanding reflex irritability). All of this was no doubt laying the essential groundwork for perfect SAT scores and admission to Stanford or my alma mater, Yale. (Q. How do you know when a man has gone to Yale? A. He'll tell you.)

The route to the stellar Apgar was, however, sinuous and strewn with obstacles. Considering the fine result, I don't want to make too much of this, but sweet Caleb did not pop out spontaneously in Birthing Room C. It was more like hiking into a box canyon with options diminishing as the trip progressed.

When True was ten centimeters dilated Bernice called Dr. Green who, good to her promise, appeared within fifteen minutes. She assessed that there was still about an hour before True needed to push. In fact, it was two.

But pushing yielded no result. True pushed and sweated and cried and screamed for hours in an effort to coax out our progeny-to-be. Bernice's shift ended and she was replaced by Rosa, who tried in vain to mask her concern at the length of True's labor. True had resisted the epidural despite Dr. Green's advice that relieving her pain would help her focus on the delivery, but after four hours, in pain and exhaustion and full of fear, True consented to the shot.

After eight hours, True's contractions, which had been strong and regular, began to ebb. Her muscles were simply tired from this goal-line push. Dr. Green, who had been a tireless cheerleader throughout the process, expressed concern for the baby and asked for permission to attach a fetal monitor. Perhaps if birth coach Marcy Lu was there giving birth, she would have had the will to refuse this dispiriting intrusion of high-tech medicine, but True and I were in no position to argue with Dr. Green, and she threaded in a small wire to relay unequivocally our precious one's heart rate and breathing.

The hopeful news on the monitor was that the young Master

Fourchette was breathing and beating like a baby starling and there was still time for True to marshal her strength and push him out. But after ten hours of effort True's baby-expulsion mechanism was finally tapped out. Dr. Green confronted us with what we sensed already.

"You tried as hard as anyone could, True. Now's the time to think about your health and the health of your baby. It's time to do a Caesarian."

I think True was glad to be relieved of the responsibility as was I. It could be argued we had given too much to begin with. Almost instantly a hospital orderly arrived, collected True onto a gurney, and wheeled her off into a nearby operating room. I stood frenzied in the hallway outside as nurses and an anesthesiologist zoomed past me.

After a fifteen-minute eternity of hovering at the door I was startled by the cry of a newborn. My chest began to heave and tears filled my eyes. My exclusion was unbearable. What could they do to me if I just burst through the doors? Then a nurse emerged with a warm smile on her face.

"Mr. Fourchette? Would you like to see your new son?"

"Is everything okay?" I asked as I followed her into the room.

"Your boy is fine and big and healthy."

True was supine on an operating table, draped in green cloth with an anesthesia mask hiding her face. Dr. Green was bending over her midsection. Something wasn't right. From what I knew about Caesarians she didn't need to be unconscious. I felt discomfort in the pit of my stomach. Dr. Green, sensing my distress, turned to me and spoke from behind her surgical mask.

"Everything's fine. We had to put True under a little deeper because I have a little repair work to do."

True isn't a truck and I wasn't mollified by the notion of "repair work."

"Your wife is fine. Don't worry."

My gaze was stuck on True when a nurse tapped me on my

shoulder. I turned. She held a tiny, wrapped newborn in her arms.

"Here he is," she said with a coy smile.

This moment has deeply etched my memory. The tiny, pink person I saw seemed quite perfect except for the clamped extension of umbilical cord extruded from his navel where the swaddling parted. Caleb was surprisingly unwrinkled (a benefit of the C-section), moist and glistening from the womb, his brown/blue eyes open and roving unfocused. Then his gaze seemed to fasten on me. I know according to the neonatologist establishment that's unlikely, but that's how I saw it. I was interrupted in my reverie by the voice of Dr. Green whose hands were busy at work inside True's draped midsection.

"Does he have a name?"

"Caleb," I replied, choked with emotion. Up to now the name was just a name.

Dr. Green looked to the nurse and directed her. "After you weigh Caleb and get him cleaned up, maybe Dad would like to hold his son for a little while."

Dr. Green then turned to me. "True had some fibroids that were holding the womb out of position. That's why she couldn't deliver. I'll be another fifteen minutes here straightening things out, but there's nothing to worry about. Then we'll bring her up to her room and let you know as soon as she wakes up."

The nurse holding Caleb asked, "Would you like to hold your son?"

I looked at Caleb, tiny and perfect and ours. My preconception was that True would be on the bed in the warm confines of the birthing room. I would be holding her left hand tightly, lovingly. On her breast would be nestled our newborn son, contentedly napping after his recent strenuous journey. Nurses would pause at the door and admire the perfection of our triad. But True was out cold on a hard table and a stranger in a green smock held our baby. This was not fair to True. The mother has a deserved primacy. He should be first with True, then with me. But this would have to do. I think processing may have made me slow to respond. I nodded to the nurse.

"I'll meet you in the nursery in a few minutes," she said.

I found the nursery a few doors down and was ushered by a nurse into a separate, smallish room with a few throw rugs over the linoleum floor and a wooden rocking chair in a corner. I waited a few minutes looking at the generic landscapes that decorated the walls, and then the nurse returned with a baby—not any baby—my baby, wrapped in white cotton. She presented him to me with a warm smile as she addressed the swaddled infant.

"This is your daddy, Caleb. Say hello."

I took him from her, uneasy and overwhelmed. The nurse spoke to me calmingly.

"That's good. Support his head. That's fine. Would you like to sit down with him?"

I sat in the rocking chair and immediately began to rock. Rocking seemed primal, right and easy. His eyes were closed. He stretched in a kind of a yawn and his tiny arms and fingers extended. There was an ID tag around his ankle with his name on it. Caleb Fourchette. The nurse offered me a bottle.

"You can feed him some sugar water if you like."

Sugar water? Is that really a healthy choice? What would True want? What would Marcy Lu say? I will just go with it. I am in good hands.

"Will he take it?" I asked dumbly.

"You can see. I know he'd rather have mama's milk but he'll get that soon enough."

"Is this his first drink?" I asked in wonder.

"This will be his first."

Oh my God. This is your Daddy bringing you your first sustenance out in the world. This may appear to be a mere disposable bottle with sugar water, but it is a holy rite and a sacred ritual.

I brushed the rubber nipple across his mouth and he reacted instantly, reached for it with all of his tiny body. He opened his eyes and he began to suckle.

"He likes it," the nurse exclaimed.

He certainly did. He was an incredible sucking machine. I cradled the bottle at a comfortable angle and I slowly rocked some more. Emotion swept over me. I felt like I had just trudged through a high pass and looked out to find that life was spread out endlessly in front of me in a giant, expansive valley. Tears rolled down unwiped, unabated. I continued to rock.

"That's your daddy," the nurse said softly to Caleb as she retreated to the doorway to leave me alone with my son whose eyes, however new and unfocused, seemed to gaze lovingly at me.

Chapter 5

I am propped against the arm of Nick's dirty beige sofa with my feet up, feeling somewhat better under the mild beneficence of ibuprofen. Around me are books and almost nothing else. Double stacked in shabby, mismatched tumble-down bookcases, piled high on the floors and on windowsills and overflowing the file boxes that are strewn around the room. If there is any order to them, it escapes me. Nick enters with a book in a raised hand and an expression like he has never seen a book before as he presents it to me with a lilt. It is a hardback copy of *The Million Dollar Mermaid*, Esther Williams's autobiography.

"What is it?" I ask, dutifully assuming the position of the unworthy pupil to his master teacher. I know that the book came out about four years ago, was a brief bestseller and made a small sensation with chapters on her love life and a revelation about Jeff Chandler's cross dressing. A clean copy sells for about five dollars on Amazon so I don't know why he's showing it to me.

"Look!" Nick says proudly as he opens the cover to reveal Esther Williams's oversize, feminine signature. I respectfully examine the flowery script on the title page.

"She never signs. She had one little signing at Brentano's when it came out and that's all," says Nick. "And it's a first," he adds pointing to the tiny words "First Edition" under the publisher information on the opposite page. "There are two signed copies on AbeBooks. The cheapest is eight hundred dollars. The gay boys love her. She's like Mae West in a bathing suit."

"Where'd you get it?"

"She signed it for me. I been trying for six months."

"But you said she never signs," I say, rising ritually for the bait as Nick's face widened into a Cheshire Cat grin. "You use the cancer thing?" I ask.

One of Nick's favorite ploys is to send the book in the mail with a fan letter and a picture supposedly of himself, but really of a cousin who had contracted Hodgkin's disease and was bald and emaciated from treatment. In the letter Nick proclaims how much of an inspiration (famous author's name inserted here) has been to him and how it would fortify him in his fight against his Stage IV cancer if only he could occasionally open the book to see the signature and be reminded of the author. This worked in the past with both Lauren Bacall and Lillian Gish, but I know that flinty Katherine Hepburn remained immune to Nick's charms to the end.

"Nah. They're getting too many sob stories these days. I mean there's real competition out there and there's nothing some of these scum won't do to get a book signed."

I examine the signature until Nick pulls it away.

"So what did you do?"

"All right. But don't tell anybody."

"Who would I tell?"

"I'm not kidding. I wouldn't want this to get around. I'm telling you and nobody else."

Is he sincere? Is he telling only me? One thing about Nick is that I never quite know. He is an onion with alternating layers of sincerity and duplicity and you never know what you might find in the core and I am nowhere near experiencing Nick's aromatic core.

"I know this Bev Hills hairdresser, Rupert, who sometimes gets me some of the Taschen art photography books—you know, like the erotic wrestling stuff and the fetish stuff—he's got a source and he gets them for me sometimes for cheap. I don't ask him where they come from, but sometimes he gets me a hundred-dollar book for ten bucks. He wears nipple rings under his shirt. I wouldn't bend over in front of him but he's an okay guy. He's always bragging about his celebrity clientele. But they're all from TV which I don't watch on account of I'm so busy and I like DVD movies better. He tells me their names and I never heard of them. I know he comps them just so he can say he cuts their hair as if somebody cares. So one day I'm picking up the small Helmut Newton portrait book from him—ten bucks which is not that great a price 'cause the book is devalued lately and you're lucky if you can get fifty for a copy even though Newton's been croaked for years and he tells me in the course of a conversation that he cuts Esther Williams's hair. Rupert says she comes in on the second Wednesday of every month unless she's away on a business trip. She's got this big swimsuit line they sell in Macy's and Bloomingdale's and all those places."

"How old is she?" I ask, trying to form a picture of what she might look like not on a diving board.

"She's eighty-three in February. So I say that I'd be interested in her signature and he says she's coming in the next Wednesday but that she's a pretty crusty old broad and she doesn't like being bothered. I ask him what time and now he's getting nervous. I mean what's he got to be nervous about? She's eighty-three and he cuts her hair for free anyhow. What's the big deal?"

"Just tell him, Nick," Doreen cuts in.

"So I show up Wednesday a little after eleven. He walks up to the appointment desk where I slip him a twenty and he points her out sitting at his chair. He pretends to answer the phone and I meander over in her direction."

"What did she look like?"

"Like somebody's grandmother. She's eighty-three."

"What did you do?"

"I turned on the charm." When Nick "turns on the charm" he affects an unctuous, servile, rodent quality. No doubt there are some people who find his Dickensian persona pitiable and respond kindly. Most simply scan for an exit. "I ask her if she's Esther Williams and she nods yes and then I tell her how much I love her movies, but I'm trying to come up with the name of one."

"*Million Dollar Mermaid*," offers Doreen.

"Thanks for telling me now." He scowls at Doreen and then continues his story. "But I can see she's not warming to my routine. And then I tell her that my wife won't wear anything else but one of her swimsuits cause of the way they fit and the way they're made. That goes over a little better and I think I'm getting her and I say that it's this amazing coincidence 'cause I have a copy of her book in the car which I have read cover to cover and it'd mean so much to me if she were to sign it." He paused.

"So?" I prod reflexively.

"She looked at me like I was some kind of worm that crawled into her nectarine. And she says that she gets a zillion requests so she has a policy that she doesn't sign any more. She says she's sorry. Like I care she's sorry."

"So what'd you do?"

"I don't know. I just keep talkin'. You know me. Brain wired straight to my mouth. I started talking about how I saw her on Turner Classics in some swim sequence with big blue pools and how great she was, but I could see that was going nowhere fast. Then Rupert comes back and he got real nervous and twitchy about what was going down. And I guess I must have been talkin' too much and then I start telling her about Doreen and about how good the swimsuit fits and I was thinking about maybe telling her Doreen has got Hodgkin's or something, but I had the feeling that nothing was gonna work. She's definitely getting this pissy kind of look on her face. So I tell her again how much I would appreciate it and Rupert's saying, like, 'It was nice of you to drop by, Nick,' and starts pushing me out the door. But I'm sticking it out. And then she says out of nowhere 'I wouldn't sign a book if you came in wearing an Esther Williams swimsuit.'"

"Tell him what Rupert said," says Doreen.

"So Rupert says, 'Sure you would.' He's got this big faggy grin on his face. 'How could you say no to that?' he says to her.

And she smiles like out of the corners of her mouth. So before she can change her mind I say, 'How long you gonna be here?' She doesn't answer, but Rupert says she's gonna have to spend a half hour under the dryer and then he's gonna have to comb her out. Maybe forty-five minutes."

"You didn't?" I say.

"I jump in the car and run over to Macy's in the Beverly Center which is a couple of blocks from there and I find the biggest size Esther Williams swimsuit and I buy it. It costs sixty bucks, but I figured I can return it any time."

"You can't return swimsuits," Doreen adds sagely.

"What do you mean you can't return swimsuits? I got it at Macy's for Chrissakes."

"You can't return swimsuits. It's a law. It's unsanitary."

Nick looks to me to adjudicate. He knows I went to college and for him that qualifies me to settle the issue.

"I don't know. I think maybe Doreen's right."

"Are you kidding me? I spent sixty bucks on the fucking thing."

"Did you wear it?"

"Of course I wore it."

"He wore it in front of Esther Williams." Doreen affirms proudly.

"I put it on in the car. I was parked out on San Vicente Boulevard and I had to wait until there was nobody walking on the sidewalk and then I scrunched down in the seat. It was made out of some kind of stretchy stuff so it kind of stretches to fit, but it was murder getting it to cover my balls. I had to like scrunch my nuts back inside. I got myself all squeezed into this thing and then I marched into the salon with the book and the pen in my hand. Rupert's combing her out. Everything in the place stops. She looks at me like the freak that I was, but you can get away with more in a Bev Hills beauty salon than you can in a whorehouse in Bangkok, so she kind of chuckles and takes the pen and she signs it. And then I walk out—Jesus fucking Christ, Doreen. Are you sure I can't return the suit?"

I laugh and it feels like daggers going into my bruised, maybe broken ribs. "Did she say anything?" I ask, attempting to speak without actually moving my distressed diaphragm.

"She said, 'You look good.' I don't think she was being sincere."

"She's got millions," Doreen says in a Doreen-style non sequitur.

"That's 'cause she's smart," says Nick. "Some of them actresses from the forties now they're living in studio walk-ups in Van Nuys, but Esther Williams—she had brains to go with the looks."

I wonder if Esther had invested in the internet. I imagine that her investments are limited mostly to bonds, blue chips and real estate. As she dives confidently off that high board that is life I believe that she is endowed with the preservation skills and wisdom that belonged exclusively to a previous, superior generation.

Outside I hear the buzzy sound of a small motorbike in the driveway. The little engine shuts off with a hiccup. I look up at Nick, he rolls his eyes. "Shit!"

"What?" I ask.

Nick goes to the window, looks out, and then turns to me.

"It's fucking Helmet Head."

"He knows where you live?"

"Last year I Craigslisted some discard inventory out of my driveway. He showed up."

Someone knocks insistently at the front door and Nick leaves the room to answer it. I overhear the conversation.

"Kak pozhivaete?"

Although I can't see from my sofa perch, I know from the voice that its origin is a short guy with nervous, darting eyes wearing a beat-up, half-dome motorcycle helmet clumsily spray-painted red, with dirty curls of stringy, dark hair spilling out from its perimeter, and the chinstrap flapping loosely at his neck. The ensemble is always completed with a ratty army jacket, greasy work pants and worn-out sneakers. He wears the helmet whether he is on his bike or off, indoors and out, but he never, as far as I can tell, fastens the chinstrap.

"I don't speak Russian," says Nick coolly.

"I thought your parents were Russian."

"Yeah. But I was born in New Jersey."

"You should learn it."

"What do you want, Hector?"

Hector, we assume, is his given name. It is the only alternate to Helmet Head that I have heard. Other book scouts say that Helmet Head wears his fiberglass chapeau to bed each night. It is also said but unsubstantiated that Helmet Head is a twice-convicted felon, a candidate to be locked up forever under California's three-strikes law if he gets caught out of line with the law in the smallest way. Also, he has a compulsive twitch that emanates from around his chest and moves to his shoulders. It's kind of like an oversized shrug, and it seems to appear unheralded every several minutes if you are unfortunate enough to be in his presence long enough to notice.

"I heard about Ralph."

"I told him not to go to Anaheim," says Nick grimly.

"Did he say what it was like down there? Was there good stuff?"

"I didn't ask."

"I heard they had unsorted bins down there."

"I wouldn't know." I know Nick is trying to close the door on him.

"Unsorted" means that nobody has gone through and pulled out the good books. On the bright side of sorted bins is that they put ex-junkies and winos on the early morning sorting duties and mostly what catches their eye are big coffee-table books, which mostly aren't worth anything anyway. A big old, omnipresent Abrams art book on Matisse with appealing large pictures sells for about four bucks on Amazon and you lose two on the shipping.

"So where is he? That's his car out front, right?"

"He's lying down."

"So he didn't say anything about what it was like?"

"I gotta go, Hector. I gotta pack my orders."

"Oh yeah, sure."

"I'll tell him you were concerned about him." But Helmet Head already has his foot in the entry and pushing forward, sees me on the sofa.

"Hey Ralph! I heard you had trouble in Anaheim."

I see him but don't want to engage him. Nobody in his right mind ever wants to engage Helmet Head. Nick intervened for my sake.

"He's resting, but he's okay. I'll talk to you later."

Helmet Head ignores Nick, calls to me. "So was it the big guy with the buzz cut? They think they own the fucking place down there."

I try to summon appropriate hostility as I respond.

"I don't feel like talking now. Okay?"

Helmet Head, uncharacteristically, seems to accept my rebuff. He backs away.

"Sure, Ralph. You get yourself together, man."

He exits my field of view. I hear the door close, then Nick returns.

"What a fucking fruitcake he is," opines Nick.

Sometimes I wonder how Nick talks about me after I have gone.

"He speaks Russian?" I ask.

Nick ignores my question as he perks up his ears, listening for the sound of Helmet Head departing.

"Take a look and make sure he's leaving," he says to Doreen.

"Why don't you?"

"Because I asked you." Doreen sighs and walks to the window just as we hear the sound of a kick starter and then a moped dropping into gear.

Helmet Head is a mystery to other sellers. Where he lives, how he sells his books and where he came from are all subjects of conjecture but no one has hard knowledge. He shows up on his moped at every Saturday morning garage sale and library sale. With wild-man eyes he will rudely push his way to the front. Most people give him a wide berth.

"He's a fucking thief, you know," says Nick to me.

"What a fruitcake," echoes Doreen.

"Did you lock Ralph's car?" Nick demands of Doreen. She hesitates because she hasn't and Nick shakes his head with conviction. "Jesus fucking Christ!" He goes to the window, stares outside at my Volvo with the spare tire on the back wheel.

"I hope he didn't fucking take anything."

Chapter 6

True's father had been a family doctor in Rapid City, South Dakota. He was a saint of a man who healed the children of struggling farmers and sometimes took his pay in tomatoes or chickens. I always felt humble in his presence. True's mother died in an automobile accident when True was fifteen. Her father never remarried and as far as anyone knows remained loyal to her mother.

Just as True's father didn't seem impressed by my prep school and Ivy League credentials, he didn't seem at all deterred by my dark complexion. True said that when she first told him about me, she felt obliged to tell him of my mixed heritage. She said she sensed a hint of hesitation, but not a word of complaint, and then he said that he trusted her judgment and looked forward very much to meeting the man she judged worthy of her affections.

Five years ago, shortly after Caleb was born, True's dad was diagnosed at sixty-six with pancreatic cancer and died within a few months. There was a tearful and touching memorial service at the Lutheran Church attended by phalanxes of dedicated friends and grateful former patients. I stood stalwartly at True's side and, as the good husband I was, helped nurse her through the depression that followed his death. The house and a rental property were sold and True split the proceeds with her older brother, Adam, a barrel-chested ex-frat boy lawyer who lived in Denver with his family. Adam was always uncomfortably cordial with me as if I were a guilty client that he had agreed to defend. It was clear he didn't like me for his sister and that color was undoubtedly part of the equation. I wondered what the conversation was between True and Adam when she told him we were getting married. Although he had yet to deal with the possibility of having a partially black niece or nephew, I believe he regarded my having any control over his white family's inheritance as financial miscegenation.

True received a total inheritance of about three hundred and eighty thousand dollars. On the advice of True's family banker, we placed the money in high-yielding CDs and treasury notes with our joint names to ease inheritance burdens in case one of us should die. The accounts required dual signatures for withdrawal. At the time, it was not difficult to get yields of 8 and 9 percent, although inflation ate up much of it.

It was a difficult decision to take money out of this account for a down payment on the house, but we took comfort in the belief that True's father, the Good Doctor, would have wanted us to do so. We had been happy in our apartment in Brentwood, and the rent was moderate, but with Caleb it was much too cramped. And it didn't have an outdoor place for him to play.

The money had appreciated to about three hundred and ninety thousand dollars; two hundred and thirty-five thousand remained. It was a nice nest egg. If it continued to appreciate it would help pay for Caleb's college education and our retirement, or perhaps help Caleb buy a nice little house when it became his turn. After feeling like adolescents for most of our grown-up lives, we were finally adults. We had Caleb, a home, and over two hundred thousand dollars safely tucked in the bank.

There was always a trace of discomfort when it came to True's father's money. We both acknowledged that it was more hers than ours, but she showed little interest in managing it, and clearly True looked at me to take responsibility for it. I think it is fair to say that she trusted me.

By the fall of 1999 a book called *Dow 36,000* was quickly surpassed in Panglossian optimism by a new book entitled *Dow 100,000* which promptly took over the top spot on the bestseller list. Today, these books sell for a penny on Amazon and there is no shortage of available copies.

Red Hat, a software company that packaged and sold Linux, a gussied-up version of a free, public domain operating system, had an initial public offering at $14 a share and finished out the week at $85. On September 3, feeling lucky, I bought fifty shares of QQQ, a basket assembly of the most popular NASDAQ technology stocks. I bought it with money from our regular account, which was mostly fueled by my earnings, and had about seven thousand dollars in it. On September 4, the NASDAQ gained 108 points, its largest one-day point gain ever. I was on a roll.

I calculated how much a $5,000 investment would appreciate at my current rate of success in the market. Of course I couldn't expect it to go up 5 percent every week (compounding to a surprising 1,200 percent annually, or half a billion dollars, for the reader without a nine-digit calculator handy) as it had done for me lately. I wasn't greedy, however. I could easily settle for 1 or 2 percent a week.

We hired a sitter and I took True out for a celebratory dinner of lobster with coconut curry sauce at Chinois, her favorite food splurge. We usually found that no matter what the surroundings, the conversation centered on Caleb with occasional forays into topics of work or friends or politics or shopping.

This night I had an additional topic in mind. I planned to update her on our financial situation. Taking on a paternal air, I expounded on our portfolio.

"I know you have a limited tolerance for talking about this stuff, but I wanted to have a little money talk."

"You've been making us rich," she said with a smile as she dipped crusty, fresh bread in the sweet lobster sauce. "That's why we're eating at Chinois. What else do I need to know?"

"I want to take 20 percent of the inheritance money and invest it. Even though there's been a big run-up, I think there's some life in the stock market and I think we can make some gains."

"What if it goes down?"

"There's always some risk. That's why I want to limit our investments to 20 percent and I only plan to buy stock in pick and shovel companies."

"What are 'pick and shovel' companies?" she asked. Although True was broadly educated and well informed in many areas of academic and practical pursuit, she was never embarrassed to admit she didn't know something.

"They're the companies that have products to sell. Like Cisco makes routers."

"What is a router?"

"Internet hardware. Things they need to buy to expand it and make it run. Even if eBay disappears, there will be other websites and an internet and they'll need the equipment and the physical means to keep it going. And then there's Microsoft and Intel and Oracle and Apple—"

"Apple? At least I know what that is. Jessica has an iMac and it's really cute."

"The term 'pick and shovel' is from the merchants who sold tools to the miners. Only a few miners hit it big, but the men who supplied the gear always made out."

"And women? Did women supply the gear, too?" She said mock-piquant. True sometimes tempered her feminism with irony.

"I'm sure they did. I'm sure women found some product to offer all those horny miners and they probably made a tidy, consistent profit."

"The stock market makes me nervous."

"So did buying a house. So did getting pregnant. But they were right, weren't they?"

"What would Dad think? He worked so hard for that money. He sacrificed so that he could pass it on to his children."

I wish she hadn't said that. I know that even deep in the ground Dad still believes that even a high-yield certificate of deposit is a needless and profligate speculation when compared to a comfortable passbook account with the small town bank that served him well for fifty years.

"If he had invested some of it, there might have been more for you and your brother."

True blanched. I wish I hadn't said it. I knew I had violated her sacrosanct view of her family with loose talk about filthy lucre.

She recovered. I know she didn't want to spoil our evening out. "I just don't... I just don't want us to be too money crazy. Okay?"

"This isn't being money crazy. It's planning for our family's future."

"I know you're right. It's just that I have been raised to equate money with work. I'm not comfortable getting it out of the air."

"I am working. There is effort involved. I spend time learning and researching. I don't throw a dart at a board."

"I'm sorry..."

"It is for us and for Caleb. It is for education and security."

"I'm old-fashioned. I admit it."

"College will be expensive if Caleb decides to go to an Ivy."

She takes a bite of lobster to end the conversation.

Chapter 7

Nick pokes his head into the living room as I daydream on his sofa. "I got fuckin' eighteen orders. I gotta start packing." I realize I have been on his sofa longer than I anticipated.

"Oh shit," I reply. "I have to do mine."

Amazon requires that sellers ship within two days of the receipt of an order. I could wait a day or even two, but it's good business to please your buyers with a shipment that arrives ahead of schedule. It makes for good feedback. I may have many failings, but I can say with pride that I have excellent Amazon feedback. When I am feeling low I can click on my feedback page and bask in the comfort of approbation.

"Almost like having my lost original; precisely as described, well-packaged, and I got good follow-up emails between order and receipt. Thanks, Terminalbooks!" Rated by Buyer: grisha

"OMG, this company is the best! I HIGHLY recommend them for anything! They are absolutely perfect" Rated by Buyer: John

"the book I ordered was used but is in excellent condition. it arrived quicker than i expected (from california to pennsylvania). i would order from this merchant again without hesitation." Date: 07/23/2004 Rated by Buyer: John B.

I start to get up from Nick's sofa and a sharp pain hits me in the ribs. I fall back to assess my disability. Nick is already in the back room he uses for storing books. "Hey, Nick. Can you give me a hand?" I call out to him. Doreen appears in the doorway, and then approaches.

"You should rest, Ralphie."

"I gotta get my orders out." I try again to get up.

She hesitates and then offers a hand as I swing to my feet, smarting in my rib cage. I say my thanks and goodbyes to Nick and Doreen and make my way out to the driveway where the Volvo is parked. In the cargo area the slashed tire sits loose where Nick placed it on top of several file boxes full of books. I open the driver's door grabbing the top edge to brace myself as I slide in behind the wheel. My side doesn't sting as badly as I had anticipated. Maybe the rib isn't broken. The car starts willingly and I back out using the rearview mirror rather than turning my body to look. I'll deal with the tire tomorrow.

Back in my apartment I feel better. One of the many strengths of my small business is that the obligations are always manageable. My tasks are clearly defined and achievable. In advertising I was a hapless toreador chasing a darting red cape being whirled by whim-driven clients. In the bookselling era of my life one foot follows nicely after another. Right now I must fire up the computer and see how many orders I have.

Eleven orders. Most of them are for academic trade paperbacks in the fifteen-dollar range, but one is for a copy of *Howard Hawks, Storyteller,* an out-of-print paperback in a scuffed and disarmingly artless black cover that I found a few days ago on a picked-over shelf at the National Council of Jewish Women thrift store on Venice Boulevard. Even with my slim book-scouting experience I know that film buffs crave this out-of-print title. I listed it for eighty-five dollars and it sold today to a Rachel Darby in Myrtle Beach. I have learned through my business that there are cineastes in every pocket of the country. I sell books about how to market your screenplay to places like Plano, Texas and Hibbing, Minnesota. And while it often surprises me when I send a treatise on Boethius to a small town in Georgia, it has been my experience that serious books about history and the classics mostly go to the East Coast.

At a gross of $227 in sales I'm slightly below par for the day, but I'm in the game. At the computer I generate a list of books to pull off the shelves and packing slips.

I have about two thousand books in my garage—give or take—in fifteen cheap white particle board bookcases, neatly arranged along the walls and in a back-to-back central island.

List in hand, I remove my eleven books from the shelf. When I do this I always have a gnawing apprehension that a sold book will be missing from the shelf and lost. Today eleven books are all here. I am relieved.

Back inside I place the books on a long folding table near my supplies, an assortment of bubble mailer bags (sizes #1 through #6), plastic sleeves in two sizes, tape, lighter fluid for dissolving and removing gooey price sticker residue, a razor blade scraper for prying off old labels, several varieties of erasers, scissors and pens.

I place a book inside a plastic sleeve along with a packing slip, making sure to write "Thanks (Kevin, Julie, Huang, Ricardo, Susan, etc.)" on a blank portion of the paper, to give it the personal touch that will garner good feedback. I tape the bag closed and insert it in the bubble mailer, seal it, taping the edges to make sure it doesn't pull open. I write the buyer's name on the envelope and weigh the completed package on a small digital scale and note the weight on the pull slip that I will use to generate a postage label on my printer. I affix the labels to the correct packages and take them to the post office sorting station (where the mail carriers pick up their mail) on Colorado Avenue in Santa Monica. I realize this all may sound like dreary rote to you, but these are the details that form boundaries and structure in my current life and I am truly thankful for the restraint and support they provide.

At the Colorado Avenue sorting station, the postal worker takes my box of packaged and labeled books from me. He's Korean, in his thirties.

"How's business?" he asks with a pleasant smile as he takes and sorts the packages into their appropriate larger bins.

"Not bad," I respond. Not good either, but I'm not here to chat.

My rib stabs me as I bend to enter the Volvo, but overall I think my condition is improving. I drive the two miles back to my apartment. As I exit the car I look again at the file boxes of books from Anaheim. Most still sit underneath my flat tire. I should take them back inside and upload the titles to Amazon. I open up the back hatch on the Volvo, and then try to push aside the tire. My midsection smarts and I just remove one box that is already free.

Wait...wasn't this the box that had my shiny, sixty-dollar textbook *Literature and Language* in it? I'm sure I packed it here, along with the book on Sufism and the book on Islam and the book of Heinrich Kley illustrations. That textbook was the only book in the whole lot worth more than a twenty-dollar bill.

Sucking in my pain I shove aside the tire and pore through the other boxes, looking for the orange sheen of the jacketless textbook cover with a generic picture of an autumn meadow. I can't find it.

Wincing in discomfort, I place the boxes on my little luggage cart and wheel them into the apartment. Carefully I go through each box, looking for the missing *Literature and Language*. It isn't there.

My heart starts to pound. Was it Buzzcut? Did he rifle through my books during my brief period of unconsciousness? I couldn't imagine it. Buzzcut was a bully, but not a plunderer. Who else? The Mexican lady said I was out for "tres minutos." Did someone at Volunteer Veterans remove the precious book in those three minutes? Who among the shoe-gatherers and salvagers-of-ancient-keyboards would have known that this was the pay-dirt book?

Is anything else missing? I try to visualize the original treasure. My copy of *Value Investing* with the birthday inscription to Robert is here. The various ten-dollar spiritual books seem to be here.

Maybe Helmet Head. He might have had time before Doreen went outside to lock my car. He is the most viable suspect.

Oops. Where is *The Old Man and the Sea* that I got for Caleb?

I don't see it. It's not there. This doesn't make sense. If two valuable books were missing, then I would suspect foul play. But a valuable book and a worthless book? A current textbook with a high Amazon ranking and a ubiquitous old novel? There is too much randomness here to ascribe purpose. Hmm...Wouldn't that phrase go nicely on my epitaph?

Chapter 8

On March 14, 2000 the total value of outstanding shares of Priceline.com hit $17.7 billion. At its close of $131 a share, that made the startup airline ticket seller worth more than American, Delta and United Airlines combined. Remarkably, Priceline was selling a paltry $40 million a year in tickets, and losing money on every ticket it sold. Its total physical assets consisted of a few rooms full of computers and a few floors of eager twenty-somethings — callow and overpaid MBAs and computer nerds. Its IPO, which was originally issued at $16, finished its inaugural day up 425 percent at $68. Was it worth $16 or $68 or today's $131? Clearly it continued to have value if you owned the shares and there was some naive optimist willing to pay more than you had paid. In every transaction, there had to be a greater fool.

On Colonial Avenue two blocks down from our sturdy Mormon house was a glass, spruce-and-white-stucco, modern cube-on-cube structure with a Japanese garden in front. Protruding noisily among the mostly postwar bungalows that lined the street, it was a sign of the rising tide of gentrification. The old timers on the block thought it was pug-ugly. Most contemporary houses on this side of town are the cynical postmodern aberrations that refer only to the irony of modern materials — turrets made of chain link and that sort of thing — and not their beauty. This house was elegant and classically formed with Bauhaus simplicity. Through the large windows I could see a white Saarinen tulip table and matching chairs. I admired the house and wondered who lived there.

A sports car usually sat underneath a fitted green cover parked in the driveway. I intuited from its curvy shape and wire wheels that it was a Jaguar XKE. It was sexy under wraps, like Charlize Theron in a bathrobe. One spring day in 2000, I left the office early and drove my new Volvo down Colonial Avenue toward our house, eager to get back to True and Caleb. I noticed a shiny, bulbous powerboat shoehorned onto a galvanized trailer in front of the modern house. A man in his early forties, nicely tanned, with a neatly cropped beard and wearing Nike sandals, cargo shorts and a French T-shirt was hosing it down. From its telltale *w* hull shape I knew that it was a Boston Whaler, a vaunted and expensive East Coast fisherman's craft with a walk-around cabin and a flybridge. Two giant new Yamaha V6 outboards hung off the transom. The fiberglass topsides gleamed and water from the hose formed droplets over the heavy wax that remains after new boats are popped out of the mold. I slowed to admire it.

The man lowered the hose in deference to me and the Volvo. I came to a stop and lowered the passenger side window.

"Nice boat. Is it new?" I called through the window with a neighborly smile.

"Came in yesterday. Two months on back order."

"Thirty feet?"

"Twenty-nine six," he replied. An accurate estimation of a boat's size is a secret handshake of fraternity between boat owners. His look became welcoming as I admired the Whaler. I would guess it cost close to a hundred grand.

"They just trucked it out," he said. "The factory's in Florida now. Brunswick bought 'em out, but they're still all-hand laid up like they used to be in Massachusetts. You fish?"

"Not really. Occasional trip to Cabo. I'm more of a rag man." He nodded as I patronized him with the vernacular that power boaters use for a sailor but that sailors never use among themselves. "I live on the next block," I added. "Mitchell Fourchette."

"Chuck Firestone."

Firestone? Was he a tiremaker heir? He had the aura of old money about him. That would explain the house and the toys although Bel Air or Hancock Park would be a more likely venue for a real Firestone.

I stepped out of the car to fully take in the Whaler. He seemed pleased to share its features—the composite, hand-laid, foam-cored fiberglass hull, the self-bailing cockpit, the twenty-four-gallon bait tank and the patented Boston Whaler "reverse-chine" bottom design. We climbed aboard to check out the pressurized hot and cold water and the thirteen interior lights. Belowdecks reeked of the acrid smell of new fiberglass. I admired the teak cabin sole and then I remembered that Caleb was home waiting for me to go biking with him. I thanked Chuck and left.

The following weekend while I was reading the *New York Times* and True was feeding Caleb lunch in the kitchen, there was an unexpected knock on the front door. I opened it to find Chuck on the doorstep.

"I spotted your Volvo in the driveway so I figured this was your place. You wouldn't happen to have a couple of hours? I had a new instrument package put on the Whaler and wanted to check it out, so I'm looking for somebody who can drive while I play with the calibration."

I had been looking forward to the Sunday paper and my family, but the notion of planting myself atop the flybridge and commanding the resonant power of the twin Yamahas was seductive.

True and I had plans to go to the farmers market, but she seemed pleased for me and Chuck assured her that we'd be back before noon. He said he had already put the boat in the water and it was tied up at a public dock.

I would have liked to take Caleb. I knew it would be a thrill for a six-year-old to ride on the big boat. But calibrating nautical instruments was serious, grown-up work and Caleb would be a distraction so I didn't ask Chuck if Caleb could go along.

The ride over to the marina in Chuck's big, fully optioned, leather-scented Chevy Suburban didn't take long—just enough time to move along the rudiments of acquaintanceship. I could hear in his voice the familiar cadence and tone of Eastern society—maybe Long Island.

"So where do you work, Mitchell?"

"I'm a creative exec at Sather and Knowlton. They're an ad agency."

"What are you working on?"

"Trek bicycles is our major account these days. What about you?"

"Humble stockbroker."

"Where?"

"Just a little independent brokerage in Century City. We do mostly money management on a few big accounts and some trading for the house."

"That sounds good."

"Yeah. I used to toil in the fields at Merrill Lynch in New York and this is a lot more satisfying."

"And the market's good." I added with a conspiratorial smile.

"Boston Whaler good."

The boat was tied to the public dock with rope so new and supple that it felt like cashmere. Powerboats have about the same appeal to a sailor as motorcycles have to a sports car owner—they're a quick thrill, but nothing you'd want to indulge in long term. Anyone who chooses to spend more than an hour or so pounding his kidneys on the afternoon chop has to be a masochist. Chuck's offer for a brief go-round seemed perfect.

We set out into the channel that leads into Santa Monica Bay. The boat had a speedometer (in marine parlance a "knot meter") that uses a tiny paddlewheel under the boat to measure the speed of water rushing by. It also had GPS that could read out speed. Both systems are subject to minor inaccuracies. The paddlewheel needs to be calibrated to be trusted, and one can do it either by comparing it to the GPS readout (not accurate after the first decimal point), or by running a course of a fixed length using a stopwatch to measure time in both directions and then computing the speed in knots by dividing seconds into nautical miles. The timed mile is the failsafe mariner's method, and since proper boating is a celebration of obsessive compulsion, we were going to run the half-mile fixed course marked by poles on the rocks of the channel breakwater and convert time and distance into speed.

My job was easy. He ran the stopwatch and called the marks while I steered a straight line and watched to keep the knot meter at a steady 5.00 knots. We did six passes. He adjusted the instrument on the first four and the last two were confirmatory.

He acted diffident about his background, but after breaking the ice and telling him of my Eastern roots, I learned that he was raised in Greenwich, and had gone to Deerfield Academy and to Dartmouth.

"Deerfield was good for me," he confided. "I still have friends from Deerfield. I don't have a lot of fondness left for Dartmouth."

Chuck didn't say whether he was a descendent of tire maker Harvey Firestone and I wasn't about to ask. I think I remember that the Firestones gave to Princeton and not Dartmouth.

In Chuck's presence I felt a pang of the same discomfort I remember as a nominal black person at Hotchkiss School—an insider and outsider at the same time. Privileged by having attended one of the East's most prestigious prep schools but always feeling the uneasy guest.

Afterward Chuck invited me for a quick drink at the bar of the California Yacht Club in the Marina where he had a membership. Among a spattering of well-to-do nautical barflies in a milieu of captain's chairs with polished brass name plaques, trophy cases and yacht club burgees he managed an air of elite diffidence to the surroundings.

"What kind of clients do you have?" I asked him.

"They're pretty dull, really. We don't take management accounts under a half mil and we only do it if we totally control all the transactions, so it keeps the loudmouths and bozos pretty much at bay. It's mostly older clients with too much money who are looking for a good return without getting their hands dirty."

"Well, I bet they're happy now."

"Even in a good market, we always outperform so the answer is yes. And we have our own company portfolio which is doing quite well. Everybody in the market is a winner these days which naturally makes me nervous. You invested?" he asked.

Of course I was invested. The bartender was invested. The parking lot attendant was invested. In 1999, everyone was invested. And we were all pleased as punch with ourselves. It was like being a Chicago Bulls fan in the Michael Jordan days.

"A little bit," I said with false modesty. "Pick and shovel tech companies. Medium caps mostly."

"That's good." He nodded paternally. "You making out?"

"I'm doing fine." I tried to mask how terribly proud I was of myself. I was doing fan-fucking-tastic.

"You know I shouldn't say this—"

"No, that's okay."

"Look. Take it for what it's worth. It's a rising market. And it will probably keep on going for a while. But it's not going to last forever."

"I know that." I thought I did. It had always been part of my plan to take my original stake off the table and play with winnings only.

"I know everybody and his brother is making money right now just like I am. But in the end it's really an insider's game. And I don't mean just logging on to *stocksynergy.com* and pimping for stock tips. It's fat right now and everybody's feeling good. But when it gets thinner, you'll be playing against guys in the know, guys like me, and it could get tougher. It will get ugly."

"I appreciate that." (Note to myself, what is *stocksynergy. com*?)

"I shouldn't have said anything. It's just that I like you. It looks like you've got a great family. I wouldn't want to see you get hurt."

"I'll be careful."

"Enough said. My partners call me Eeyore."

I got home in time to accompany Caleb on a short bike ride around the block. True made sure his little helmet was fastened tight before we left and stayed home to cook dinner. Caleb and I rode down Wasatch Street, right on Colonial, right again on Palms and then back home. When a poodle barked at us from behind a fence Caleb was startled for a second, then giggly.

Chapter 9

I see Nick's car parked outside of Book Trader in Redondo Beach. I want to talk to him and I pull into a parking space nearby. Book Trader is a storefront on a narrow street in an area with lots of surf and motorcycle shops. It is one of the few book stores that have survived since Borders and Barnes & Noble and, later, Amazon devoured what was left of the independent bookstores landscape. I look over the two-dollar used-book rack out front and quickly find a book on yoga I know I can sell for twelve dollars.

Online bookselling is one more predator nipping at the heels of brick-and-mortar stores, but Bunk Petersen, Book Trader's proprietor, has never been anything but kind and cordial to me. The same couldn't be said about his sister and partner, Sally.

"Hey, Ralph," Bunk greets me. "I heard something about you getting beat up in Anaheim."

Bunk is in his early sixties, but he approaches with his grip on a walker, the result of early onset Parkinson's.

"You okay?"

"Yeah. Just bruised and a little wiser."

"Nick's in the back. He told me."

"Yeah. I saw his car."

Bunk has boxes of books in a shed behind the store. He takes them in from long-established sources and sometimes doesn't even open the boxes before letting a few preferred online booksellers rummage through them.

He notices the book in my hand. "Find a treasure?"

The synergy of my relationship with Bunk is that he doesn't like selling online. As a bibliophile he finds no pleasure in the impersonal transaction. To him it's the difference between owning a restaurant and selling frozen dinners. Because he only carries clean and unmarked inventory and prefers to sell books

77

that actually interest him, a lot of titles that might bring good money on Amazon were chaff for him. This was our point of intersection.

For example, I can bring him a copy of *Frank Lloyd Wright: Inside and Out*, a nicely illustrated but common coffee table book on a tony subject worth only about six dollars online. Because it's such an appealing book, it will sell for twenty on Bunk's shelf. In exchange, he'll give me an unattractive accounting textbook that would never move in his store, but that I can sell for thirty.

"Hey, Ralphie," he says, putting down his book and walking toward the back, expecting me to follow. I do, passing through Sally's hard stare. She regards me and my business as a waste of her brother's valuable time. He goes to a stack of books on the floor near the back door, picks up a large book.

"You know this?"

It's a book of Miro lithographs. It says *Volume One*. There are three more volumes in the set underneath. I don't know it but I know I should.

"Where'd it come from?" I ask, unable to formulate a smarter question.

"An estate in Pasadena," he says. As an established and reputable dealer with a physical store, he has access to estate sales that I can't muster. The high-end estate brokers call Bunk to preview estate libraries because they trust him to pay a fair price. The sleazy brokers may look for someone who will kick back to them for a first look, but that isn't Bunk.

I thumb through the crisp pages.

"There are thirty-six original lithographs inside the set," he says. "That's where the value is." He is pleased to be my mentor.

I turn the heavy pages and stop on a full-page lithograph. The colors are bright and beautiful. The sharp image looks very much like Miros that I have seen in museums.

"Really nice," I say with conviction. He's pleased that I like it. I'm honored that he chooses to share it with me.

"I'm gonna go in back," I say.

I go out the back door and find Nick outside the metal shed foraging through a couple of moving boxes. I'm uneasy about my agenda. When I inquire about the missing books I don't want to seem suspicious of him, even if I am. Although we are friends, we understand the larcenous nature of the business, and our trust is layered over a bed of mistrust. Underneath I believe Nick is entirely capable of stealing another bookseller's books. In fact, I wondered later why he chose to announce when I was on his couch that he noticed that my car was open and that he hoped Helmet Head didn't take anything. Could that have been disingenuous of him? If so, the benefits of our relationship are still greater than the price of a few books. Let it lie for the moment.

As he digs through the boxes, Nick's constantly darting little eyes catch me before I speak. He looks briefly surprised, and then grins at me.

"Hey Ralph. How are you feeling?"

"I'm okay."

"That's good. Doreen was worried about you."

"No. I'm feeling a lot better. Thanks to you and her. I appreciate it."

Nick nods, reaches into a box and pulls out a small paperback, *Little Essays Toward Truth* by Aleister Crowley.

"What do you think?" he queries me. Everyone is a mentor today. That suits me fine. I pick it up and look at it. The copyright is ten years old. It's lightly worn. It doesn't look valuable. I know Crowley has some cachet among book collectors and early editions might be worth a lot, but he is in print in many editions and this one doesn't seem noteworthy.

"I don't know."

I pull out my phone.

"Not good enough, my friend. You won't find it in there."

I have a feature in my phone that allows me to quickly check the price of books by feeding it the title or ISBN number, but it's not very useful for antiquarian or first edition books. He places the book in a small pile he has started. Clearly he considers it to be of value and he'll negotiate with Bunk for it. I decide this is a good time to ask my question.

"Hey, so I'm missing some books."

"What are you talking about?"

"I think from my car. I'm thinking maybe Helmet Head took them...when my car was in your driveway. Remember, I forgot to lock it."

"What books?"

"I'm not sure. But I had a fifty-dollar textbook that was something like *Literature and Language* and a book about Sufis—"

"Sufis?"

"Yeah. You know. The religious sect?" He nods. I continue. "And a Heinrich Kley art book, but I don't think it was worth much."

"You think he took them?"

"I don't know. I'm sure I had them."

"You were pretty out of it, Ralphie."

"No. I know I had them."

"And that's it?"

"And an old copy of *The Old Man and the Sea.*"

"Hardback?"

I nod. I see from his eyes he's on to something.

"How old?" he continues.

"There are millions of old ones out there."

"You didn't look inside it?"

"I threw it in the box."

"You didn't look at the publisher's page?"

"No."

"What if it was a first?"

"It wasn't a first."

"It's a classic novel. You always have to look at the publisher's page. Always."

"I mean what are the chances?"

"Did it have a dust jacket?"

I nod.

"Fishing village on the front dust jacket?"

I nod again.

"Village in brown?" Yes again. "Cover is blue?" he goes on. "Uh-huh."

Nick continues to press.

"Was Hemingway's picture on the back of the dust jacket?"

"I don't remember. I think so. Maybe."

I look at him for guidance. I don't know if it's good or bad if Hemingway is on the back of the jacket. I have a sinking feeling.

"What color was the photo?"

"I don't know. Wasn't it black and white?"

"Was it tinted blue?"

"What do you mean, 'tinted blue'?"

"Not black and white. Had a bluish tinge."

"I don't know."

"Think."

I try to remember. When I picture the cover in my mind's eye, the photograph does indeed have a bluish cast.

"What if it did have a bluish tinge?"

He pauses a moment for effect, then says gravely, "If it had a bluish tinge, then it's a 1952 book and it's maybe gonna be a first."

"It wasn't a first edition," I say. I don't know what I prefer. Do I want to find out the book I had and lost was a first edition? "There are a million of them out there."

"Okay."

"I mean, what are the odds?"

"Was the picture blue?"

I think hard. I can see it in blue in my mind, but I don't know if I'm making it up.

Bunk ambles over from inside. Nick brings him up to speed.

"Ralphie found maybe a first edition *Old Man and the Sea* in Anaheim and Helmet Head stole it out of his car."

"We don't know it's a first edition," I say.

"If it's a first it'll have the Scribner's seal and a letter A on the publisher's page," Bunk offers.

"I never saw the publisher's page," I say.

"But why else would he bother to take it? Helmet Head knows books," Nick offers, shaking his head.

"No, he doesn't."

"He's a fucking iceberg, Ralphie. He's all under the surface."

"I won't let him in the store," says Bunk.

"I don't know that he took it," I protest.

"Fine. Forget I said it."

"What's a first edition go for these days?" I ask, trying to sound diffident.

"What was the condition?"

"I don't know. Pretty good."

"Dust jacket, too?"

"I don't think there were tears."

"First edition, first printing?" Bunk, now interested in the conversation, responds.

"Okay. Say first printing."

"You don't want to know," Bunk offers as he rolls his eyes.

"Near fine? No autograph or inscription? At least ten thousand," Nick says.

"Shit."

Sally appears at the back door. Bunk fills her in on the discussion. "Helmet Head stole a first edition Hemingway out of Ralphie's car."

"Oh no!"

"We don't know it was a first edition," I say. I know, however, that a book scout's myth is being born here and now, and that I am in no position to stop its momentum.

"We won't let him in the store. He's such a creep. What can you do? Can you call the police?"

"Good luck with that," says Nick with a sneer.

"Does anybody know where he lives?" I ask. Helmet Head knows where Nick lives. Maybe they have reciprocity.

"Probably under a bridge," says Bunk.

"Nobody knows," says Nick. "He just appears like a cockroach. What would you do if you knew where he lives anyway?"

"I don't know."

"There's a plan for you."

I look at my watch. I have to pick up Caleb.

Chapter 10

It was on a Monday at the agency that I was supposed to be thinking about a series of television spots for Carswell Automotive Group, a regional network of GM dealerships. Rick Carswell is its aggressive young owner. We usually shunted local and regional clients to smaller agencies, but Jerry Seligman, my boss and a senior VP at the agency, asked me to woo them. Carswell had just bought out dealerships in Santa Barbara and Palms Springs, and had a modicum of real cash to spend. Not only that, but Rick was a likely choice to be the next head of the GM Western Regional Dealers Association, a marketing cash cow now aligned with a competitor agency. Rick would be entrée into that account.

Rick's little empire had been started by his dad. In the sixties, Carswell père used to appear on local TV stations dressed up in a caveman costume standing in front of a line of cars with price stickers. He would announce the price and a buxom cave girl would exclaim to the camera, "Stan is such a wild man!"

No doubt Rick in his Italian suit carried some discomfiture about his heritage, although the car agency was doing undeniably well. He came to our firm because he was a fan of the slick Nissan national TV campaign that the agency had shot with a lot of cutting-edge visual effects in Monument Valley. At the end the car morphed into a puff of smoke. But Rick was savvy enough to know that Nissan's budget of four million for three thirty-second spots was clearly out of his reach. And paying even a fraction of that would make his dad spit up lunch in the clubhouse of his Palm Springs golf retirement community.

I liked Rick and I had anticipated the problem. We talked about it over lunch at Drago. He was right that he needed corporate-looking branding—he needed to tie the dealerships together and give the impression of trustworthy solidity without sacrificing the approachability and friendliness associated with a local agency. Anything cheesy would undermine that message. I had the agency's best artist rework their logo and I planned to hire a dulcet-toned public radio announcer to do narration that would emphasize Carswell's fifty years in the business. I knew a talented young director recently out of NYU Film School that would work for a quarter of what we paid the famous movie director that did the Nissan spot. There was a new computer graphics company that worked on inexpensive PCs that, for pocket change, could nearly approximate the wizardry of the Nissan ad. I had a strategy for ad buys on regional cable that would give him the most bang for the buck and groom him as a client. I was on my game.

Sitting in my office on Monday morning, while musing on a concept that would (as we in the ad business sometimes say) *whisper loudly* "Carswell Automotive Group," I thought about my encounter with Chuck Firestone. He may have had friends from Deerfield, but I was an uncomfortably shy teenager and had few remaining connections to Hotchkiss.

As a matter of policy, I think Hotchkiss would have preferred a darker shaded Negro than me. When I appeared for my admissions interview I could sense the interviewer's disappointment as he looked at my father's mocha skin and then at my lighter café-au-lait complexion. No doubt he was on the prowl for deeper browns to better offset the snowy whiteness of his crop of ninth graders. But my Scarsdale public school grades were good, my manners were well honed by proper parents, and there was a commendatory note in my file from the coach of the Hotchkiss sailing team (I was a local champion in Optimist dinghies at our yacht club and a Junior Olympian). Even better, Hotchkiss wouldn't need to dig into the scholarship fund, yet could still include me in their minority count.

If I had any doubt of how Hotchkiss regarded me, however, it was made clear when I arrived for the first day at my dorm, Coy Hall, an old, two-story, Spartan brick building. My roommate was already there and unpacked, sitting on his bed. His name was Elwood Johnson. He was from East Baltimore and his skin was a deep, dark brown-black. He looked at me in my polo shirt, khakis and Docksiders with a cocked, inquisitive grin.

"You a brother or what?"

"My dad is black."

"Well, I guess this here must be where they keep the niggers then."

It turned out that there were five black students counting myself in the incoming class of two hundred. The other three were given white roommates. I can't help but think that I was matched with Elwood as payment for the uppity insult of wearing a Brooks Brothers suit to my admissions meeting. My father was angry (what was the point of going to prep school except to further distance oneself from the Elwood Johnson sort of culture?) and wanted to speak to the headmaster to make him change my roommate, but my mother prevailed. She said she thought it might be a positive experience for me to have the opportunity to interact with a bona fide inner-city black person in totally safe surroundings. I think she didn't want to make waves.

Elwood was an "ABC" student, part of the "A Better Chance" scholarship program that was meant to troll for promising inner-city kids from dead-end environments and give them a leg up by putting them in prestigious prep schools. Andover, Exeter, St. Paul's, Groton and Hotchkiss were all subscribers.

Elwood had academic talents, but he was also a former junior member of a violent street gang called the Tree Top Pirus or "TTPs." His language and demeanor had a lot of the street in them. He said "axed" instead of "asked" and "nigger" was exponentially his favorite word although he was canny enough not to use it in class. He was a certifiable math genius. He had gotten an unheard-of perfect score on the SSAT prep school math entry exam and immediately was placed in senior calculus despite being also assigned to remedial writing classes.

Although he was a total fish-out-of-water, his social charisma was astonishing to me. Even the social register types fought each other off for his attention. He ran for freshman class vice-president and won. With the zeal of an ex-con telling scared-straight stories, he regaled wide-eyed preppies with tales of drug dealing and revenge killings in the streets of East Baltimore. I wondered how much was actually true. Although I made the varsity sailing team, garnered a coterie of sailing friends and was middling social, he was the shining star of Coy Hall room 18.

One day when I came home late from a sailing regatta in New London I found him sprawled senseless on his bed. A paper bag and several tubes of airplane glue were on the floor. I was afraid he was dead or comatose and I shook him vigorously. He woke up with a start.

"What the fuck, man?"

"Are you okay?"

Clearly from his vacant eyes he wasn't, but he shrugged and denied.

"What the fuck? I'm fine."

Although some of the younger kids sometimes smoked pot in the woods behind the school and I had heard a few stories of cocaine among upperclassmen, glue-sniffing was acknowledged by everyone as both dangerous and déclassé.

Elwood looked down and saw the empty tubes of glue and the paper bag and clumsily gathered them up. He and I both knew that Hotchkiss has an ironclad honor code and that if I didn't report him I could be expelled.

This may surprise you considering my current state of moral laxity, but I took the school honor code very seriously. Not just because of the expulsion threat, but because the simplicity of the code relieved me of the burdens of equivocation. As a junior sailor, one is expected to act in a "Corinthian" manner. If one breaks a sailing rule while racing, it is one's duty to notify the race committee. Some racers do. Some don't. When I was eleven years old, I was leading the pack of thirty Optimist dinghies in the final big race of the season, the Long Island Sound regional junior championship. While rounding a mark of the course, a large inflatable buoy, my rudder just barely kissed the mark as it bobbed up on a swell. Nobody saw the infraction but me. Without hesitating I chose to re-round the mark, losing twelve places in the race and thereby losing the champion's trophy. I was devastated to lose the championship, but content with my decision not to burst my moral boundaries. I was not a perfect young man, but even at that young age I understood the lasting comfort and strength one derives from following the rules and doing the right thing, even when nobody is watching.

"If you tell anybody about this I will kill you. That is not pussy-preppie-repp-tie chitchat. I will fucking come at you, Oreo, and I will kill you. You know this is true."

Nobody had ever called me Oreo before. I think of myself as more homogenized than an Oreo—more like a maple cookie.

Did I think he would really kill me? Probably not. Maybe. Was he scarier than the honor code? No question. Might he have benefitted from a drug intervention brought on by my betrayal? Possibly. Nevertheless I kept my mouth shut, reluctantly ignored the honor code and lived. I also applied for a single room and when a diplomat's son transferred to school in England, my name came up on the waiting list. When Elwood didn't return for sophomore year it turned out that in his summer at home in Baltimore he was involved in a dispute with a rival gang and was caught nearby in a car full of guns shortly after a drive-by shooting. When the school heard about it they sent a lawyer to petition that he be tried as a juvenile. The headmaster wrote a letter on his behalf. Because of the letter and a school-provided lawyer he was given probation while his less connected buddies went to jail. Hotchkiss at least had the good sense not to offer him his old spot in the class.

Still at my desk, I tried to banish thoughts of Elwood and concentrate on the NASDAQ account, but my mind had difficulty making the transition. As mind sorbet I checked my portfolio on the internet. Pretty much an average day in the market. NASDAQ was up about one and a half percent. An auspicious beginning to a ninth straight week of advances. I clicked on the view that would allow me to see how much each of my stocks had gone up.

Intel was up almost two points to $67. Apple, my new darling, had climbed three and a quarter to $80. Qualcomm was at $67. I bought it two months ago at $39. So far on this day I had made about three thousand dollars, several times what Sather and Knowles paid me. Perhaps I have been spending my hours at the wrong job.

Thoughts of watercraft filled my head. Not stubby, noisy, smoky powerboats but tall-masted, slender sailing yachts. I imagined my hands resting on the expansive, coxcombed wheel of a sixty-foot ketch. I experienced a familiar sense memory as little kicks of water turbulence fed back to the wheel from the rudder below, like a baby sending signals from the womb to a pregnant mother.

I reached for my keyboard.

I remembered what Chuck had told me and typed in the URL for www.stocksynergy.com. The home page was straightforward but not artful and littered with box ads for investment newsletters and portfolio gurus. I found topic headings that included "Big Board," "NASDAQ," "Penny Stocks," and "Mutual Funds." I chose NASDAQ which led me to an A-Z menu for names of stocks. Just for fun I looked for activity on the Intel forum.

From: Wavygravy
Subject: Intel Mid-Day Line
Intel is up 4¼ from intraweek moving average and should cross
150 by the end of the month. Any pullback to under 120 and
I'm in.

That would be good. I got in at 70. I've almost doubled. 150 would be more than doubling my money.

From: Biggercap
Subject: Intel Mid-Day Line
I don't expect to see it down to 120 again in my lifetime—until
of course when it splits! J

Splitting... That would be nice if it split.

From: Diddler
Subject: Intel Mid-Day Line
Intel is having a major problem delivering Celerons to Toshiba.
This is well known among friends who work for Toshiba America
and they are rejecting about 20% of the chips that Intel ships.

Maybe I should sell my Intel and take my profit. I had boasted to True that we had almost doubled our money in Intel. I didn't want to be made a liar to True. I could sell now and still be a hero in her eyes.

From: WallyW
Subject: Intel Mid-Day Line
You're behind the curve, Diddler. The Toshiba Celeron problem
is old news, reported in a bunch of chipmaker trade publications
two days ago. Toshiba is less than 1% of Intel's gross. I'm
looking at 180 by the summer and then a split.

To my mind credibility rested with WallyW. I decided to let my Intel ride for the moment.

Having dodged the Intel bullet I wandered to the J's. I had been eyeing JDS Uniphase. I didn't own any, but had been considering it. The upside was that it qualified as a pick-and-shovel company. In fact, it was even better than pick and shovel. It was infrastructure. Everybody knew that in a world of "convergence," where our computers and televisions and telephones were all to be part of the same system and reside in the same box, the delivery network was key. Broadband communications. Fiber optics. Exactly what the product was I couldn't tell you precisely, but I knew in my gut that JDSU was going to be one of the prime constructors of the internet superhighway, getting rid of those meddlesome bottlenecks. JDSU had the critical mass to command the market. Like Cisco did with routers. Remarkably enough, I could say the word "router" with such comfort to my office friends that I was almost convinced I knew what a router does.

While I had been modestly doubling my money in Intel, JDSU had skyrocketed from $15 to $150 in six months. And now it was about to eat its competition, with a plan to buy its smaller rival, SDL. Of course I knew it was volatile compared to the stocks I had been buying, but look what a little risk taking had gotten me. Larger risk could mean only larger rewards.

I pulled up the Seymour Schein Investments page. I used Seymour Schein because it was a ubiquitous, hungry, booming national discount brokerage and trades were much cheaper than traditional brokers like Merrill Lynch and Morgan Stanley. I logged in with ID (Adman) and password (utopia). (Don't bother to try them—the account is long dead.) Other passwords I have used are destiny, salvation and resurgence.

JDSU was down four points at $194⅛. A sign of weakness or a dip and perhaps a buying opportunity? I checked the consensus of analysts' reports. Of fourteen analysts following the stock, twelve thought it was a "strong buy" and two worrywarts thought it was just a "buy." Nobody advocated "hold" or "sell." The six-month target price was $250, but this was an era when targets were always moving, and always moving upward.

There was only seven thousand dollars in the cash account, and to add to it would mean that I would need to get True to cosign a draft from our bank to the brokerage. But I had a margin account which meant I could automatically borrow money from Schein to buy using my equity in the stock as collateral. A hundred shares would cost over twelve thousand but I didn't have to put it all up. I had a good feeling about JDSU.

I put in a good-until-cancelled margin order for a hundred and fifty shares at $102—five dollars under the current price, hoping that the train hadn't already left and JDSU might never see $192 again.

Two hours later, I was straining to noodle a Carswell TV ad concept, but all that came to mind was young Rick Carswell dressed in his dad's caveman costume.

An email from Schein popped on my screen informing me that my order for three hundred shares had been filled at $191¾. I abandoned Carswell immediately to go to the Schein website to check the current price. When I found it was now down to $188 I got a pinched feeling in my gut.

Chapter 11

I muse about Hemingway in Cuba as I sit parked in the pickup line at Jefferson School. True drops Caleb off in the morning on Thursday (our switch day) and I pick him up in the afternoon. That way we don't have to see each other during the handoff. Sunday mornings, when I drop him off at her house on Colonial Street, are more awkward. I park in the driveway and let Caleb out, making sure that he has all of his school things in his backpack, and then I watch him go to the front door and ring the bell. True gives him a big showy hug without a glance in my direction. I know she'll quiz him later on what we did together. If we went to the Space Museum, she'll suspect I'm pandering and trying to buy his allegiance. If I take him to odd neighborhoods with me while I look for garage sale books, she'll enter into her scorecard one more affirmation of my neglect.

I doubt that Hemingway waited to retrieve his children after school. I read that one of his three boys became a transsexual. That would be fitting payback to homophobe "Papa" for spending his time dodging bulls in Pamplona and fighting marlin off Key West rather than showing up early like me for a good spot in the K-3 pickup line.

Jefferson School turns out to be not so bad. Caleb's kindergarten teacher, Mrs. Mirisch, took a liking to my shy and well-mannered little boy. Also, a resolute new principal is running a turnaround operation. Under her leadership the school has been cleaned up, largely with co-opted neighborhood parent labor and money. I spent a Saturday with Caleb and families painting away graffiti on the cinderblock wall of the school that faces the back alley. I contributed some large and shiny books to the school flea market to be sold for a dollar or two each and received the nodding approbation of the PTA chairwoman.

The school bell rings at three on the button and, five seconds later (I instinctively count down from the sound of the bell), I hear the crescendo of youngsters scrambling headlong to the school perimeter. I spot Caleb in the throng. His eyes search and then land on the Volvo. With a broad grin he radiates primal pleasure as he sees me. He runs akimbo toward the car. I get out and greet him with a fatherly caress on the shoulder, open the car door for him. He has a slender face with nicely chiseled, delicate features and rich dark brown eyes. His complexion is fair like True's family but I gave him his soulful dark eyes.

He holds something he made out of a paper plate. I can't quite make out what it is supposed to be, but it has eyes, a mouth and pointy yellow cardboard ears glued on at ten o'clock and two o'clock.

"It's a owl," he says as he offers it proudly to me and I examine it.

"*An* owl," I correct him with a paternal smile.

"*An* owl," he parrots back. Someday he will be a teenager and resent being corrected by his dad.

"Can I put it on the wall?" I ask.

"Which wall?"

"Where we eat. Near the table."

"Okay."

"If you want. I could do a better one."

"I like this one."

"Then you can have it," he says with a shy blush.

"Thank you." I take it from him and place it carefully on the back seat of the Volvo.

I help him buckle his seat belt, making sure it doesn't catch him under the neck. I quickly flush from my mind the potential consequences of a collision with the seat belt riding under his neck. Caleb's lifeless body, a deep purple bruise under his Adam's apple flits through my brain. Sometimes it is as if my thought path wanders through the hallways of a suburban multiplex theater and from the dark hall I mistakenly stumble into the theater that shows a grizzly slasher movie on the screen above me. I look up at the screen where I see heads are being lopped off, race to the exit and then I must ploddingly retrace my way through the labyrinthine gray hallway to the light romantic comedy for which I bought a ticket.

"T-ball at four," I say. I know he won't be pleased. Caleb is not an athlete. For that matter, except for sailing, neither am I. He doesn't complain, which only makes me feel like more of a bully for dragging him to this court of scant pleasure. But it is in his best interest I tell myself. Caleb needs to coordinate his young reflexes and he must learn the team ethic to prepare him for high school, because as we all are painfully aware, high school is the last stop in social progress.

"Can we get Twisters?" he asks. He believes he is doing me a giant favor by going to T-ball and the Twister is his *quid pro quo*.

No need to negotiate. I'm proud that he prefers an original Twister (soft-serve ice cream mixed in a blender with your choice of cookie and candy pieces) at funky old Foster's Freeze to the poseur McFlurry at McDonald's. What can I say? He is an old soul.

At the park ballfield on the industrial edge of town, sated after having had a medium Twister with Reese's Peanut Butter Cups and Oreos mixed in, Caleb is pushed into the on-deck circle by his coach for the Santa Monica Meridians (the local appliance dealer who initially bankrolled the uniforms chose the team name for an inexplicable reason). Nearly all T-ball batters will get on base as six-year-old infielders rarely can make the throw to first for an out. Since the ball sits on top of a tee, there are no strikeouts. To make sure the game ends finitely, the rules dictate that the inning is finished after each player has had one turn at bat. The first kid at bat on Caleb's team pops one past a napping shortstop and he's at second base in a flash.

When it is Caleb's turn (near the end of the roster) he dribbles a small grounder down the first base line directly to the first baseman who traps it and touches the bag. Caleb doesn't seem to be bothered at all when he's called out and returns to the bench wearing a benign, goofy smile. Whether it turns out to be an asset or a liability for him in his life, it seems he will not be tortured by the remorse and recrimination that dog a man with a fiercely competitive nature.

The last member of his roster dinks a single, but the inning is over nonetheless. To his credit, Caleb looks around and notices his teammates putting on gloves. He finds the flimsy, Chinese-made fielder's glove I bought for him in the sale bin at Big 5 and ambles distractedly out to deep left field where he is left-fielder number two. An eleven man T-ball roster allows for two players to cover each of three sections of the outfield (there is no pitcher), and the coach places Caleb far enough back that he would never actually come in contact with a live ball unless Barry Bonds were to arrive at the plate (or should I say "tee"). Caleb is perfectly pleased not to have the performance anxiety that would accompany any real possibility of having to field a ball and throw it to one of the bases.

Left-fielder number one, the son of a litigator, crouches with cheetah-like attention. He is ready to attack any long balls that might come his way and to incidentally cover any territory that might remotely be considered Caleb's (for the sake of the team, of course). My progeny looks up at the sky, perhaps scanning for birds in flight, then down to the ground, maybe looking for odd crawly things. Then he picks absently at a scab on his wrist. All the while he is completely unmindful of the young batter about to address the ball that sits poised at the top of the 30-inch tee.

I am on the peeling bleachers and settle in for a long inning. By choice I am at the end of an empty row, distanced from a gregarious gaggle of parents and their condescending suggestions about how I might work with Caleb to help him build confidence. I could never explain without sounding neglectful that Caleb's approach to T-ball is not simply a matter of confidence. I tried explaining his gentle spirit once to a beefy sportsmother as she nodded in a patronizing way that was code to me as mock sympathy for Caleb's incipient gayness.

Fortune smiles on Caleb as only a couple of Jaguar batters manage to get past the infield. One well-hit ball is easily scooped up by the litigator's son who throws smartly to third base where the uncoordinated Meridian third baseman bobbles it and the runner, at the insistence of an overwrought parent acting as third base coach, trots home for what must have been the fortieth run. There is no scoreboard but the parents on the other end of the bleachers assiduously keep the tally.

When the last hitter on the other team hits a bouncing single, the inning is over. The Jaguars, our estimable opponents, slide on their gloves and head out to the field as the Meridians trot in. Except Caleb, who simply stands there. He remains in place as the Jaguars left-fielder number two takes his position next to him. Parents titter. I feign unconcern under their sideways glances. The coach, Larry, a pleasant-enough, out-of-work sitcom writer, yells out to him.

"Hey Caleb!"

Caleb looks at him, but stands statue motionless.

"Time to bat!" Larry yells good-naturedly.

This time Caleb shakes his head in the negative, holding his body straight like a stick.

"Caleb? Come on in, kiddo!"

Caleb stands his ground. The Jaguars coach looks impatiently to Larry. I watch as Larry sighs and walks out in Caleb's direction. Caleb hasn't moved, even with the apparent urging of the rival second left-fielder. I hear a mother's whisper in the bleachers next to me.

"Maybe he peed his pants."

I want to tell her that Caleb has a very strong bladder. Perhaps there are bladder control problems in her family, but not in ours. Not that I know of. Larry reaches Caleb, and says something to him, but Caleb shakes his head. Larry looks imploringly to the stands, finds me. Under the gaze of the team and the other parents I walk from the bleachers onto the field. When I reach Caleb, Larry and the other young fielder back off to give us some father-son space.

"You okay, Caleb?"

No response.

"Your team's at bat. You're supposed to come in."

"There's a bee," he says with a look of panic and urgency.

"What?"

"There's a bee."

"Where?"

"Out here."

"Where?" I look around and don't see a bee.

"He was here."

"He must be gone."

Caleb isn't a particularly fearful child, although this must make him sound that way. Up to this moment I didn't know that he was afraid of bees. He has never been stung to the best of my knowledge. He is phobic about needles and I suppose that bees similarly have something sharp that violates your epidermis.

"If he was here, he's gone now."

"He's here! He's here!"

"You can't stay here, Caleb."

"Yes I can!"

"Do you want me to carry you in?"

I ask this question only to prod him to move. But he doesn't respond, just looks up hopefully, wide-eyed.

"Do you want me to carry you in front of everybody?"

He nods. "Yes."

"Really?" I ask.

"Yes."

If he can stand the humiliation, why can't I? I look at the tittering parents, at his giggling teammates, at the impatient coach. I reach out my arms and Caleb grabs immediately and firmly. I hoist him up and carry him off. When we arrive at the dugout he seems pleased and proud that his Dad had been there for him as he announces to his teammates with wide-eyed wonder, "There was a big bee out there."

I retreat to the bleachers and stand on the side, not wanting to sit. A couple of mothers regard me with feigned empathy.

"There's a big bee out there," I call to them. I turn to watch Caleb as he waits his turn at bat. I wonder where he carries his shame. Certainly not where I can see it. I admire him.

Back in the apartment after the game Caleb settles in on pasta shells with meat sauce, a favorite of his. I make them with a little bit of fresh Italian sweet sausage. The rest is Ragu and Ronzoni and a sprinkle of basil from a spice tin. Usually I make a point of sitting down with Caleb for a facsimile of a family meal, but tonight he sits on the floor in front of the TV and watches cartoons as I go to my computer to satisfy my nagging curiosity.

My business model doesn't include antiquarian books. Hard-to-find books are my meat and potatoes. A relatively obscure text on aerodynamics, culled for a few dollars from the estate sale of an engineer who once worked for Douglas Aircraft, for example, might sell for a hundred dollars, although I can't say the trade in these kinds of books is brisk. Amazon, where I sell, is a good place to buy and sell hard-to-find books. Signed and antiquarian books, however, are best sold elsewhere, either at venerable auction houses like Sotheby's or Pacific Book Auctions, or by reputable dealers with small storefronts in quiet neighborhoods. There are websites that specialize in valuable books, but mostly they allow dealers with actual physical stores to list their wares online. Who wants to buy a very old, very expensive book from an email address?

Typing *www.addall.com* produces a master list of rare books from many individual bookselling websites. In the parlance of cyberspace, this cornucopian indexing is called a *metasearch*. It parallels the workings of the mind, very much like a depressed person who might gather all the indignities and humiliation of his or her experience and conjoin them into an all-encompassing funk. In this particular area of computation, Microsoft would have to take a backseat to my personal operating system.

The web form appears. I know the drill. I put "Ernest Hemingway" in the author box, "*The Old Man and the Sea*" in the title box, and "first edition 1952" in the keyword box. I wait for twenty seconds while holding my breath. Suddenly there is a list of books with prices. Here's one:

> *US First Edition; First Printing, Hard Cover, 8vo, Good in good dust jacket. New York, NY, U.S.A.: Charles Scribner's Sons, 1952. An exceptional, crisp First Edition/First Printing copy in good condition with some spine sunning, crisp dust-jacket with much less browning and chipping than usually seen, a rather minute closed tear in the back, showing the original price of 3.00 and bearing Hemingway's blue tinted portrait on the back.*

"Rather minute?" Give me a fucking break. Are you trying to sound British? Try "small." Try telling the consumer the actual length of the tear, you fraud. Anyway, the big question—"how much?" BOING BOING BOING.

EIGHT THOUSAND, SEVEN HUNDRED AND FIFTY DOLLARS.

Jesus! Okay! Wait. Here's another.

> *NY: Scribner, 1952 F Hardcover Dust Jacket Included Published in New York by Charles Scribner's Sons in 1952. First Edition, contains capital "A" and seal on copyright page which refers to first edition. Book fine except for slight wearing on corners and spine ends. DJ near fine except for wearing at corners, spine ends, and joints, slight fading and discoloration on covers, spine, and flaps. DJ price reads $3.00.*

How much?

NINE THOUSAND FIVE HUNDRED DOLLARS!!

There's more. If it's flat-signed (Hemingway's signature by itself) it's worth fifteen thousand. If it's a good presentation copy (personally inscribed, best to a famous person) it can be worth thirty thousand. I never thought to look inside the book. It could have been signed. This cannot just pass.

I normally avoid Helmet Head. If, on a Saturday morning when I am cruising garage sales, I see his decrepit motorbike leaning precariously on its kickstand with plastic shopping bags dangling from the handlebars, I move on. He's never not trouble.

At a church rummage sale he will shove to the front of the line of people waiting to get in when they open the gate. When the sale begins he pushes his way to the books and elbows away anyone bold enough to get close to him. He then grabs big armfuls of books and dumps them in a pile in a corner. He doesn't have a smartphone price scanner (HH having a price scanner would be the book scouting equivalent of Uzbekistan having the H-bomb) so he slowly studies and sorts the books that he has cached, outlasting anyone else who might have an interest in one of his selections. An hour later when the initial flurry of customers has subsided and he has made his final selections, he leaves his discards scattered willy-nilly on the ground and takes his purchase to the cashier. That's where the real fun starts.

"Look, this one has a coffee stain on the first page here," he will exclaim as he flashes the book in front of the blue-haired church lady cashier.

Used to dealing with the tireless haggling of old Russian babushkas she may not be easily fazed by a would-be negotiator. Her mistake.

"Well, they're two dollars each, and if you don't want it, that's fine. You can just put it back."

But that's not where it ends. Not with HH. "And this one's

got scotch tape marks on the back cover. At Saint Anne's they only charge a dollar a book, but these books all have problems and you're charging twice as much."

"As I say, you don't have to buy them." She tries to look away from him, toward the next customer. Of course there's a line building up behind him, and people in line are rolling their eyes to each other. That's only encouragement for Helmet Head.

"How about ten dollars for the pile?"

"There's fifteen books there."

"They're junk books."

"Some people will want them. Nobody is telling you to buy."

He holds up a book and waves it.

"Do you actually think this book is worth two bucks? I thought the Methodist church was supposed to be honorable."

"There are people waiting here."

"Do you think it's fair for a place of God to ask two bucks for a book that's full of coffee stains?"

"I'm sorry. We have one price."

"Well how much do you think it's worth?" He leans over the table and his halitosis wafts over her.

"I think it's worth two dollars. If you don't—"

He reaches for his wallet and slaps a ten and a five on the table.

"Fifteen dollars. Okay? That's fair."

Here's the thing—half the time the woman will take the offer. Just to get him out of there. There are people waiting and he's scary and he smells. And if she doesn't take it, he'll stay and harangue her until some brave guy from the church comes over and sticks out his chest and tells him to leave. Of course that isn't the end of it. HH won't leave on request or command.

"This sale is open to the public and I'm here to buy something," he insists. He continues to intimidate and wear them down. It's his playbook. Sometimes the only thing that ends it is a volunteer pulling out a cell phone and dialing 911. That elicits a final offer from HH. At that point, many find it easier to just accept. HH can then fill his plastic bags with books and ride off on his motorbike to his next victims.

What my esteemed peer actually does with his booty is a subject of speculation among booksellers. Where, for example, does he keep his stock? Is there a landlord that actually rents to him? Does he have a computer and an internet line? If he just resold his books to the local bookshops, we would all know about it, so he must sell online, but not even Nick knows if he sells on Amazon or eBay or Alibris or what. He is a mystery wrapped in an enigma wrapped in a scuffed helmet and dirty leather jacket.

Chapter 12

The *buy and hold* stock strategy works only if you accept the basic premise of markets. If you choose to buy 100 shares of Apple listed at $34, a seller is glad to unload 100 shares at $34. It is the equilibrium of the desire of one person to buy and the desire of another to sell. What you own is by its nature sensibly priced by a democratic market consensus that is, as a whole, better informed than you. Buying and holding implies that you have made a trade that is reasoned and conservative but optimistic and you are willing to stay tough through the sometimes cruel vicissitudes of the market with the belief that your company has lasting value and will ultimately prosper in a developed economic environment.

I believed that, as a couple, True and I would be classified as *buy and hold*. I was twenty-eight and True was twenty-six when we married. We are both acceptable-looking examples of our species, but not movie star material. We are average tall. I am six feet. True is five feet nine inches. Our educations were roughly equivalent; she has an advanced degree, but my BA came from Yale. Our values of family, honesty and worth came from the middle mainstream. Neither of us came to the partnership with more than a few thousand dollars of personal savings. My wound-up wit was countervailed by her easygoing candor. We loved each other. We felt we were made for each other. There is a part of me that despite everything still feels that way.

If you are a young man and you think that the woman you have won as your mate is somehow a spectacular deal, beyond your most optimistic expectations and not to be passed up, you have probably miscalculated. It is the nature of life's marketplace that a golden-haired woman with an alabaster tummy and perfectly poised breasts who holds her own on Ukiyo-e and Jimi Hendrix, plays a good game of tennis, and cavorts puckishly with her devoted golden retriever will ultimately reveal herself in other ways that will bring sense to the value of the original deal. Perhaps it will be a previously masked propensity to bipolar behavior, or an inability to bear children or a fear of travel. In coupling as in the NASDAQ, if it appears too good to be true it probably is.

Also, the principle of *buy and hold* presupposes a mature market whether applied to equities or to partners. In a different time one might have assumed that most people who participate weren't rash, ignorant or crazy. In the year 2000, when every supermarket checker and fry cook had an online trading account it was easy for anyone of middling substance like me to take on the confidence of an elder statesman. While in 1998 I might have been buying shares of AT&T or Johnson & Johnson whose prior owners might have included retirement funds and college endowments, in 2000 I could buy shares of a new technical incubator company that were previously owned by a Hollywood talent agent whose considered reason for selling was for a down payment on a Lamborghini. Conservative money managers would no doubt consider him a greater fool than me. I had a feeling of opportunity probably akin to that of a young capitalist in perestroika Russia at the awakening of the free markets. To those without vision who said at the time that the 2000 tech market was chimerical, I would say, "What isn't?" In 1999 the NASDAQ shot up 86 percent from January to December. Meanwhile some old-schoolers wondered how Cisco ($12 billion in sales and $2.1 billion in profit), for its fiscal year ended in July, could have a market capitalization as big as Exxon Mobil and Wal-Mart Stores combined ($350 billion in sales and $13 billion in profit).

There was a simple retort to the few remaining investment Luddites: Cisco and its techno-kin companies were growing at rates not seen since the beginning of the industrial revolution and one could no longer compare them to any classical model.

History was simply not a useful guide. Cisco had a mere $183 million in sales and about $40 million in profit in its 1991 fiscal year. Analysts predicted that by 2001, one decade later, its sales would be close to $25 billion and its profit better than $4 billion, a hundred-fold increase.

One didn't need to be a financial analyst. Investing in the market just required a willingness to understand and embrace the logarithmic nature of the rate of advance of technology. As proof of my point, the relatively conservative investments that I had made were bearing plump and delicious fruit. My JDSU had me worried when I bought it at $192, but it split again in the beginning of March and was now selling at $124 for a split share. I had made about $8000. Qualcomm, which I had purchased at $612 only a month earlier, had risen smoothly to $736 and then split at four for one. The diluted shares quickly rose to almost $200 and because of the leverage of my margin purchase I was up a quick $10,000 on just this one trade.

Trying not to be giddy, I decided that if the market were to show any signs of weakness, I would pull out my profits and buy a ten-year CD for Caleb's college fund. God knows how much Yale or Stanford would cost in 2016. Although I believed that in the long term the tech revolution would continue to buoy the market upward, I also considered that the market might get ahead of itself. I resolved to remain vigilant.

I bought True a small lapis pendant on a gold chain. Other than her wedding ring I had never bought her a single piece of jewelry. I had gotten her sweaters and a bicycle and flowers and other things, but jewelry was off our radar. For my taste those baubles had once seemed too small and too expensive. I saw the pendant in the window of an antique store on Montana Avenue when I was walking by. It was in an Art Nouveau style, which I knew True liked, and was striking with a shiny black background. It was a nice feeling to know that I could afford it. I walked in and asked the clerk to gift-wrap it without even mentioning the price ($600), as if I were some movie star or CEO. In return for my diffidence I was treated discretely and deferentially. It was exhilarating.

I presented my gift to True at breakfast the next day. She opened the box and her face lit up. I helped her put the chain around her neck and she streaked to the mirror in the front hall.

"It's gorgeous. It's just gorgeous."

"I'm glad you like it."

"This isn't about anything, is it? I mean you didn't do this because something's wrong."

"Of course not."

"You're not doing this because you've taken on a mistress?"

"You are my mistress."

"I know this was expensive."

"It's all relative."

"To what?"

"How much I have and how much I love you."

"And…"

"I love you a lot, and we've been doing well in the market."

"Well, I didn't do anything. You did all the work."

"Yeah, my back is a little sore."

"I am a little worried. If you're doing well, then you should put that money aside for our future."

"I will. I am."

"You swear."

"Of course I do."

That was my plan. To put the money aside for our future. No matter how much I made in the market. I didn't want anything to change. I wanted to continue working. I wanted True to be able to continue teaching or raise Caleb or both if she chose. I just wanted the security to be able to make decisions that weren't driven by money. How much money would be enough? We are not talking Malibu beachfront property and Ferraris. Just enough to know that things will be covered and that Caleb will never have to take care of us in our old age. I had a rough figure of two million, which could then be put into tax-free bonds and annuities. I didn't mean to stay in the market long term. I never had the hubris to think that I could win forever. A bull market can't last indefinitely. And that was why it was so important to act right away.

Peter Lynch, the celebrity fund manager and investment guru who drove the Fidelity Magellan fund to angelic heights, advised individual stock investors to buy businesses they understand. If your supermarket chain gives you better service than the other markets, perhaps you should buy some of their shares. If you think General Motors has a good-looking new lineup of cars, buy stock in GM.

Frankly, despite my newly minted expertise, Qualcomm and Cisco were difficult businesses to understand. Qualcomm made chips that had something to do with cell phones and communications. I knew that cell phones needed their chips. Cisco made routers. I knew routers are required for the internet, but I couldn't tell you why one router was better than another or that another company wouldn't come along and make a better router than Cisco and take away their business.

JDSU was another story. It built fiber-optic cabling for high speed data connections. Having swallowed up a dozen smaller companies in the last year they were the largest fiber optic company by far. As the internet continued to explode, the inevitability of the need for more bandwidth that could only be supplied by a new infrastructure of fiber optic cabling was a simple model to understand. Copper phone lines were incapable of handling that inevitable volume of traffic. Nobody else had the technology or the capitalization of JDSU. Everyone would have to come to them.

JDSU had traded as high as $137 after its last split. It was backtracking a little bit now and selling in the high 120s. This was clearly a good time to buy. With fifty thousand dollars invested I could control eight hundred shares.

I didn't want to make this big a step without informing True, though I was concerned that discussing it with her would make her uneasy. I would need her to cosign the withdrawal. I asked in bed that night. She had a book out and was preparing for her class the next day.

"I want to invest some more."

"Okay."

"I want to invest fifty thousand from the account."

"You mean fifty thousand besides what we've already invested?"

"Yes. I think we've done really well, but this is a good chance to get some money to put aside for Caleb's education."

"What if we lose it?"

"I don't think we will. But it's possible we could lose some. There are risks." Full disclosure was important and it helped to bind my own anxiety.

"That's a lot of money."

"I know." True doesn't respond and I fill the dead air. "But I wouldn't do this if I didn't think it was a good thing."

Another long pause and then she replied.

"Can I think about it?"

"Sure. But I do have my eye on one stock and timing is important."

"Okay. Just let me think about it in the morning. Will you take Caleb to preschool? I have to meet with a student before class."

"Okay. Do you want to know more?"

"No. I trust you. I just want to think about it tonight."

In the morning Caleb woke me up by jumping on the bed and giggling. True passed through the bedroom already dressed for school.

"I'm off. I want to beat the traffic. And Caleb needs breakfast."

"I want a waffle," said Caleb. The world started to come into focus for me.

"What about what we talked about last night?" I asked, hoping she hadn't forgotten.

"Okay."

"Okay what?"

"Okay do it. I trust you."

"That's all?"

"I don't know anything about the stock market and I guess that's because it really doesn't interest me. Half the faculty can't talk about anything else but how much money they've made in the market and sometimes I do feel a little jealous. I think you have better sense than any of them and I think you'll do fine."

"Do you want to know any more about it?"

"Just shower us with money. I have to go."

"I need you to cosign a check from the nest egg account."

"I have to go."

"I might want to buy today."

"I'm late. Sign my name. If you give him a waffle, make sure he eats fruit."

I can sign her name pretty well. I have probably done it a dozen times, always at her behest. True gave me a peck on the cheek, picked up Caleb for a big hug and a smooch, then grabbed her briefcase and disappeared out the door.

I made a toaster waffle for Caleb and put a cut-up orange on a plate. I also made him drink his milk. I had raisin bran. While Caleb waited for me at the door I pulled the Wells Fargo checkbook out of the desk and wrote a check for $50,000 to Seymour Schein Investments, signing first my name and then, using a cancelled check with her signature as a crib, signed True's name. I took Caleb to preschool and drove from there to the Seymour Schein Investments office in Century City where I deposited the check in my trading account, handing it to the woman behind the desk as if I handed out $50,000 checks all day. In turn she acted like she received them all day, scanned the bank code in a little reader and then entered the amount into her computer and gave me a receipt.

When I arrived at work I closed the door to my office and pulled up Schein on the computer screen. The Wells Fargo check had already been credited to my trading account. I searched for JDSU and found that it was trading at $125. That was a midpoint in its trading range from the last week, but overall it had trended down from its $135 plus range the week before. The stock was slightly depressed. The stats gave no indication why it was down but there is a tidal rhythm to stock prices.

My fear at that moment was that I might have hesitated too long. The trading day in New York was already half over. The ticker showed it selling at $126¾. I could buy it at market, which is ten dollars under yesterday's trading price, or I could try to eke out a few more dollars by specifying a good-until-cancelled lower price. If I was a day trader turning over huge volumes and making several trades a day, a dollar or two saved would be important. As a mid-term trader it wasn't as crucial. Nonetheless I decided that since it was True's and Caleb's money and I shouldn't be cavalier with it, I put in a good-until-cancelled order for 800 shares at a maximum of $122, a healthy, perhaps wishful, discount off the current ticker price. I half-expected it never to go down that low. Then I waited, trying to pay attention to my several messages from clients.

Immediately I wondered if maybe I should have just bought it at market price. What if it shot up to two hundred in another two weeks and then split again and I never bought in? My parsimony could cost me thousands. What if there was a piece of unexpected good news about JDSU on the ticker? It would climb from here and never get to $122 again. I logged into my account intending to mend by cheapskate ways, but at the very moment I logged in, my email dinged with a message from Schein. Its header was "Order Filled."

I navigated to my account and saw that indeed the buy went

through at $121 7/8. The good news was that I had owned it even cheaper than I had hoped. The bad news was that the stock had been moving downward so quickly that there wasn't enough of a pause on the way down to peg it at my $122 price. There were two and a half hours left in trading today. During that eternity I watched the stock travel down to a truly frightening $114 at noon and then move incrementally back up until at the closing bell it was $122¼—up twenty-five cents from purchase. Most importantly it closed while on the move up. That momentum was likely to continue at the opening of the market tomorrow.

But I tempered self-congratulation with humble resolve to be content with what fortune brought.

Chapter 13

The quality of the morning light in Santa Monica is defined not only by the stillness of the air before the sea breeze kicks in, but also by the angle of the sun. Fine particles of dust float undisturbed to subtly refract and reflect the golden early sunshine. I especially like the way it filters through the window onto Caleb as he eats granola with milk and peaches at the little table. I watch him from the kitchen where I engage in one of my favorite child care rituals—making him a sandwich for lunch. This is one of Caleb's several favorites—cheese and cranberries on whole wheat bread with a daub of sweet honey. I slice it, place it neatly inside a clear plastic sandwich bag and add it to his lunch box along with carrot sticks and a cup of yogurt.

I hustle him into the Volvo and take him to Jefferson School, collecting a sweet smack on the cheek before leaving him. It's Thursday and True will pick him up later. It is two hours until the thrift stores open, and I kill about an hour at Starbucks near the marina. Bicyclists tend to congregate there because of its proximity to the bike path, and I look forward to eyeing athletic young women in Lycra shorts. Of course it makes me horny, and that makes me think of Angela. I should wait for her to call. I know that if I can be patient there will be a voicemail in her little girl voice asking me what I am up to. I try not to call. It is better if I wait. I dial anyway. And then Angela's receptionist comes on the line.

"Westside Accounting Services. This is Stacy."

"Hi Stacy. It's Mitchell. Is Angela available?"

"Hi Mitchell. I'll see." I hear *Sex in the City* in Stacy's tone when she answers. Even though she's just eighteen and a student, I think Angela tells her saucy details about us. I imagine Stacy now holding up the phone to Angela, wiggling it and grinning, silently mouthing my name.

Angela has probably also confided to Stacy that Angela's ex-husband could never get her to orgasm. In fact, in the last year of her marriage, Angela's husband couldn't have an erection unless they went to a sleazy motel and watched porn first. Their marriage counselor essentially threw up her hands at the problem. Angela and Mr. Limp-Dick separated a year ago.

Since meeting me, Angela has been singularly orgasmic. Which is to say that she has one big orgasm, and then, like a drunken john, she flops over, panting and spent. I, however, need to work harder for my orgasms. I would say my average with Angela is the same as the median outfielder's batting average. But Angela is tall and sleek and athletic and beautiful. She does crunches at Gold's Gym for at least two hours a day and her stomach is flat like a teenager's, her butt is delectably tight, and she has firm, natural apple breasts.

"Mitchell. Don't you have other, important things you should be doing?" she teases.

She made the initial contact to me online from Match.com. Frankly, I was surprised. In her picture she was hiking with her dog on a trail at the top of Mulholland Drive. She had a bright smile. Her bio said that she likes the outdoors, Disney Hall and ethnic restaurants. What she neglected to mention is that she is clinically, pathologically, irretrievably passive-aggressive. It was a mistake for me to call first today. I will pay.

"I mean sometimes it is disturbing to me that you are so available."

Why do I subject myself to this transparent aggression? I think you can guess.

"I could try to make myself less available if that would please you." I sensed she liked it when I parried.

"I would always want you to be honest with me."

"Would you know?"

"With you, Mitchell, I would know."

"Do you want me to bring anything tonight?" I ask, desperate

114

to neuter the course of talk.

There is a long pause. As if to imply that she had forgotten, but I know her game. She hasn't forgotten. Space in talk is power for her. It is, however, my kryptonite. She out-waits me without half trying.

"It's Thursday." I can't keep myself from saying.

"Of course I know it's Thursday. It's 'big O' day. I have it on my calendar. There's an 'O' there. It's a big one." She is drawing me in with her charm preparing to land the sucker-punch. I try to forestall it.

"Do you want me to pick up something on the way over?" I often choose ingratiation as a weapon. There is some paradoxical power in that. I know already that she'll give me dinner, and she likes to take care of everything herself. Afterward we will together satisfy her needs and perhaps mine.

"No, don't do that. But Mitchell..."

"Yes." I can handle whatever she delivers. The body is worth it, and the company keeps me on my toes.

"Would you mind if I asked you not to wear the yellow shirt. The one you wore last week? I don't know, but for some reason it makes you look... I don't know"

"I won't wear it."

"Kind of smallish. I mean not that you are... Anyway I've got to go."

"I'll wear blue. That's bigger." But she has already hung up leaving me with nothing but a dial tone and a hard-on.

There are seven or eight thrift shops on the west side of the 405 Freeway and north of Washington Boulevard, which is the area I try to cover. Most open at ten, but new books are usually not on the shelves until later in the day.

The employees that run things are vaguely aware that some of the books might be valuable, but their knowledge is limited and, to the average twelve-stepper who sorts these things, a big coffee table book with pictures of custom Harleys or of fancy window treatments is what is valuable and will be marked up to seven or eight dollars. These remainder-table books are worth a couple of dollars on Amazon, but a small, soiled book about optics and prisms might be worth two hundred and will get stamped ninety-nine cents. The first book scout who sees it will grab it like a frog snags a fly. That is why it is important to be there when the books are shelved.

There are no rare volumes to be found when lazing about the house and any morning it is key to get out and place myself in the path of scouting fortune. This is more than a normal morning, however. I want to recover my Hemingway. Midmorning at a local thrift store is a grazing field for Helmet Head.

HH's best quality is that he's easy to spot. It's helpful when you want to avoid him. But today, I have driven past the Goodwill on Santa Monica Boulevard and the UCLA Hospital thrift shop on Sawtelle and, fueled by thoughts of the missing ostensible first-edition Hemingway, I am relieved to see the decrepit Yamaha leaning like a battle standard up against a utility pole in front of the National Council of Jewish Women thrift shop on Federal Avenue.

I pull into a nearby parking space, get out and walk toward it. The seat fabric is torn. Brown latex foam sprouts from the cracks. A film of dirty grease covers the motor and the rubber on the foot pegs is worn to the metal underneath. The plastic supermarket bags hanging from the handlebars are stretched with the weight of books. I look in the store window. There is no sign of HH. I peer into the bags and notice a few obsolete computer books. A red temporary registration certificate is attached right above the license plate, held in place by tattered and yellowing clear tape. My missing book is likely at the address on the certificate and finding where Helmet Head lives would be the first part of a plan. But the paper is creased and the ink is blurred from rain.

I squint and strain and then I am brought up short by a voice—his voice. It's slightly guttural, and even though it has a patina of civility, I intuit a subsurface of threat.

"Looking for something?"

I realize too late that I'm not ready for this encounter. HH, strap swinging metronome-like from his helmet, continues over my apoplexy.

"Are you looking at my registration? Something interest you there, Ralphie?"

Should I engage? The perennial question. Should America have invaded Iraq? It is not a question of whether the provocation is serious enough to merit a response. It is a question of self-interest. Will a response serve my interests? Will I be closer to my missing book if I engage now, or will I be farther away? Will I be bogged down in an endless and inescapable quagmire?

"I was looking for you," I say, trying to turn the conversation to my offensive.

"Why are you reading my registration, Ralph?" HH persists, referring unabashedly to the elephant in the room as crazy people are wont to do.

"After I got back from Anaheim and Nick and Doreen were taking care of me, remember you came over?" I continue, trying to deflect his challenge.

"Are you looking to find out where I live?" he persists.

"Maybe you were curious about what I picked up in Anaheim and you took a look at a couple of the books while you were in the driveway," I offer, acting diffident as if theft were a natural and not notable activity.

"Why would I do that?" he replies. For the moment I have at least won the battle of topic. It's encouraging. Perhaps dialectic is possible.

"There are some books I'm looking for."

I don't want to show my hand yet by zeroing in on the Hemingway.

"So why are you looking at my bike?"

"I'm missing some of the books I bought in Anaheim."

"What does that have to do with me?"

"I thought you may have seen them."

"Why would I have seen them?"

"Because over at Nick's I saw you were looking at my stuff."

"So why were you trying to find out where I live?" Uh-oh. Back at square one.

"Listen. It's not a big deal."

"Well, obviously it is a big deal."

"Not really."

"You know for a person in this particular business, you can be painfully transparent, Ralph."

"Is that a compliment?"

"Do you think it is?

"No." I am tempted to say, "No, Mister Helmet Head," but I bite my tongue.

"It's a post office box anyway...the address," he offers, pointing to the registration.

"I don't care where you live. I am wondering if you have any of my books and I would just like to get them back if you have them."

I map out a strategy and continue.

"There was a textbook that I'd like to get back. I need it for a customer. If you have the same title I'll pay. I'll pay retail for it so I can fulfill the order."

I will let on like what I really care about is the textbook and hope that will lead me to the Hemingway. Perhaps he isn't aware of its value. Of course it's hopelessly naive. But I can't go forward without a plan and this is the best I can do for now.

HH advances toward his bike, straddles it and raises the kickstand.

He kicks the starter.

"Is this because I am in possession of certain facts?"

"I don't know what facts you're talking about."

"The government tells us that the steel in the towers melted and that's why they came down. Steel melts at 2700 degrees. Jet fuel burns at 1200 degrees."

"That's very interesting. You didn't happen to see my book?"

"Doesn't that make you curious?"

"I'm curious about the book."

"Who do you work for, Ralph? Maybe I should be looking at your registration. Maybe it's from Langley, Virginia."

It's his exit line. He buzzes off wearing a smirk which he won't even deign to send in my direction. I don't know if he's serious and I don't know how to react. Does he really think I work for the CIA? Is he delusional or merely larcenous and clever? Regardless, I have lost the advantage.

I was asleep under the comforter in Angela's bed the morning of 9/11/2001. It was a little before 6 AM in Los Angeles. She was up early and already pumping on her Stairmaster in the living room with the TV on when she saw footage of the first plane hitting the North Tower. She woke me up and together we watched in awe the second plane crash into the South Tower. Nobody knew what it meant. Possibly an imminent wider attack, war and even nuclear conflagration.

I went into Angela's kitchen and called True who was just waking up and didn't sound pleased to hear my voice.

"Turn on the TV."

"Mitchell? What do you want?"

"Turn on the TV."

"What for?"

"There's some kind of attack."

"What kind of attack?"

"Two planes just flew into the World Trade Center in New York."

"What do you mean 'into it'?"

"Two planes. Two towers. They crashed into them."

"Oh my God!"

I hear some fumbling with the phone and then the sound of

the news from her TV.

"I can come over."

"Oh my God! How could two planes do that?"

"I can come over."

"Oh my—" An instant of call-waiting deadness interrupts the line. "That's my brother calling me. I've got to go. Don't come over." She hung up. I returned to Angela and the TV. She was sweating hard on the Stairmaster as the commentators speculated on what comes next, and the sight of her firm muscles on her taut, tan waist below her halter top vied for my attention to the unfolding event. I remember on that morning I felt a burgeoning fear that fate would have me spending my last moments with the wrong person.

With Helmet Head out of my grasp, I am uneasy for the rest of the day. I continue on a perfunctory thrift store route and return home to find an unremarkable group of orders. I pack with lassitude and deliver them to the post office.

If I knew that the missing book was a real first edition, then I could face my situation with undiluted anger. But what if it is really just an ordinary old copy? Perhaps the blue tinted jacket is just an aspirational false memory.

Hopelessly stuck in my thoughts, I drive to Angela's apartment to divert myself with a different sort of dialectic. There was a brief period at the beginning of our relationship when Angela would come to my apartment, and then there was a time when we would trade off venues, but now I only go to hers.

Angela lacks a sense of pace in sex. When she rides on top of me, as she gets more excited and gets close to orgasm, she starts to move too quickly, and she passes right over and past her personal narrow window for fulfillment. Unless I intervene, grabbing her hips, slowing her down, forcing her to build slowly and purposefully to the anticipated ecstatic moment, she will bypass it entirely and collapse in a withered and unfulfilled heap.

I bring an inexpensive Cabernet. She presents farfalle with sun-dried tomatoes and capers and a spinach salad. This fosters an unnecessary illusion that this isn't just about fucking. Afterward, I am always amazed that we manage to fill the conversational void. Tonight we each offer up some morsels about travel to Europe, both employing the first person singular, speaking as if we traveled alone, when in fact we were each with our former spouses. We decide to leave dessert and go to the bedroom, not so much out of a breathless need for sex, but to shorten the conversation.

"Are you all right?" she asks, as we lie on the cool percale. She has orgasmed mightily. I didn't get close. But her concern has to do with a tightness in my demeanor that transcends sex.

"I'm fine."

"I came like church bells," she offers. It is, I suppose, offered as a compliment, but its context is predictably Angela-centric, about her and her bells. She snuggles up under my arm, in an approximation of tenderness she no doubt saw in a French movie.

"Is Caleb all right?" Although she has never met Caleb, she knows that he is at the top of the list of things that might concern me.

"He's fine."

"And the ex?" Even I resent the diminution of True to *the ex*.

"Nothing new on that front."

A pause. She lifts her head up and grins widely, as if I am an infant in a crib and will respond reflexively. I don't. She takes her hand with its lovely, long manicured fingers, and its lithe arm, and slowly traces it down my chest to my pelvis.

"Don't make any promises you don't intend to keep," I say. She slips lower and begins her work. It leads me to believe that an air of alienation might have its rewards with Angela. Perhaps I should learn to fake ennui. But I'm too transparent and she's too perceptive. I stir as her head follows her hand.

"I can't find a book I bought."

"That's too bad," she says as she works me with her hand.

"It could be very valuable."

"Well, what happened to it? Your book." She warms to her work, as do I.

"I think maybe it was stolen."

"How valuable is it?"

"Maybe thousands…"

"Do you know who stole it?"

"Somebody took it out of my car."

She steps up her efforts at my midsection, perhaps in an attempt to distract me from my pain.

"What about the police?"

"I don't think they can help."

Her pace accelerates. My mind is like a nickelodeon flashing alternate images of HH and Angela.

"Can you get it back?"

"I will try."

"I have faith in you, Mitchell." She reasserts herself with vigor, transferring her duties to her lips.

I explode in her mouth. She swallows with a big grin. This is a first. She has never, ever swallowed. To some men, this is supposed to be the *ne plus ultra* of sexual gratification. God knows why. To me there is something ominous about this moment, as if she perceives I am a hapless soldier about to leave for the front. She dabs the corners of her mouth with the sheet.

"You are such a naughty boy for making me do that," she says with a grin, and then lies back next to me. Even though I sense this night is different, I know I won't stay. She turns on her side away from me, my cue to leave, and I do, pausing to admire her near-perfect ass.

"Don't get used to it," she offers, still not looking at me as I leave.

Chapter 14

It is 2 AM when I arrive home to turn on the computer and check my sales. Nothing special on the order list—a few ten-dollar books. I shower, brush my teeth and then go to my small bedroom. There is a bed, a table and a lamp, nothing else and all very basic. All our former furniture resides with True. Window shades and no curtains. Sometimes I think I like to live simply like a student, but more often the regression is merely demoralizing.

I fall on the bed and turn out the light. I am extremely tired, but doomed to fight my demons for a short spell as I lay in the dark. I think of errors I made. In judgment. In character. I wonder how Caleb will be marked by the experience of the separation. I think of the missing book and the futility of trying to recover it. Move on. Move on. I try to clear my mind, first by thinking of the color blue in abstraction. But I see my book and then HH's motorbike, all in blue, and then I riff on various motorcycles I have ridden, trying purposefully to move into more calming territory. I travel purposefully into sense memories, trying to abstract them from their context—the feel of the motorcycle throttle on a Honda I once owned as a student. I find that for me the abstraction clears the mind. I twist the handgrip, and then I imagine the feel of its diamond rubber pattern and so on until slowly I am Morpheus borne.

The doorbell rings. Not in my dream, but in my living room. I stir. It rings again. I look at the clock and it says 4:14 AM. This can't be good. I forget my dream, but the dread I feel is either a continuation of the dream or the certainty that when your doorbell rings at four in the morning, nothing good will follow. I drag myself to my feet and walk toward the door.

I open it on the chain, peek through the crack. It's Helmet Head. Oh shit!

"Hey Ralph!" he says with patently false cheer.

My stomach suddenly feels like it's on a down elevator.

"What the fuck are you doing here?" I ask.

"I don't know why you think I'd steal anything from you, Ralph."

"It's four in the morning."

"It's not so hard to find out where somebody lives. I found out where *you* live."

I look to see if he holds a gun or a knife. His hands are empty. His fingernails are cracked and dirty.

"What do you want?"

"You're projecting, Ralph. You're projecting all the anger and all the failure you feel inside onto me."

"You are nuts and get away from my door."

"To acquire wisdom, you need to be able to recognize truth, regardless of the source."

"The steel in the towers didn't have to melt. They soften enough to lose strength at a thousand degrees and I'm going back to bed. I looked it up." I start to close the door, but he puts his foot in the open space.

"You think it's a joke? You think that the country has been taken from us is a joke?"

"I'm not laughing."

"You can liberate yourself, you know."

"Would you get your foot out of my door, please?"

"You have so much. I have so little."

"Give me my book."

"I don't have your book. And if I did, it wouldn't fix the problems that you have."

"Take your foot out of the door or I'm calling the cops."

"So where's your kid?"

This hits me like a falling piano. What does he know about my kid?

"What are you talking about?" I stammer, trying to think of when he could have even seen me with Caleb.

He cranes his neck to look inside. "I guess he's sleeping. Don't want to wake him. Guess I'll be going."

He has a sickening, sociopathic grin on his face as he removes his foot from the door. I close it and wait several seconds to hear his motorbike start and drive away. I return to bed, but it takes an hour to get to sleep.

In the morning, I drive over to see Nick, hoping for guidance. I find him prowling in one of his storage sheds crammed with hundreds of books, searching for a missing volume in a stooped space designed for garden tools. There are some things I could teach Nick about inventory control. He has over 30,000 books and no SKU numbering system to keep track of them, which means he has to sort them by titles and authors and subjects, which in turn means that when he gets an order, maybe 10 percent of the time he can't find it and has to refund the customer.

"You know the Flammarion catalogues *rayzonay*? You know... *Toolooverpant*?" Flammarion is a French publisher. He means "*raisonée*" and "*tout l'oeuvre peint*," but although his French pronunciation is bad, he has knowledge of the actual books. I, on the other hand, know from prep school French how to pronounce the title including the rolled "*r*".

"I had most of them. I sold the Raphael book and I can't find the motherfucker."

He pores through a musty file box of art books that are part of a series detailing the complete works of European painters, not finding what he wants. Sweat drips along his cheeks in the hotbox of a shed.

"Helmet Head came to my house last night," I tell him.

"What the fuck for?"

"I don't know how he even found out where I live."

"I know this miserable fucking frog book is here..." He continues rummaging.

"He scares the shit out of me."

"What was he doing?"

"I think he was trying to scare me."

"What does he care about you, Ralph? He's got so much crazy crap buzzing inside his head he's got no room for you."

"I had a sort of a confrontation with him yesterday morning."

"A confrontation? I thought you were a smart guy."

"You were wrong."

"Jeez, Ralph. You don't want to go rattling Helmet Head's cage."

"I want my book back."

"Well, maybe you're just fucked. Maybe that's all there is to it."

"I need the money."

"You don't even know that you got a real first edition. Look, I know how it is…things start to go south on you and then you start ruminating and you start thinking like I couldn't have gotten in this place if I didn't have enemies and you start putting all your attention there…"

"The other side of that is you hang around and be a patsy and everything in life continues to fuck you over until you're dead."

"It all leads to the same place, Ralph. Doesn't it?"

"Where do you think he sells his stuff, Nick?"

"How do I know? Maybe on the moon."

"EBay?"

"Probably."

"How do I find his store site?" I ask.

"If he's got your book, you could search for it."

"I already have."

"Well, he probably hasn't listed it yet."

"Somebody has to know his last name."

"Jeez, Ralph. I don't know if his first name is really Hector."

"You know he speaks Japanese? I heard him at some garage sale where he talked to the sellers in perfect Japanese."

"How do you know it was perfect?"

"It sounded perfect."

"Maybe he was raised in Japan."

"Except his Russian is perfect, too."

"Can I give you a little advice, Ralph? You know how you're always asking me for advice?"

"I am?"

"Yeah. Sometimes you act like a little kid, wanting to know about this book or that binding or whatever, or where to go. Remember, I told you not to go to Anaheim?"

I nod. He's so right.

"So let it go, Ralph. Just let it go."

I nod again as if he's the sage. In fact I believe he is, but I know also there is something restive in me that can't be quelled. It's not just that I have been challenged by the loss of the book, but also that I am deep-inside thirsty for battle. But just for this moment, I will let it pass.

Chapter 15

To observe the arrival of the new millennium, True, Caleb and I drove north up Interstate 5 to Pearblossom, to watch the stars under the clear, cold, high desert skies. Nobody seemed to really know for sure how one appropriately honors a new millennium and there was pandemic nervousness—not only about the possible catastrophic effects of the computer glitch dubbed Y2K—but about how to celebrate after a thousand years of anticipation. Even grandiose plans by movie stars and captains of industry to spend the millennial moment in 747s flying directly over the international dateline while drinking champagne with a hundred of their closest friends seemed to ring hollow in the cosmic momentousness of the event. There were a couple of parties from the agency to which I was invited, and True had a bid from some faculty people who wanted to reserve a large table at an Italian restaurant in Encino, but neither of us wanted to celebrate without young Caleb, the genuine heir of the coming millennium.

I think True and I were both a little extra spooked about the year 2000. True's Dad had died a few days after the New Year in 1999, and there was something in the chilly, declinated-sun, post-Christmas feel of the day that recalled the day we received the phone call from True's uncle announcing the death of her saintly father.

We found a patch of desert ground off the side of a dirt road and laid down a tarp and a pair of sleeping bags that we zipped together. We brought Caleb's stuffed animals, Moncrief the monkey and Mr. Dog the beagle, to help him feel secure. We packed raisins, marshmallows, apple juice and graham crackers for Caleb and a ten-year-old bottle of Moet and some smoked salmon with crackers and capers for us. And then we all snuggled into the sleeping bag under the canopy of the Milky

Way. If the whole scene reeked of Spielbergian sentimentality, it was still wondrous and powerful to me.

I had a Casio digital watch that I had synchronized to the US Naval Observatory's atomic clock through its website, and I could mark the second that we entered the year 2000. We decided we would avoid the hype that inevitably would come from listening to the radio, even the dulcet NPR. It was best just to be with each other and with the moment.

My little secret was that my consciousness was bifurcated for most of the evening. Yes, I did locate Orion's belt with True's assistance and we both got caught up in pointing it out to Caleb.

But another conversation was aggressively competing for space inside my brain as we urged Caleb to try to find the Big Dipper—a conversation related to Y2K and the safety of my investments. A few months before, there was widespread fear that the old mainframe computers that govern so much of our infrastructure—electric power grids, telephone switching, financial databases—would be brought down by an international digital aneurysm because of their inability to transition from the opening digits 19 to the digits 20 as we passed from 1999 to 2000. It seemed like a stunning lack of foresight—a mass clapping of hands to large foreheads. In many cases, the computers were so old that the young software designers didn't even speak their language and computer engineer oldsters who spoke the moribund programming language of Fortran were dragged and herded out of retirement to coax some sense into the reprobate old mainframes. As of New Year's Eve, the predictions of the pessimists were being discounted. Neither Y2K nor the stock market would brook any pessimism. And I was betting my bankroll with the optimists.

Meanwhile the NASDAQ had finished out 1999 at a stellar 4069, up 85.6 percent. The Dow Jones Industrial Average was up a comforting 25 percent for the year. The vaunted and ever-giving JDS Uniphase was performing a celebratory splitting of its shares once again on December 31. So as I snuggled under the stars with my family unit, I had reason to feel optimism as we entered the new millennium.

I had bought fifty shares of Qualcomm a week before at $612 a share. Qualcomm, which made communications chips, was selling for $25 a share in March, but several analysts had pegged a target of $1000 for middle 2000 and if recent experience was to be any guide, targets were always upped long before their arrival date.

I bought the Qualcomm shares from a margin account I set up with the earnings of my earlier investments. Otherwise, I would have had to transfer money from our central account and needed True's signature. She would have given it if I asked, but it seemed simpler to use the margin account and I didn't want to worry her. I waited by my computer watching the price, hoping for a dip. It was, however, on an inexorable rise, and when it went from $603 to $615 I regretted not having jumped in earlier. I resolved not to miss another opportunity.

I put in an online order with Schein at market price and in an instant I received confirmation of the purchase of fifty shares at $614¾ plus a $29 commission. That's a total of $30,766.50. But when the stock goes to 1000, which even conservative Paine Webber says it will, then my investment would be worth…it takes a moment…wait…

"There it is, there's the Big Dipper," said True to Caleb, interrupting my calculation. The young prince looked up to the sky where True pointed.

In round numbers, fifty shares are worth $50,000 and the profit on that is $19,000 and change. And on margin, I only had to put up $6,000. Which really means a 300 percent profit on my investment.

Caleb focused his attention for the moment in the general direction of the northern sky. I tried to finish my counting as I smiled in response. Nineteen thousand is a year of college.

Four more deals like this set aside in CDs and I'd have college knocked. Task completed, I lowered my head to Caleb's shoulder and followed his pointing finger to the area of Ursa Major and the Big Dipper. While in this position I found it irresistible to put my lips on his sweet neck and blow a raspberry. He giggled and pulled away. I grabbed him and repeated. I could have done it forever, but True asked me to stop.

"I'm giving him an astronomy lesson," I replied.

"Let's just be quiet and enjoy the solitude. Okay?"

I stopped, but Caleb's eyes seem to plead for more.

"He wants it," I begged.

"Resist," said True.

I withdrew from the beloved neck. Silence crept over us. A shooting star flew across the sky. I looked to True and we acknowledged it with a glance. Before long I counted down on my Casio the seconds that ended 1999 and we toasted the New Year with champagne and kisses. After exhausted and over-stimulated Caleb had fallen deeply asleep, we put his head on a pillow and covered him with a blanket. True and I made love slowly and silently in our zipped-together sleeping bags under our heavenly canopy.

Chapter 16

It is Saturday morning and as I weigh Nick's advice from the previous day to let go of my anger at HH, I am in the car, tracking down a yard sale far up one of the canyons north of Sunset Boulevard in Brentwood. It was advertised with just a small hand-lettered yard sale sign on a telephone pole on Sunset and didn't appear in the paper or on Craigslist so it won't be ravished early by the Craigslist herd. It's a good neighborhood, moderately upscale and dotted with book-laden UCLA faculty. It's promising.

I drive three miles up winding roads to a pleasant hillside house where a family is shedding old sets of dishes, faded dhurrie rugs, and (drum roll) their daughter's high school textbooks—a shiny pile four feet high. They are pristine, as if she had never opened them.

It is not uncommon in upscale Brentwood for a private school child with divorced parents to have three sets of books. One for the mother's house, one for the father's, and one for the school locker—an indulgence that may seem nonsensical to most, but it neatly relieves the inevitable migration of a book to the wrong house and the consequent nuisance of having to retrieve it from a hostile ex-spouse. Let me not be judgmental of others in this matter and we will see how many books Caleb will have. I dread it.

Father and stepmother stand cheerily out front, enjoying their dress-up roles as smiling and solicitous neighborhood retailers. Feigning indifference I wander over to the books, trying to determine how old they are. If they're current editions, they can be worth $50 to $75 each. If they're out-of-date they're worthless. Being glossy and new is a good sign. Newer books have brighter graphics, with banners announcing CDs and DVDs inside and passcode numbers for entry to supplementary websites. The newest ones have barcodes for thirteen-digit ISBN numbers, as opposed to the earlier standard of ten digits. But the only way to determine for sure if they're valuable current editions is to look them up in my cell phone database.

I open the first one. It's three years old. High school texts don't update as often as college texts, and a three-year-old book has a good chance of being current. There are at least twenty of them here. I pull another one off and look at the publisher's page. It's a year old. This could be good for me.

"How much for the books?" I ask with flat affect, trying to mask my interest. The husband turns to the wife.

"How much for the books, Cher?"

"I don't know. I think Jessica said five dollars," she replies.

Five dollars each could be painful if a big percentage of them are outdated editions and worthless. If they were a buck or two each I could easily buy the lot and afford to toss the rejects after I looked them up.

"Where is she?" he asks.

"Sleeping, of course." She turns to me with a shrug that says, "Teenagers…what are you gonna do?" I nod in sympathy.

I try to speed it along. I have other sales to go to, but if these books are current editions, they could make my day. About fifteen books times sixty dollars. Nine hundred bucks.

"How about forty for the lot?" I ask. If only half are up to date, I'd still be in my sweet spot with a ten-to-one profit.

"I think she said five each," was the pleasant, but unyielding reply. I see I'm going to have to go through them individually and weed out the ones that are outdated and worthless.

These people don't need to bargain. For the few dollars it will bring them this transaction should really be about getting the books out of the house.

"You want to wake her up and ask her?" he asks his wife.

I'm blindsided and squirming. Everything I have learned from experience and from Nick's tutoring tells me to close the deal immediately before good fortune reverses itself.

I am too late. Mayhem announces itself with the buzzing sound of a motorbike approaching. I turn to look as Helmet Head pulls up, parks and dismounts in a single fluid motion. He heads straight for the books.

I plant myself in front of them and pointedly re-examine them, making a pile. This is lingua franca for all booksellers that the books are spoken for. You make a pile, it's your pile. End of story. He reaches over me and examines one of the books.

"Those are mine."

"Just looking."

"So where is my Hemingway book?" I say to him. Much to my surprise he has the politic to ignore me. I think of Helmet Head as being engagement personified.

"How much for the books?" he asks the father, still ignoring me. I wince and look in appeal to the man, but he also pretends I am not there. In his eyes I am the troublemaker who is making him wake up Jessica.

"Five dollars apiece."

"How many are there?" his chapped lips demand. Without waiting for an answer, he counts them. Sixteen. He reaches for his back pocket. I'm apoplectic. This isn't just outrageous. This is like shitting in the bed or coldcocking an old lady. It is beyond the pale.

"These are my mine," I protest, to HH and to the husband.

The husband smirks. From the first he didn't like me. It's plain he prefers the unkempt and threatening Helmet Head to me in my khakis and polo shirt with a genuine embroidered Ralph Lauren polo pony. Me, who has charmed the most feckless and demanding of corporate execs, selling them lackluster ad campaigns as if they were Steve Jobs and I was Chiat-Day.

Why doesn't this husband recognize his brethren? I can only guess that he senses that I am in some way a doppelganger. I am too much like him, and therefore, in what he perceives as a damaged state, I am too close to his own fears about himself. To identify with my diminished position, would be to be linked and tainted with it. Better to side with the crazy, behatted guy with the grease stains on his pants. I am being vanquished by Helmet Head and suddenly I feel heavy, like the world is turning upside down in slow motion.

"The price was five dollars. You said you didn't want to pay that," the husband replies. The wife, who was about to go wake up Jennifer, thinks better of it and returns.

Helmet Head pulls out his wallet and starts peeling out cash.

"I was here first!" I protest, and reach for my wallet.

Helmet Head ignores me like I'm trash. He counts the money. "Ninety bucks. Right?"

I reach for my wallet and fumble for bills. "Here! Here's ninety dollars."

Both men ignore me. I appeal to the wife.

"When I am negotiating it isn't fair to give the sale to somebody else." She averts her eyes from me, embarrassed by my pathetic entreaty.

I have this dream. I am at the helm of a giant supertanker (I know that in reality modern ships use little toggle handles to steer, but in my dream I am at a big ship's wheel) and we are headed inexorably toward a far-off obstruction—a reef, a shore. I can't quite say. I know that I am aware of the approaching disaster and desperately try to turn the wheel to avoid it, but the mass of the ship is so great and the inertia so insurmountable that I have only a very small effect no matter how frantically I spin the wheel. My dreams are rarely subtle and a ten-year-old could interpret them.

I turn to Helmet Head.

"You're going to regret this!"

"Is that like a threat?"

"This man is a thief!" I say to the husband.

The husband takes Helmet Head's money. "You had a shot and you didn't want to pay the price. It seems fair to me."

"You don't understand. There is etiquette about this. You never undercut the first buyer."

"Etiquette?" he asks, wide-eyed. "You're kidding me?"

"He's a crazy guy. He doesn't follow the rules. He steals."

As HH gathers the books he speaks to the woman as if he was the corner grocer and she was a regular customer. "Ask him if he works for the CIA."

The inanity of his remark seems to bounce off as I look to her in a final appeal. Her face is a frown reserved for me.

"I think you should leave, now," she says, as if she's fearful I might do something bad.

Helmet Head is trying to put the books into bags so he can hang them off his motorbike. He gives me a sideways glance.

"Really," she continues. "This is making me uncomfortable and I would like you to leave our property."

She looks to the husband for support and he crosses his arms and looks sternly at me. Certainly he can intuit that I am a father and a husband and a former executive who earned six figures. I went to fucking Yale. I can't just *leave*... Not without the simple validation that I deserve. That I earned. That should be the minimum.

"I'm sorry. My wife would like you to leave."

"Why? Does she think I work for the CIA, too?"

"Just leave. Okay, buddy? I don't want to have to call the cops."

Out by the curb HH starts his bike and pulls in his kickstand. He salutes them with a conspiratorial wave as he pulls out. There is no reason for me to drag this out any longer. I let escape a half-assed, semi-amused chortle, but I fool no one, and I begin to leave.

As I slink off I notice plastic bags hanging from HH's handlebars bearing information that might be useful. I make note of it without giving myself away. I pledge to myself that I will track him down to his lair and recover my Hemingway.

Chapter 17

When HH scooped up the textbooks in Brentwood from under my nose I noticed that two of the bags that hung from his moped had the name "Trapper Shack" printed on them along with a logo of a brick building that looks like an old-time jail. This could mean nothing. Plastic bags migrate before they end up in landfills. I don't know that HH actually got the bags from the Trapper Shack, a landmark liquor store on Main Street in Venice, the traditionally reprobate beach town south of Santa Monica. The Trapper Shack is "old Venice," which is to say pre-gentrification Venice, before the advent of hip clothing shops, upscale eateries and concrete art lofts that start at a million. A few wooden wine racks stacked with twenty-dollar-plus bottles acknowledge the yuppie invasion, but the bulk of Trapper Shack business is still malt liquor, jug wine and six-packs for the street alcoholics who are drawn to the action of Venice's lively and decrepit nearby boardwalk.

I park the Volvo at a meter and put in money under the jealous scrutiny of a homeless man seated on the sidewalk next to his shopping cart. I enter the brick-front store. A half dozen security cameras strewn about the ceiling flash admonition with little red lights. A muscled and tattooed young Latino man nods efficiently at me as I enter.

"Good morning," he says with a baked-in smile. I nod fraternally and seek out a bottled water from the cooler. I am totally vamping. I should have a real plan, but I don't. I put the bottle on the counter.

"A buck-fifty," he says.

He snatches up the two singles I place on the counter and throws back two quarters.

"Have you seen Hector?" I proffer matter-of-factly.

He doesn't respond at all to the query.

"You know Hector with the moped and the dreds?"

His look is vacant. Perhaps he needs more detail.

"Helmet."

A short beat, then—

"Oh, Hector with the helmet? What about him?"

Pay dirt.

"Does he live around here?"

The clerk retreats a bit. I may have pushed too hard. This is not an information store any more than it is a bottled water store.

"Sorry," he says and turns away. I scramble for conversational entree.

"Because a piece of his bike fell off and I wanted to give it back to him."

I can't believe I said something so dumb. The clerk turns back to me. I have his attention. "A piece of his bike fell off?"

"Yeah, some kind of cover thing. I think maybe it goes over the battery or something. It could be hard to get another one. You know?"

He's dubious. I need to clinch it.

"Why don't I give it to you and you could give it to him next time you see him," I say, bluffing recklessly.

He hesitates and then scowls.

"I see him hanging out over on Electric someplace."

"Is that where he lives?"

"I don't know. I see him over by Electric and Westminster. At the moped guy's place."

"What moped guy?"

"Over in a garage on Westminster and Electric."

As I exit, my cell phone rings. It's True's number. She rarely calls and never with good news.

"What's up?" I answer, not in a mood for opening pleasantries.

"Caleb has an earache and is running a fever. I want to keep him here tonight."

Caleb was scheduled to be at my house and I am supposed to

pick him up from school this afternoon. He is prone to earaches.

"What's his temperature?" I ask, trying to be matter-of-fact and resisting the urge to regard this as a ploy to drive our prize deeper into his mother's arms.

"It's a hundred and two now."

"Did you give him Tylenol?" I ask. I know she did. It is my way of having a stake in the process.

"I've been giving him Tylenol and Dr. Levy prescribed Ceclor for him."

"What's Ceclor?"

"It's an antibiotic."

"I thought he gave him ampicillin last time."

"He said Ceclor. I think Caleb's a little better."

"Don't you have to go to class?"

"I got someone to cover me. Anyway, I think he should stay in one bed tonight. Is that okay? Mitchell?"

Of course it's okay. This is a reasonable accommodation of schedule that should be easy and normal for two separated parents who love their child. I don't have a problem with this. True's previous dirty dealing makes me feel as if I need to be rigorous about boundaries because of the mistrust that she has chosen to foster. But I acquiesce.

"Okay. Just keep me posted. Let me know if he needs anything."

"Okay."

I click off and continue to my destination. Just south of the corner of Westminster and Electric I see behind a decaying wooden fence an old bungalow court painted a peeling, grimy gray. I park a few doors down the street and walk up. Weeds, old bicycles, cracked flower pots, rusty barbecues and decaying doors landscape the open area behind the gate. I look around for HH's moped, but it isn't there. A path around the side of the buildings leads to the service alley. It is littered with trash and broken bottles and smells of dog shit.

In the alley, a dumpster blocks my view of a dilapidated apartment garage with five single doors that face the alley. A glance in the dumpster shows that it contains the detritus of transient living common in Venice. Old clothes and towels, porn magazines, underwear, broken toys, ancient cell phones, dishes, lamps, chairs. This is not my first dumpster experience. Once by chance I noticed a five-hundred-dollar cache of architectural monographs in a dumpster by an office building in downtown Santa Monica. Since then I have not considered myself too lofty to poke through a promising steel container.

But this downscaled dumpster lacks potential and sticky juice has seeped from leaky garbage bags onto most of its contents. Besides, I have my eye on a partially open door in the garages that face the alley. As I approach I hear right-wing talk radio emanating from inside.

"What is it about the liberals that they always have to believe the worst possible thing? There's an army of scientists out there that haven't been brain damaged by organic carrot juice yet that will tell you if there is global warming that it's just a natural process and no matter how many catalytic converters we put in and make cars twice as expensive or put batteries in them or whatever it's like a drop in the bucket. And killing the economy will not help the environment. Poor countries can't protect the environment. Just look at Haiti! I mean if the world is going to end and we're all doomed, do we have to act poor? If Armageddon is as close as they say, let's at least go out driving in style!"

I advance toward the open garage and glimpse tires hanging on the inside of the door—skinny moped tires. At least a dozen hang from hooks and nails. I can barely see into the shadows of the interior.

"What I can't stand is all the negativity and the whining. I mean this country has solved every problem so far, haven't we? We are still here. Richest, free-est nation in the universe? You think we haven't put stuff worse than this down before? What about 9/11??

Mopeds are stacked from front to back. A guy with a huge, quivering beer belly hanging over fleece Nike shorts and a T-shirt that reads, "I'm the One You've Got to Blow to Get a Drink Around Here," stands over a workbench and bangs with a rubber hammer on a wheel rim. His jaundiced legs appear to be depilatory-smooth and he sports a pompadour and a Lenin goatee. Pink feet with scraggly brown toenails rest on loose flip-flops. His pale, pasty face suggests to me a likely pederast. Don't ask me why. In the abstract I don't know what pederasts look like, but I know one when I see one. Struggling to erase the picture in my mind of a wispy twelve-year-old boy poised at his fly, I nod personably. He nods warily back.

"Is Hector around?!" I yell over the inanity coming from the radio on the workbench.

"I haven't seen him!" he says, goes back to his hammering.

"You know where I can find him?!"

With a frown he makes it clear that I am interfering in his colloquy with the radio fascist.

"What for?"

"Does he live around here?!" I ask, trying to fill the pause before it is subsumed in the radio rant. I know it's the wrong question the instant it leaves my mouth. Too much too soon.

"Nope." He goes back to hammering.

"You think he'll come by today?"

All I get back is a cold stare. I try another tack.

"You work on his bike?"

"Whose bike?" he says without looking up.

"Hector's."

"Why don't you ask him?"

"Is there a reason you're being such a prick?" I say as I feel my censor suddenly toggle off.

"It suits me." He smirks.

Which is the greater humiliation? To be dismissed by scum or to be dismissed by nobility? The former unanticipated insult or the latter anticipated one? I don't know. I turn to leave as he continues hammering without looking up.

"You look like trouble. I don't want a part of it today. Okay? I've got enough trouble."

I look like trouble? The hammering pederast thinks that I look like trouble? Part of me would like to prove him right but I resist and remove myself to the alley.

I still don't have what I need. I don't know if this is where HH lives and keeps his books. Best to pretend that I'm gone and look around a little bit while hidden from view. It shouldn't be rocket science to locate a helmet-ensconced sociopath in a smallish beach ghetto. Perhaps a little more shoe leather will do the trick.

I return to the dumpster for another look-see. I am outside the pederast's field of vision. Elevated by a nearby milk crate I lean over the edge of the bin and study the archaeology of its contents. A couple of old mops, some flattened boxes, the leaky garbage bags, a broken folding chair, a number of retired wine and beer bottles, a worn-out roll of carpet, a stack of old car mags. *What is this?* A brown plastic bag and inside a small cache of books? I lean over to retrieve it, my feet lifting nervously off the crate as I extend to grab the bag.

A half-dozen books are inside—tattered and stained sociology textbooks. Are they valuable? No. They are out-of-date editions and badly worn. They could very well be the leavings of HH after he bought a pile of books for a few dollars and then discarded the rejects quickly as he can't carry worthless items with his limited carrying capacity on the motorbike. It's not much to go on. I am no closer to finding him and his lair, even if these are his former books.

A couple of old moped tires sit against the side along with a broken rim and twisted fender. Also I see a few small boxes with labels from motorbike parts suppliers. I scan the boxes. Most are addressed to "Venice Moped Repair" at this address on Electric Avenue. Some read "Ed Summers, Venice Moped

Repair." Presumably Ed is the portly pederast. Then I see an outlier address. It is from "AJ Motorcycle Parts" in Stockton, California. It is addressed thusly:

Hector Matthey
5118 Martin Luther King Boulevard
Los Angeles, CA 90012

Who is Hector Matthey? Is he our Hector? What are the chances? Let us say that Hector ordered a part via the internet—maybe a new brake pad—and then brought it over to well-known babyfucker Ed Summers to install. That would make sense. How many customers named Hector could Mr. Summers have? How many Hectors were in your high school class?

To reach the box I have to balance most of my torso over the edge and then extend my fingertips to snare it, all the while avoiding falling headlong into the stinking bin. With the box in hand I head for the moped garage. When I arrive I find Ed in the back of the garage pumping air into a tire. Broadcast demagoguery continues unabated.

"Would someone please explain to me why there is a ten-mile hole in the fence between Arizona and Mexico when this was supposed to have been finished a year ago. I mean what good is it to have a fence if there's a ten-mile hole in it? I have seen some fat Mexicans, but nobody that won't fit through a ten-mile hole."

I call out to him.

"Hey Ed!"

He looks up, surprised that I know his name.

"Is 5118 Martin Luther King Boulevard still good for Hector?"

His expression tells me what I need to know.

That 5118 Martin Luther King Boulevard is in an African-American neighborhood. In fact, the wide swath of Los Angeles south of the Santa Monica Freeway and west of La Cienega Boulevard that surrounds MLK boulevard is a black neighborhood, including Baldwin Hills, Crenshaw and Leimert Park, and of course the former Watts, now referred to as South

Los Angeles.

In 1983, long after the death of Martin Luther King, Jr. and before Governor Ronald Reagan finally recognized a Martin Luther King holiday, Los Angeles belatedly joined with other cities in naming a street after the inspirational leader and orator. It was the great co-option. What was once Santa Barbara Boulevard (Saint Barbara, the patron saint of artillerymen, was beheaded by her father who God then struck by lightning—could not a prescient God have more simply prevented the whole mess from happening in the first place?), became Martin Luther King Boulevard, formally ghettoizing the seedy collection of decaying storefronts and decrepit housing with stoutly barred windows that lined its wide asphalt. For local politicians the consecration was a thrown bone to keep a simmering black populace at bay, easily outweighing any possible slight to the ancestry of artillerymen. Two decades have passed since the Rodney King riots, and despite empty spaces and cheap rents, the big chain stores still redline the area. It is a mixed blessing never to see a Chili's or a Target or Staples. For me, MLK is a place to go for good barbecue ribs once or twice a year. Why Helmet Head would choose to live there (if he does) is a mystery to me.

My coffee-and-cream complexion feels alabaster white as I wait for a traffic light in my Volvo while in the next lane four T-shirted and tattooed young urban warriors in a lowered, black Camaro with giant wire wheels blast gangster rap loud enough to make my sun visor buzz. My sideways glance is returned with calculating sneers.

I pass small storefronts in withered, flaking, flat buildings displaying handmade signs that declare medical supply stores, wig stores, fried catfish parlors and, of course, houses of prayer. Many houses of prayer. Large and small, storefronts and converted supermarkets, mostly with proud declarative names emblazoned marquee-large at their entrances—The Ajalon Temple of Truth, the Heavenly Vision Baptist Church, the Messiah Missionary Church of Redemption, the Pilgrim's Hope Tabernacle, the Children of Zion Hope and Salvation Congregation.

On a Sunday, no doubt, there is a lively and celebratory scene here—dress-up and flowers and standing at the entrance exchanging pleasantries with the minister, rounding up the kids and helping grandma into the car in the crowded parking lot.

Today it is Woodstock the day after. Food wrappers, soda cans and bits of newspaper that sometimes aggregate in little piles. Buildings are made barren by chain-link barriers and cracked tarmac with grass growing in the cracks. Letters have fallen from signs. Brown glue spots mark the missing letters of the "Abys_nian _aptist Chur_h."

I can't find 5118 Martin Luther King Boulevard. Numbers are not neatly painted on the curbs as they are in Santa Monica, and houses and storefronts are most often numerically anonymous, by preference or neglect. But 5345 is a standout with a big number over the door of a small, but shuttered storefront that declared itself on a sign as:

The Pan African Black Fact and Wax Museum. Repository of black history and culture for all to enjoy!

That was definitely a place to which I should return some day when they are open, if they are ever open again.

Then 5084 MLK is Danny's Liquor and Convenience Outlet. I have inadvertently passed by 5118. In the previous block I noticed an un-numbered and amorphous group of beige stucco boxes that were set back from the street and fronted with a chain-link fence. I presume it was once a small shopping center, maybe in the sixties. It must be within this small complex that I can find 5118 and perhaps the Helmet Headed fugitive. I turn around.

Weeds a foot high poke through weathered asphalt littered with abandoned cars and supermarket carts. I still can't find a street number on any of the buildings. Adjacent to the empty and abandoned storefronts of a low stucco structure is a two-story box-like building with lettering on the otherwise unadorned wall that reads:

RAY OF LIGHT MISSIONARY BAPTIST CHURCH
REV. DR. JAMES ALBERT LIGHTFOOT, PASTOR

The letters are comfortingly complete and untarnished. There is no front entrance, but I park and walk around to the side where I find a large double door and several cars (clean windshields, current license plates) parked on a small lot. Sitting on the edge of the lot, leaning against a pole is a familiar black Yamaha moped with plastic bags hanging from the handlebars.

At a lull in traffic from MLK I can hear the voices of a gospel choir singing inside the building. I am drawn to it. On the door are the numerals "5116." Close enough. I try one of the double doors and it opens. I enter into a large reception area. Despite the cheap wood paneling and linoleum floor I am clearly in a church—one that has been carved out of what was once a large retail space.

A table in front displays literature with titles like *The Truth about the Devil; Confirming and Defending our Faith in the 21st Century; Train Up a Child in the Nurture and Admonition of the Lord*. Several stacks of plastic chairs are piled nearly to the ceiling. Another set of large doors, now closed, presumably lead to the sanctuary. The music, however, comes from elsewhere. I follow the sound.

Not my brother, not my sister, but it's me, oh Lord
Standing in the need of prayer
Not my brother, not my sister, but it's me, oh Lord
Standing in the need of prayer
It's me, it's me, it's me, oh Lord
Standing in the need of prayer
It's me, it's me, it's me, oh Lord
Standing in the need of prayer.

The singing is boisterous and beautiful, full and rich. It seems to come from down a hallway that leads off this reception area. I pass down a long hall with beige walls lined with pictures of what must be Pastor James Albert Lightfoot, a portly and energetic-looking middle-aged black man most often dressed in church robes, sometimes in ensemble with members of the congregation but often with celebrities, including one with Magic Johnson's hand draped over the shoulder of Pastor Lightfoot. That photo bears Magic's signature. At the end of the hallway the singing becomes loud.

Not the preacher, not the sinner, but it's me, oh Lord
Standing in the need of prayer
Not the preacher, not the sinner, but it's me, oh Lord
Standing in the need of prayer
It's me, it's me, it's me, oh Lord
Standing in the need of prayer
It's me, it's me, it's me, oh Lord
Standing in the need of prayer.

I enter a large open doorway that leads into a meeting room/ cafeteria and the choir. It is a mixed chorus of about twenty men and women dressed in street clothes, arranged in a corner of the room near the coffee urns. In front of them, the choir director waves cadence. To the side a woman plays an old upright piano.

They are all black people except a short white guy with long, greasy black hair in the second row, two from the end, singing his heart out. This is the first time I have seen Helmet Head without his helmet. Essentially naked. Although his exposed locks are oily and irregular, they are pulled back into a tight ponytail and his face seems shaven and scrubbed. He wears a checked shirt and clean jeans. In this context he looks a little less crazy and a little more like a reformed indigent—a chronic inebriate who has just been outfitted and made over by the volunteers at a downtown mission. I lock eyes with him for a second and then he turns toward the choir director as he takes a half a step forward to sing solo as the rest of the choir hums in counterpoint.

Not my mother, not my father, but it's me, oh Lord
Standing in the need of prayer
Not my mother, not my father, but it's me, oh Lord
Standing in the need of prayer

His voice is a high tenor, surpassingly smooth, perfectly on key and ethereally, eerily beautiful with a modest and tasteful trill. Other choir members close their eyes reverently as they breathe in its melodious magnificence.

I am, of course, stunned. The choir finishes the stanza and the song in rousing, toe-tapping enthusiasm.

It's me, it's me, it's me, oh Lord
Standing in the need of prayer
It's me, it's me, it's me, oh Lord
Standing in the need of prayer.

Chapter 18

The morning after I bought the 500 shares of JDSU, I needed to be in the office for a 7 AM conference call with marketing managers from Chrysler/Mercedes, who were located in Michigan and Stuttgart respectively, to pitch a tie-in with one of our clients, Turtle Wax. We wanted them to share the cost of our print and TV spots if we featured a Dodge truck. These arranged marriages rarely work out, but I was bending to the wishes of our client to pursue it.

I left for the office just after dawn on the morning of April 4. In April, LA skies are free of June gloom—the clouds that are drawn in from the ocean in early summer. There was a refreshing dew on the ground. In the front yard True's irises were blooming. I hopped in the Volvo and turned on the morning NPR news for the short commute to the office. Cardinal O'Connor of New York had died. My mother was a fan of his. Also Vice President Gore had said at a speech the night before that Governor George Bush of Texas would gut social security if elected President. I made a mental note to be wealthy enough not to have to worry about that possibility. I was waiting for the news of the market opening a few minutes earlier. I didn't have strong expectations, although I felt there might be a slight upward tick—maybe ten points at the open. The update came on as I pulled into the Sather and Knowlton parking lot.

"We're having a substantial selloff this morning. The Dow opened down 315 points at 10,684 and the NASDAQ had dropped 442 points at the open and was at a six-month low of 3891. They are hovering around those numbers right now with the Dow at 10,701 and the NASDAQ at 3902. The selloff doesn't seem to be related to any particular news, but rather a general unease in the market and profit-taking for some investors."

Oh my fucking God! Where is JDSU? They mention Apple and Cisco and Intel, all down about 10 or 15 percent.

I wound up mumbling to myself as I drove. "It will come back. It will come back. It always does. Just hold on and don't panic. The important thing is to be calm, hold fast." The market had been choppy for a while. Certainly this was a big retreat, but there was every reason to expect it to come back. For all I knew JDSU could be bucking the trend. Apple and Intel were bound by the number of people who were willing to shell out for computers and it is possible we have reached the other side of the parabola on demand. Not so for broadband. It was newer and hotter. Broadband was just on the beginning side of its ascent. Investors couldn't be so shortsighted that they didn't see that.

I had to open the office myself and turn on the lights. It was a few minutes before seven when I unlocked the door. I went to my office and turned on my computer. As I waited for the boot-up my phone rang with the conference call operator.

"This is the AT&T conference operator. Is this Mr. Fourchette? We have Mr. Solaris and Mr. Morris now. Are you ready to join?"

Shit. They were already on. Starting to sweat, I clicked the browser icon on my desktop as I spoke.

"This is Mitchell Fourchette. I'm ready."

I exchanged pleasantries with Dodge's Solaris in Auburn Hills, Michigan, Turtle Wax's Morris in Westmount, Illinois. They apologized for getting me up early. Meanwhile my browser's home page came up. In the right top corner was a window with stock averages and the NASDAQ was at 3760—down almost 500 points. It hit me like a punch in the gut. The conference operator came back on.

"Misters Fourchette, Morris and Solaris? Mr. Lieb in Stuttgart is delayed a moment but he says he will be with you shortly."

Oh Jesus. I forgot what we were even supposed to be talking about. I pulled out my file that had a copy of the proposal and mockups of the print ads. I tried to think of my pitch. Maybe

Morris would pick up the slack for me. Why in the hell did we even have to talk to Stuttgart on a fucking small-time ad barter deal on a fucking American Dodge truck?

I look at the Dodge file, but I have an eye on the NASDAQ ticker on my monitor. The numbers are in red to drive the point home. 3780! Morris and Solaris are talking about basketball while we wait for Lieb. The previous night the Lakers had begun the playoffs by beating Utah. Being in LA I know I was expected to add local color about Kobe and Shaq. Screw it. I was shutting up. I clicked onto speakerphone and then hit the mute button.

I tapped "JDSU" in the lookup box under the ticker. A couple of seconds later the window came up with the current price of $102¼. Oh please no! I had lost sixteen thousand dollars. I could never tell True that I had lost sixteen thousand dollars of her dad's money. Wait! Wait!! Wait!!! The low was $82 and now it was $102. It was on the rise. The worst was over. I refreshed the screen and the number moved to $103. I had just made back $800! I would survive this. It was not the first time I had a setback. Relax. I remained silent while the guys talked basketball. It was a cinch that once Germany joined the conference the basketball chitchat would be over.

"Did you see Karl Malone try to shoot a layup over Shaq just before the half and Shaq just fucking stood there in the key and grabbed the ball out of the air with one hand like it was a goddamn tangerine?!"

"They need like a separate league for guys who weigh over two-fifty. He's gonna wind up hurting somebody."

I opened my Schein account page, put in my password and navigated to "My Portfolio." I wasn't expecting it to be pretty, but I steeled myself with the belief that however low it was now it would eventually rise.

"I bet if you lean on him, Mitchell could get you tickets up front the next time you get to L.A.—Hey, Mitchell. You still alive?"

I punch off the mute button.

"Yeah. I'm going over my notes. I got you on speaker."

Wait. There was some kind of error here. My *share balance* on JDSU was listed as zero. The *current price* column showed that JDSU had gone up a little more to $104½, but not only was it saying that there were zero shares in my account it also said zero in the *current value* column. And it said *minus $12,559* in the total net account value. How could that be?

Maybe Schein never recorded the trade. Could I have been that lucky? But I had seen the confirmation. I wasn't hallucinating. Maybe my check bounced. Maybe there was a problem transferring the funds and they rescinded the trade. Do they rescind trades? I don't know. But what was this? Qualcomm was also reading a zero balance in the *shares owned* column. How could that be? Let me refresh the screen.

"Gentlemen, Mr. Lieb is joining the conference," the operator said. "The conference is complete."

"Hello. I am sorry I am delayed. We are all here?" said Lieb in his heavy German accent.

"Ron Solaris here."

"Don Morris at Turtle Wax HQ"

I had zero fucking shares? I needed to look at the account history. I needed to bring up that screen.

"Are you there, Mitchell?"

The page was slow to load. Don's voice was a cattle prod. *Oops.*

"Sorry. I'm here. Hello everyone."

The page popped up. It listed the five hundred shares I had bought at $122 yesterday afternoon, but it said that they had all been sold at 8:05 AM this morning at $82. What? And my Qualcomm had also been sold. Everything had been sold! Did someone hack my account? Oh my fucking God! Somebody has hacked my account and stolen everything!!

"Mitchell, do you want to start things off here?"

I had been robbed! And there was a negative balance in the account!

"Uh…guys. I have an emergency here. I have to reschedule."

"Are you all right?"

"I'm really sorry. I'll call to reschedule."

I hung up the line before anyone could say anything else and dialed the Schein 800 number. I had to pass through two voice menus to get to the trading desk and then I needed to key in my account number and password before I could speak to an alleged human being.

"Mr. Fourchette? This is Daniel Ames at the Seymour Schein trading desk speaking on a recorded line. How can I help you?"

"I think somebody may have hacked my account."

"Can you give me your account number please?"

"You just made me key it into the phone. Are you telling me you don't have it?"

"For verification purposes, I need your account number and your social."

Of course they weren't the enemy. I gave Daniel the information he required and I resolved to act calmly in my best interest.

"Let me pull up your account here." I heard the tapping of keys—a hopeful sign. The tapping of keys and the display of pixels could lead to a resolution.

"I should have 500 shares of JDSU and 200 shares of Qualcomm and it says they've been sold and my account has a negative balance."

I felt like I was telling the oncologist that they must have my biopsy mixed up with somebody else's.

"I'm looking at your account here and I see that you bought five hundred shares of JDSU at one hundred twenty-two dollars yesterday at fifty percent margin. It appears that JDSU fell quite a bit yesterday and that your account was liquidated."

"What do you mean liquidated?"

"Sold. It was sold to pay your margin deficit."

"You sold my shares?"

"It looks like your share value put you substantially below the maintenance requirements."

"How can you do that?"

"Do what, Mr. Fourchette?"

"Sell my shares without telling me."

"I'm sorry. It's explained in the agreement you signed when you originally chose Seymour Schein."

"That you can liquidate my account?"

"Margin accounts have very specific rules."

"Don't you have to call me before you do that? I thought you had to call me."

"It's in our agreement as well. Usually if there is time or if the account is either slightly in deficit or about to go into deficit we try to give the client a heads-up. But I see JDSU fell over fifty percent. It pretty much runs on automatic at that point."

"But it went back up. It went down and then it came back up."

"I'm looking here and I see that it's at one hundred and four dollars now."

"Then if you hadn't just run to sell my shares, there wouldn't be a problem."

"I'm sorry Mr. Fourchette. I can understand why you might be concerned."

"Is there someone I can speak to there? Can I speak to your supervisor?"

"I'll be glad to get a senior trader on the line if you'd like to hold, Mr. Fourchette. Do you mind waiting?"

"Do I mind waiting? I don't mind waiting. Waiting isn't my problem. Schein ripping me off for sixty thousand is my problem."

"I'll get someone on the line for you."

"Could you play some nice soft rock on the line while you've got me on hold?"

"Mr. Fourchette?"

"Some fucked-up watered-down version of 'Light My Fire' or something? Isn't that what you guys do?"

"Actually I don't think they play music when we go off line."

"Whatever. Are you in San Francisco?" San Francisco is their headquarters. I don't know why I asked or why I cared.

"No, I'm in St. Paul, Minnesota."

"Well, how does it feel to be fucking somebody from two thousand miles away?"

"I'm going to put you on hold for a minute so I can get a senior trader."

None of this was going according to plan. He was supposed to tell me that there was a computer error on my account and I was supposed to be agreeable and complimentary. Meanwhile the second line on my phone was blinking and I know it was Mr. Turtle Wax calling to ream my ass. What would I tell True? Someone clicked in on the Schein line.

"Mr. Fourchette? This is Alan Seligman, senior trader at Seymour Schein. How may I help you?"

"You can put back the sixty thousand dollars into my account."

"I understand your account was swept after you failed to meet the house margin requirements. I'm sorry about that."

"Is St. Paul weeping?"

"Sir?"

"Or does St. Paul think it's very amusing?"

"St. Paul?"

"Minnesota."

"I'm in San Francisco, Mr. Fourchette."

The San Francisco main office. That had to be good. Maybe they were taking me more seriously.

"What can I do to get my account balance restored?"

"Restored?"

"My money back."

"I have gone over your trades and everything seems to be in order. I'm afraid there's nothing I can do."

"What if I go to the SEC?"

"You should feel free to do what you feel is right, Mr. Fourchette, but I think the agreement between you and Schein is pretty clear and we are both legally bound by it."

"Maybe I'll find a lawyer who would take issue with that."

"That would be your decision. I know that it must be painful."

"You do?"

'Yes sir."

My phone line started blinking.

"You know I have a call waiting on the other line."

"Would you like to call back later, Mr. Fourchette? I can give you my direct number."

"Do you think this is amusing?"

"No sir. I don't think it's at all amusing."

"Do the words 'class action' have any meaning for you?"

"Sir?"

"I get the feeling I'm being patronized and I think I want to consult with my attorney right now."

"That would certainly be your prerogative, sir."

"My other line is blinking."

"Yes sir. That's what you said."

"I know what I said."

"Yes sir. It would certainly be your right to consult with an attorney. Do you have a copy of our agreement? I could send you one."

"Do you think Seymour Schein wants his customers to be treated this way?"

"You mean Mr. Schein himself?"

"Yes. Your overlord—Mr. Schein himself."

"I am trying to be courteous, Mr. Fourchette."

"Would you like to explain to my wife and child what happened?"

"Sir..."

"Maybe you would like to tell my son that his college money has been taken from him."

"I would just like to remind you..."

"You can tell him Seymour Schein took his college money."

"I'm sorry, sir. But I need to remind you that there is a negative balance on your account right now of twelve thousand five hundred and fifty-nine dollars and you'll need to make it up by Monday."

"I'm going to take the other line now."

"Sir?"

I hung up. I stared at the blinking light on the phone until it ceased. I could call a lawyer, but I knew in the end I was screwed. In my heart I knew that the margin agreement was airtight. Even if I could have found a lawyer to start a class action suit, it would be years to fruition and my biggest concern at the moment was what to tell True when I got home.

I could lie. I could simply not tell her. I could try to borrow the money from somewhere to put it in the account. Just the original $60,000. Or perhaps a few thousand less. I could live with telling True that I hadn't done as well as I expected and had lost a few thousand dollars. But a bank wouldn't give it to me and there was no one in my phonebook that would make a loan like that.

I was paralyzed for several minutes. People began to trail into the office. I closed my door and an image of Chuck Firestone appeared to me. I didn't know what he could do for me. Maybe he would take pity on me and tell me that he had a lot of money sitting in the Firestone family trust and he would be glad to lend it to me at bank rates. Maybe he would just give it to me. I would resist his charity, but he would insist and finally I would relent for the sake of my family. It would have been helpful if I had his phone number. He had given me his card but I misplaced it.

I racked my brain for the name of his company. What did it sound like? Sounded like *foot...suit*.... Never mind. I did a web search for him in Alta Vista. (2000 was BGE—before the Google era—and there was no Google search.) I typed "Charles Firestone" in the search box and got a number of hits—most of them stupid and useless as was the norm for BGE. I did, however, come up with his name on the masthead of Roos and Selvin Investment Management. A little more work yielded an estimable address in one of the Century City towers and a telephone number. I called, gave the operator my name and he came on the line quickly.

"Hey, Mitchell. What's up?"

"Sorry to bother you, Chuck. I've got a problem and I need some advice."

"About what?"

"About the market. I think I may have screwed up. I need somebody to talk to."

"Do you want to stop by?"

"I don't want to interrupt you."

"No sweat. Come after the market closes. I'll block it out, man."

"Thanks."

"You gonna be okay?" I was sure he could hear the panic in my voice.

"Yeah. I'll see you around two if that's okay."

"Yeah. Tell you what. Come by and we'll have a late lunch."

He was a good guy, Chuck. I was a drowning man and I felt somehow he would be able to throw me a rope.

The office was on the twenty-fifth floor and faced the ocean. "Roos and Selvin" gleamed in stainless steel Helvetica on the marble entry wall. From a large window in the waiting room you could see the canyons of Catalina Island fifty miles off in the clear air. There were crisp copies of the *Wall Street Journal* and *Investor's Business Daily* on the Chippendale coffee table. The receptionist offered me Perrier in a British accent, but Chuck came out before she had a chance to fill the order. He gave me a hearty handshake with a shrug of comraderie and led me out the door to the elevator.

"What happened, Mitchell? Did the market bite you in the ass?"

I nodded sheepishly. He regarded me with the air of an old trench warrior eyeing a recruit on his first day on the Maginot Line.

"It'll do that."

He led me off to the promenade downstairs and to Harry's Bar where the maître d' knew him and led us to a table in a quiet corner. I told him what happened. It was painful, and as the words came out I thought about how I would rearrange the same information later to make it palatable to True.

I told him about how my small successes made me bold. I told him that if I had put more cash in the account I would be close to even right now. I told him about True's dad. After I finished, I realized I didn't know what my "ask" was. I knew he wasn't going to just hand me money. Maybe I was just relieved to unburden. I felt a little better. We were barely friends, really only neighbors. There was a long pause after I finished my story. I could see he was concerned for me.

"Something smells bad. I don't follow JDSU but that kind of move, even on a general pullback, without any significant news just smells bad."

"Are you saying someone manipulated the stock?"

"It's possible. I don't know."

"How would I find that out?"

"Ask yourself what you would do if you did know."

"How would they do it? I mean it's not a penny stock. It's not that easy to do."

"The guys who work these things are not penny stock players, Mitchell. You learned a big lesson. Maybe that's a good thing."

"I can't chalk sixty thousand up to experience. That's Caleb's college money."

"You've got a job and you've still got most of your money

intact. You'll earn the rest back."

"It will take years to save that much. And I don't know if my marriage will survive it."

"You are a very decent guy, Mitchell."

"Right now I'm just another fuck-up."

"You didn't know. Playing individual stocks is not for amateurs. If Roos and Selvin played hunches and listened to the chat room touts, where do you think we would be?"

"I realize you tried to warn me and I appreciate it."

"I didn't expect you to listen. In a bull market nobody listens. You're a human being."

"I am not feeling that way. I'm feeling like kind of an ass."

"It's an insider's game. Order an extra beer, have the hot fudge cake for dessert and then go tell your wife. She'll forgive you. She loves you, right? That's worth more than money."

"Is Schein going to come after me for the twelve thousand dollars they say I owe?"

"Believe it. With hammer and tongs."

I rested my head in my hands.

"Oh sweet Jesus."

Chuck signaled the waiter for the check.

"I'm sorry, Mitchell. I have to get back to the office. You'll get through this. I promise."

I made a shabby display of trying to take the check. Chuck waved me off. "The company has an account here."

He signed his name on the face of the check and we stood up.

"Have you got a parking ticket?"

I reached into my pocket and weakly handed it to his outstretched hand. On the way to the door he handed it to the cashier who quickly stamped it.

We passed into the concrete courtyard at the foot of the towers. I thanked him for his time and he started off toward the office elevator. I was bound for the escalator to the parking garage with no idea where I would go next after I got in my car.

"If I think of something for you, I'll let you know. Do you mind if I talk to a couple of the guys in the office about this?"

"Sure. If there's a chance it could help."

He pushed the elevator button, paused and then turned back to me as I started down the escalator to the parking garage.

"I might have an idea," he said.

I had almost made it onto the top step of the escalator, but withdrew.

"Maybe it won't work out. Do you mind coming back up?"

"No..."

"It could be a waste of your time, but I have something I want to try out on one of the partners."

"Okay."

I followed him up in the elevator.

"Look, Mitchell. I know you're in trouble. I wish you had talked to me before you did what you did. But you didn't come just for sympathy. I don't know if I can yet, but I'm going to see if there's a way to help you out. No promises."

When we got back to his office he asked if I would mind sitting in the lobby for a few minutes. I tried reading the *Wall Street Journal*, but the market optimism on the front page was about as relevant to me now as flappers and Prohibition. Ten minutes later Chuck appeared and asked me to come in. He led me to a conference room with a big center table. He closed the door after us.

"It is just possible that you are in luck. Can I tell you something in confidence?" he said.

"Sure."

"I mean it. This would be hard on the firm if it were to get out. Reputation is ninety percent of the business."

"I understand."

"Nobody's immune when the market gets tough. We're getting beaten up, too."

"I'm sorry."

"But overall our portfolio is strong and I think we'll get through this fine."

"I wish I could say the same."

"There's no sense kicking yourself. Here's the point. And here's the place where I need you to tell me that this is in absolute confidence."

"I swear."

"We got a cap call from the SEC today. Brokers have capital requirements and the market selloff really put a dent in our capitalization report. We're below our requirements and we have to sell some of our positions."

Chuck saw from my expression that this was over my head.

"It's not an uncommon event. They require us to have a certain minimum cash reserve and sometimes we have to sell off some of our portfolio we would really rather keep."

"I'm sorry," I said although I was consoled that even the smart money was hurting today.

"Last year we became market makers for a company in Baltimore called Biogram Pharmaceuticals. Started up ten years ago by some very smart MDs out of Johns Hopkins. Publicly traded since 1996 and they already make a small but steady profit from licensing patents to the big pharmaceutical companies. For a couple of years they've been doing a good job marketing an emergency artificial blood substitute that works great on large animals—horses, cows, pigs. They've started clinical trials on humans. It could be a huge deal. Every emergency room. In the battlefield. They're in stage three human trials that are scheduled to report out in a month. I need you to swear to me that you will never tell anybody what I am going to tell you."

"I swear."

"I mean it, Mitchell. I know you're a good guy and if you weren't in such trouble right now I would never be telling you this."

"I swear."

"People can go to jail for this."

"Jail?"

"Look at me. I am guessing you know the meaning of insider trading."

I nodded. Considering my current situation jail was a barely perceptible raise in the ante.

"I won't tell anyone."

"Take this as an object lesson in why an amateur investor doesn't have a chance. The clinical trials are being held in Denver, Houston and Tucson. They're supposed to be done in complete secrecy, but the truth is that a lot of nurses and medical assistants are just underpaid workers who hate their bosses and can be approached for a few bucks to let somebody know how the trials are progressing. This is how business is done, Mitchell. I'm not defending it. It stinks. It's why I hope to be out of this game and on my boat five years from now. In the meanwhile we try our best to keep up, right?"

I nodded. I wasn't sure where this was going. I can't say I was devoid of suspicion.

"I have it from a very good source that the trials are going better than hoped for and there will be an announcement very soon. The stock is around seven right now."

He pulled out a calculator, punched the keys.

"The smallest block we can sell is thirty thousand shares at seven and it would have to go up to at least nine on good news. That's very conservative if they report a positive trial. It's likely to be ten or eleven. You could pay Schein and go home to your wife with a hundred thousand over what you lost."

"Thirty thousand shares?" I was incredulous. If I were interested in investing, this was way over what I could consider.

"Blocks of thirty thousand. I think we have twelve or thirteen blocks to sell."

"That's over two hundred thousand dollars. I can't do that."

"We only sell them in blocks of thirty thousand shares. I'm

sorry."

"I can't."

"You could sell half and make yourself even, then keep the rest to see if it gets FDA approval. If it's approved it'll probably go to a hundred or more. But, truthfully, FDA approval is like hitting the bull's-eye from a thousand yards. I might keep a few shares, but I'd sell most after a positive trial."

"It's out of my league. I'm sorry."

"I don't know your situation. I was thinking maybe you had some reserves."

"I don't. I mean there is money. But I can't touch it."

"Fine then. Don't make yourself crazy. You can only do what you can do."

"When would they announce?"

"It's scheduled in ten days."

I found myself planted in the chair. I couldn't leave.

"I'm sorry," he said. He got up and moved toward the door in a gesture for me to leave. Perhaps I had overplayed my hand.

"I just can't," I said and I think I meant it. I suddenly felt gripped by the fear of what awaited me at home when I told True. I felt a tear roll unchecked down my cheek.

"Sometimes you just have to face the music, Mitchell. Maybe this is one of those times. Make a deal with the brokerage to pay off the debt on installment and make peace with your wife."

The tears flowed. I found myself whimpering. It wasn't anything like me, but I went with it. I don't know if it was just cathartic or if I was trying somehow to work Chuck. Probably both. In either case it seemed to affect him. He stopped leading me to the door. He put his hand on my shoulder. Surprisingly, my chest began to heave. Chuck sat down again, apparently moved. He spoke after a long pause.

"I'll make you a deal. I could try to find a customer to split a block with you, but that would take time. I can sell it to you on fifty percent margin and I'll see if I can get them to cut you a five percent break on the price. Needless to say, under the circumstances I wouldn't charge you commission."

Even on margin that was $105,000, nearly all we had left in the bank.

"It's just too much."

This seemed like it could be a very good deal for a guy with real money. Not me. And besides, all of this good will from a relative stranger made me uncomfortable. I couldn't help but wonder was this all really so they could meet their capital requirements? Perhaps. It was worrisome.

"Listen to me carefully, Mitchell. I don't want there to be any misunderstanding. If I do this, I have to be able to trust you."

"Do what?"

"I can open a margin account for you and walk the check over to accounting. I can tell them to put it in a corner under a bunch of old invoices and leave it there."

"Leave it there?"

"Yeah. I could make that happen. It could sit there for two weeks and not get deposited. Look, Mitchell…you know better than me there are no guarantees, but chances are that after the trial results come out that you'll just sell out your part of your position, replace the money you lost on JDSU and still have shares left."

"You wouldn't deposit the check?"

"As far as the SEC is concerned it's a reportable capital asset for the company if we have received a viable check. We can hold it for a month. It wouldn't be the first check we've held on to. It's a service brokers sometimes perform for good clients. It's a service you would never get at Seymour Schein."

"Why are you doing this, Chuck? We aren't that close."

"There is a quid pro quo." His eyes narrowed and he leaned forward and spoke quietly. *Here it comes,* I thought.

"This is only between you and me. I want you to give me a warrant to buy five thousand shares from you at ten dollars in a month from today. You hold five thousand back when you sell your shares. If the stock is fifteen or twenty or a thousand a month from today, you absolutely promise to sell them to me for ten. That is still nearly a fifty percent profit for you."

Now we are at the meat of it. He takes my surprise in stride.

"I am your neighbor and your friend, Mitchell. I am not Santa Claus."

"Is this legal?"

"Of course it's legal. But it's between you and me. We won't put it on paper. I'll trust you just as you are trusting me."

So much for good neighbor Sam. But it really made me feel so much better. Now it all made sense. He has the potential to personally make $100,000 with no risk to him and little apparent risk to me. Now that I knew what he would get out of it, and that he would also be a stakeholder, it seemed like genius. There was, however, one nagging problem.

"My check is for a joint account. Technically I need True's signature."

"Then get it."

"I can't."

"Did she sign when you bought the JDSU from Schein?"

"I signed for her."

He looked at me as if I had just solved the problem.

"I had her permission."

"You signed it… Mitchell, I am trying to help you out of a jam here. You do what you think is right. You're my neighbor. A year from now or ten years from now I'd like to be able to look up at you if you pass me on the street no matter what. You understand that, right?"

I nodded. I thought it was very self-serving for him to act as if his self-enrichment was social work, but even though there was unquestionable risk to me, this was my only opportunity and, considering the alternative, I was happy to play his game. He straightened his arms against the table, signaling that he was finished.

"Say no if you like. I'll understand. We won't have a problem selling the shares elsewhere."

There was no more opportunity for deferral here. I knew it was up to me to be either in or out. There was just the one lifeline being offered to me. I felt better that he had skin in the game. I grabbed for it.

Chapter 19

Stepping back and rejoining the other singers Helmet Head seems flushed from his performance. He basks in unambiguous admiration from his peers. He seems purposely to ignore my presence. The choir director, however, glances to me with a slight lilt of the eyebrows. I am an unexpected guest, and perhaps he hasn't determined from my skin color whether I am black or white. The director addresses his choir with the enthusiasm and charm of a preacher.

"I need a little more from the sopranos—reaching for the sky—reaching for the sky. And prayer is two syllables. *Pray-errr! E-nunn-see-yate!* We are all about making things clear, aren't we? And Hector—"

He looks at the stringy-haired white guy.

"Hector. That was inspiring. You have God's gift."

Helmet Head smiles his acknowledgment sweetly and shyly—as if he were a human being. I am dumbfounded. I almost catch his eye as it darts past me. At any moment I expect him to bolt.

I sit for renditions of "Many Rivers to Cross" and "Arise My Soul, Arise" and it is evidence of the power of the music that it almost succeeds in transporting me from my place of purpose and anger. Almost. I hear the choir director speak again.

"Just quickly let us thank our Lord because Leticia brought us a cake. What kind of cake is it, Leticia?

"It's a fudge cake," says Leticia, a large black lady in a muumuu.

"It definitely would be worth staying around for."

He bows his head and the choir does likewise. Hector bows his head the lowest, closes his eyes so tightly that there are creases in the corners.

"We thank thee, oh dear Lord, for the blessings you have bestowed upon us and we most humbly present our songs to you in the hopes that they please you and that we may be further blessed. Amen."

A chorus of amens follows and I find myself saying amen as well. I do not, however, take my gaze off Hector. I expect him to take off for the door and his moped at any second. In fact, I had worked out in my mind how to intercede between him and his vehicle.

"I'll see you Sunday bright and early and next Tuesday we start a half hour late."

The chorus quickly scatters, some going for the cake and some for the door, but Helmet Head/Hector walks head down and purposefully straight to me. If he is going to kill me, I don't think he would do it in church. I stand my ground. He stops a few feet in front of me.

"You want your book?"

"You have it?" I replied.

"Uh-huh. You want it?"

"Of course I do."

He turns and starts to leave, indicating with a slight gesture for me to follow. I do. Leticia interrupts with a wide, friendly smile as we pass.

"Aren't you having cake, Hector? I know you love chocolate."

Helmet Head/Hector replies in total Eddie Haskell mode.

"It looks delicious, Leticia. I'm on a diet today."

"You don't need to diet, Hector. What about your friend?" she says looking at me.

He introduces me sweetly to Leticia.

"This is my friend, Ralph, Leticia. Would you like some cake, Ralph? Leticia makes terrific cake."

"That's all right. Thanks," I stammer.

"Excuse us, Leticia. I have to see a man about a book," he says.

A couple of the choir people wave fond goodbyes to him as he opens a side fire exit door. It leads us directly into another section of the parking lot. He continues to walk toward the rear of the lot, passing by his moped.

"You're a black man, aren't you Ralph?" he says.

"I have a lot of black people in my ancestry."

"Wonderful people. Wonderful music."

My skin is crawling. I might be in physical danger. I don't know where I am going. I am in a neighborhood that is alien to me and arguably not safe, accompanying a crazy person who has already threatened me in my home. How badly do I want this book?

Enough for me to follow him to a largish, windowless structure behind the church. At its base is a weathered steel door. The door is conspicuously secured by an oversize stainless steel burglar-proof combination padlock on an armored hasp as well as a very robust, keyed deadbolt.

"Don't watch, Ralph," says HH as he clicks the numbers in the padlock. "Nothing personal."

"Is this where the book is?" I ask.

He pops open the lock and doesn't reply. He pulls a keychain off his belt, inserts a key in the deadbolt and opens the door. He reaches inside for a light switch, and then holds the door for me. There is a brief moment while I speculate if his plan is to shut the door behind me and entomb me. A quiet entombment might be a relief and a respite so I enter. HH follows.

I find myself in a single enormous room that resembles a movie sound stage. There is a substantial balcony/mezzanine made of raw boards that wraps around the entire room. HH busily flips on more lights and I get the full effect. All of the walls are completely lined with bookcases full of books. On the balcony are more books. It looks like a crude, Flintstone version of a grand classical English library. There are library tables in the middle and boxes and boxes full of books piled everywhere. Paintings and substantial stone and metal sculptures lie around like rocks in a garden. I am stunned.

HH grins grotesquely.

"Surprised?" he inquires.

"Whose is this?"

"The building belongs to the church. But everything that's here, that's mine."

My mouth is agape. I look at a nearby shelf. It is full of large out-of-print artist monographs. On another shelf is a pristine and complete leather-bound collection of the Harvard Classics. A twenty-volume set of the Oxford English Dictionary, a complete set of the original German Freud. I can see nearby what appears to be a collection with original dust jackets of first editions from American authors like Vonnegut and Steinbeck.

"You know you shouldn't be quick to judge people," he says.

"Where is my book?" I ask, trying to regain poise.

"I have it. It's safe."

"May I see it?"

"I'd like to hear more about your black roots."

"If it's all the same to you I'd like to get my book and go."

"You are very tight, Ralph."

I see he is not going to just hand me the book and let me go. If I retrieve it there will be a price.

"I think you have a lot of conflicts."

"Of course I have conflicts. That is what makes me a person. Can I have my book or do I need to call the cops?"

"You and I both know the cops can't get you your book back. You have nothing to prove it's yours."

"Maybe they'd like to look around here anyway. Maybe you don't have receipts for all of the things that I see."

"Are you implying that these are stolen? They aren't."

"I don't know what you do. I don't care. I just want my book. You said you had it and would give it to me."

"If you had a little more ambition, Ralph, you could have this, too." He makes a gesture to indicate the riches around us. "I know you are too fucking cultured to read an ad on Craigslist and knock on a door at ten on Friday night before a Saturday sale, but that is where the goods are. And your Christmas list probably doesn't include envelopes for the managers at Goodwill and the Salvation Army, but I gift the greedy bastards generously and not just at Christmas. And they text me the minute something interesting comes in."

"I will try to learn from your example. Could I have my book now?"

"Sit down," he says pointing to a pair of what I assume to be matched genuine Arne Jacobsen Danish egg chairs in original fifties chartreuse fabric that make a little conversation pit among the sculptures and the stacked boxes of books on the floor. Sensing my reluctance he adds, "Just go with it, Ralph."

The chairs are worth at least five thousand apiece. The president of my ex-agency has one in his office along with the other mid-century Mies and Eames trappings. HH perks at my interest.

"Nice chairs, huh? Bought them for a hundred bucks out the back door from Stevie at the Van Nuys Goodwill."

I sit with trepidation, sensing I am being funneled into a smaller, tighter pen like a steer before a slaughter. Unlike your average slaughter pen, here an original Ed Ruscha oil leans up casually against a box of books.

HH picks up on my gawking at his mass of property. "I've been at this gig for fifteen years, Ralph. I'm not a total asshole. I know what I'm doing. How long have you been doing it?"

"About a year," I respond. He smiles loftily like he's Babe Ruth patronizing a bat boy. Then his look hardens as he stares through me.

"He wants to stay, but he wants to go. He wants to score, but he wants to be fair. He wants to win, but he expects to lose. That would be you, wouldn't it, Ralph?"

I recoil a bit. He is encouraged.

"You're in dialectic meltdown, Ralph. You're too smart not to see at least two sides of everything and that means you're always at war with yourself. Am I right?"

My lack of response to his little display of garden variety fortune-telling serves as an affirmative to him. He continues.

"There's nobody worse to be fighting with than yourself. This is what I do. I separate the two me's. Here I'm one thing. Out on the street I'm another. I know in some circles people might think this is a little weird and—dare I say—schizoid, but it works. There is Hector in the street, making trouble and scoring merch, and then there is Hector at church. Everybody has both sides. You do. I just give them each their own leash and try not to let them mess with each other too much."

How crazy is this? Does anything he says have a whiff of truth? Has HH found the peace that eludes me or is this the babbling of a psychopath? There is something very alluring about living the Jekyll/Hyde life. There are parts of me that I would rather not deal with and bifurcation would be a simple and expedient solution. Would I be better off as two people instead of one? I try hard to integrate the good self and bad self, but maybe better to keep them separate and enjoy each. Don't let them cross paths. It seems strangely harmonious with my mother's formative Catholicism. Sin and later be redeemed.

"Tell me about yourself, Ralph."

"My name isn't Ralph to begin with."

"I know that. It's Mitchell Fourchette."

It stings to be identified by him. I feel suddenly naked.

"So who was the real negro in your family? Your grand-mother?"

"My grandfather... Listen, if this is just bullshit... Why don't you show me the book?"

"I have it and I'm going to give it to you. That's what I said, didn't I?"

"If you have it, then why don't you just give it to me?"

"You're talking to good Hector, remember? I'm trying to help you. You're fucked up, Mitchell-slash-Ralph. You're really fucked up, but now you're in a good place and you will be cared for. By the way I gave good Hector permission to swear in moderation."

"What are you even doing here?"

"Here?"

"Here. This place. What are you doing in a black Baptist church in Crenshaw?"

"Do you think I belong here less than you?"

"I was raised Catholic, so probably not."

"Three years ago I went to an estate sale in Glendale and it turned out to be for some Baptist minister. There was a metal storage shed in the yard and it was full of books. Theology, hymnals, bibles—a thousand JC books—a lot of totally brand-new, never read shit. Nothing rare—just a lot of average Christian books. I buy them. But then I get kicked out of the garage I rent for storage in Culver City and I don't know what I'm gonna do with them so I put an ad in Craigslist offering to sell the lot for three thousand hoping to get lucky. I get a call from some guy who says he's Dr. Lightfoot and he wants them all. I figured—"Doctor"—he must be like an MD but this black preacher dude shows up and tells me he wants the books because he's jump-starting a big church library and he wants to fill up a lot of empty shelves. He offers me two thousand and whips out a roll of hundreds. The books won't fit in his car so he makes a call and we wait for some guy from his church to show up in a pickup. We're standing around and he starts asking me about religion and shit. Tells me that God must have led me to him 'cause I'm selling him these wonderful books at such a terrific price. He doesn't know I paid two-fifty for everything. Glad to be of service, Rev, for seventeen-fifty profit and helping me clear out my storage space that I'm about to lose."

"Wait a second. How did you get the books from the shed in the first guy's backyard to your garage with a moped?"

"I pay a guy. I got a guy with a truck I pay to do it when I need it. Is this what you're fucking taking away from this, Ralph?"

"I'm trying to make sense of it."

"You're trying to figure out what to believe?"

"I don't know what any of this has to do with me."

"It all has to do with you if you're the guy who's listening and taking it in. Isn't that right?"

He is wearing me down. I consider leaving, but if I do leave, any further attempts to get my book back, even if successful, would mean a lot more than sitting for a while in a mid-century chair and listening to Mr. Bizarro telling stories. He continues.

"So we're standing there and we're waiting for somebody to show up with the pickup and he asks if I like gospel music. It just so happens that a member of my family was an ethnomusicologist and she taught me a lot about gospel music. It was like a sub-specialty for her."

I try to envision his family and I can't. I can't even imagine human beings. There are ethnographers in HH's family tree? This is rich.

"An ethnomusicologist?" I ask in wonder.

"My mother. She taught it over at the music department at UCLA."

Oh my God. Not only does he have a mother, but she's an ethnomusicologist at an esteemed university. I'm wondering how she reacts when her son shows up with his helmet and shopping bags full of old books at family dinners or ethnomusicology seminars. And then I am caught short and choke on my mean-spiritedness. How would I feel if Caleb, as a young teenager, turned angry, donned a helmet and rode a moped? Of course I would love him and stand by him. HH continues over my chagrin.

"So Dr. Lightfoot starts telling me about his church choir. Choir is like a sport in black churches. It's like football. They compete against other churches. They have events. He asks if I can sing. My mother taught me how to sing."

"The ethnomusicologist?"

"She would play things and I would listen and then I'd try to sing like I heard."

"You do have a good voice." (Why not show praise when due?)

"Thanks for the compliment, but that's not going to speed things up here."

"Just saying."

"So the reverend, he asks what my range is and I say tenor but I got a falsetto, too, and he asks me to sing and I sing a couple of bars of 'Gospel Train.' I got a good voice."

"I just said that."

"I started taking voice lessons when I was like twelve."

He notes my surprise and continues.

"Yeah. I know you're trying to catch up here, Ralphie. So the reverend's jaw fucking drops down around to his belt and he asks if I want to join his choir because their regular lead tenor just moved back to Georgia or something. I had like zero interest and told him no way and then the guy with the pickup shows up and we all start loading books. That's when I find out he's got like a ten thousand square foot storage facility next to his church that's almost empty and that's where the books are gonna go. I ask him if he wants to rent some space and he says no, but he'll give me some if I sing in his main choir."

This is all very interesting, but I try not to lose sight of my goal. I need to cajole him into turning over the property. I speak plaintively to whom I hope is Good Hector.

"Tell me what you want me to do? What do I need to do to get my book back?"

"Why don't you tell me my story, Ralph? That would save me some trouble and get you out of here quicker."

"What do you mean, 'tell you your story?'"

"You're acting like you know fucking everything. You probably know my life better than me."

"I never said that."

"Tell me about me."

"I can't."

"Why not?"

"Because you are about the biggest enigma I have ever seen."

"You want your book? Take a stab at it."

"I don't think you're going to give me the book."

"That's where you're wrong."

"I don't believe you."

"You need this book because you are desperate. I don't know what happened to you, Ralph, but you wouldn't be here if you weren't absolutely fucking desperate."

"My desperation doesn't have anything to do with whether or not you are going to give it to me. You're going to or you're not."

He hesitates, opens his eyes wide and then stands up.

"Exactafuckinglutely!!" he cries out. He paces as I stiffen, not knowing what will come next. Perhaps he will attack me. "It doesn't have anything to do with it! Does it?!"

I don't know what he is getting at. Is he being subtle or obtuse? Are we into street philosophy now? Are we getting epistomafuckinglogical?

"Do you think I'm on medication, Ralph?" he challenges out of nowhere.

"I don't know."

"Make a guess."

"I don't have any idea."

"Well, I am on fourteen." That could explain something. It could explain a lot. "Are you surprised?"

"A lot of people are on medication."

"What about you?"

"I take a few pills. Nothing major."

"Let me guess," he says. He paces a couple of times, strokes his chin, and then turns to me. "An antidepressant. An SSRI, probably second generation—not too old, not too experimental. Maybe Zoloft... Is it Zoloft?"

I shake my head in the negative. "But I'm right on the antidepressant?" he continues. I nod. He's pleased. "And it's an SSRI?" Again I nod. How many wrong answers does he have to give to end the game?

"I'm thinking Celexa." Not exactly brilliant and maybe a stab in the dark, but he got it. I nod. He grins and paces some more. I'm only slightly impressed.

"A multivitamin, a regimen aspirin, maybe an occasional Prilosec for the heartburn, right?" He's got my number. I nod and he's loving it. "And of course, for the really bad moments, when everything's closing in, and you have like the littlest twinge of panic deep in your gut, you keep a little bottle of Ativan that you ration really, really carefully, 'cause you know you could get addicted."

I don't have to nod. My face betrays my discomfort at his correctness. I know that crazy people can be frighteningly perceptive. He folds his arms in front of him in satisfaction.

"Tell me what I take. You want to get out of here? Tell me any three of my fourteen medications in six guesses and I promise I'll give you your book and you can go home."

"I thought you were going to give me my book anyway."

"I am. I figured you might want to get home sooner."

"And I thought this was supposed to be for my own good."

"It is."

"How is that?"

"You want to spend more time on this conversation or do you want to try to tell me what's in my medicine chest."

"Ativan," I say, barely hesitating. This would be the fish-in-the-barrel choice regarding any person with demons. He flushes and I am encouraged. One out of one for me.

"Aspirin."

"Just the prescription drugs, please," he replies with a snort.

"An antipsychotic..." I say.

"Which one?"

"I don't know. It's not an area in which I have major familiarity."

"Not good enough."

As I look at him, I see his eyes are yellow. His complexion is pallid and there are broken veins in his nose. I presume addiction of some kind.

"Antabuse?"

"Not even close."

"Methadone?" If not alcohol, then perhaps heroin.

"Is that really what you think? You think I am a junkie?"

"I am just guessing. I am trying really hard to play your game."

"One more miss and it's over."

"What's over?"

"This part of the entertainment."

"OxyContin," I say and get a reaction.

"That's not a medication."

"Yes it is."

"It's not prescribed."

"But you take it."

"I said I am talking about prescription drugs."

"It's not exactly over-the-counter."

"Ralph, I am trying to help you. Why are you so fucking obstinate? Give me another one. A prescription one."

"Vicodin."

"That's good, Ralph. That's good. You are smart."

So he has pain. Maybe he fell off his moped and hurt his back. Maybe a muscle relaxant. That might be a good guess.

"Naprosyn?" I ask naming what my doctor gave me when I hurt my shoulder playing tennis in my former life.

"Bzzzzzz. You lose."

"Okay. I lose. Now what?"

HH arises from his chair, motions for me to follow him as he speaks. "All right. I'll show you."

I get up and follow him into an area hidden by tall bookcases that has been designated as a kitchen area. It is basically clean, and has a mélange of quality, but mismatched appliances that undoubtedly came from yard sales. There is a shelf over the sink that has a lineup of pill bottles. He points to it with an oddly prideful look.

"All right. Here's a new one. Look at the bottles and tell me what my ailment is. Why do I take all these pills?"

"I'm not a doctor."

"I know you're not a doctor. You would never have the perspicacity to get through medical school. Tell me and I'll give you your book."

"Couldn't you just give me the book? I mean what good is it going to do for either of us to tell you what you have? Don't you already know?"

"Of course I know. That's not the point."

"Then what is the point?" I ask.

His response is to fold his arms in front of him and purse his lips.

"Just look at the labels and try using your feeble brain."

I look at them with curiosity and HH begins to recite.

"Diphenoxylate with atropine sometimes known as Lomotil, Temazepam to get me some sleep, bedtime or any other time, Fiorinal which is supposed to be useful for headaches but doesn't do shit. A couple of inhalers here—Advair and Albuterol. They're supposed to help me breathe which is always a good thing. And then I take Singulair in pills because I can't just be using the inhaler all day long. Compazine for nausea that I sometimes get dealing with jerks like you, Ralph. And Synthroid gives my thyroid that extra little spark it needs. Here's your Vicodin and your Xanax. And then there's the ones that keep me from being crazy—the Wellbutrin, the Prozac and the Risperdal—or at least enhance the crazy experience. They make kind of an exhilarating cocktail. You should try it. Beats the hell out of the pussy crap you take. You've got no idea what I went through trying to figure out the dosages. At least I'm not crazy, right Ralph?"

"If you say so."

"So...what do you think?" he asks.

"About what?" I know I am playing dumb.

"About what I've got. Tell me what I've got, Doctor Ralph, and you run home with your book."

I look at the bottles. They're regular amber plastic bottles. I look at the labels. There are a few different prescribing doctors and the prescriptions in the name of Hector Matthey are all generic substitutes for the proprietary drug. For example, what HH called Advair is actually "Fluticasone with salmeterol" with "Advair" added in parentheses.

Where I would expect to find the pharmacy logo on the label, I see simply printed in small bold Times Roman "WESTLA ACC,CA 90012." Below, in Courier, are an 800 phone number and a prescription number and dosage instructions. It's oddly bureaucratic. For some reason there is an eagle embossed onto the cap.

"What is this pharmacy?" I ask.

HH shrugs.

I rephrase. "Is this like Medicaid or Medicare or something?" Again a shrug. I know I'm onto something. But I don't think that Medicare has its own pharmacies. Maybe they do, but I've never heard of them. This is a clue. The drugs indicate a guy with multiple problems, psychological and physical. I try to make sense of it. Maybe he's a hypochondriac. But his pallid, drawn appearance, his compulsive tick and the oddness in his gait indicate that something is amiss in his body. As for his mind, clearly he needs more drugs and not fewer. If not Medicaid, then what? Is he part of some clinical trial? No—not with the confusion of fourteen different medications.

As he waits for me to guess again, I begin to understand. I will not have to kill him. Clearly what is going on is a seduction. HH is reaching out to me, but he doesn't want to be thought of as easy and I think there is something he wants me to know about him. This is all a tease to protect his warped vanity, but I suspect that in the end, for better or worse, he (and the book) will be mine.

"Is this from the Veterans Administration?" I ask, not even quite sure how the idea popped into my head. Must have been the eagle. I know it wasn't the Post Office that gave him the pills. "Are you a vet?"

He looks stricken. I have hit pay dirt. The Veterans Administration Hospital sits on a large plot of land near the Wilshire Boulevard entrance to the San Diego Freeway. It is Times Square for the walking wounded, mostly middle-aged, addled casualties of Vietnam. They crowd the bus stops and many of them panhandle at the traffic lights on the busy intersections on Wilshire. The sidewalks buzz with motorized wheelchairs and there are shopping cart encampments of homeless and forlorn veterans in the bushes on the perimeters. HH could easily be one of those men, but he is too young for Vietnam and too old for Iraq or Afghanistan.

"Were you wounded?" I persist. "Is that what this is about?"

If he wasn't wounded then, he looks wounded now. I almost feel sorry for him. Am I close to the heart of the mystery of what plummeted Hector from promising, mellifluent son of a college professor to fiberglass-domed miscreant?

"Why don't you go fuck yourself, Ralph?"

"For being right?"

"No. Because it's Tuesday."

"I want my book."

"There is no book. I was just messing with you."

"You are a lousy liar. I want my goddamn book."

HH turns away from me, walks toward the door.

"Just leave, Ralph. You're chasing air. Again." He starts to walk away.

It's not the insult that pushes me over the edge. If I analyze it I am not sure that it even makes sense considering what HH could know about me. But I am on him in a flash. I jump on his back, get him on the ground and turn him roughly over. He tries to resist, but I am bigger and stronger and I am pumped. I put my knees heavy on his chest and raise my clenched fist over his head.

"I have your book! I have your fucking book! Get off of me and I will get it."

I ease up slightly and he squirms out from under me and bolts toward the door. I leap after him and tackle him just in front of a table full of packing materials. Again I flatten him on the floor and put my knees on his sunken chest.

"This is an assault, Ralph! You can go to jail for this!"

I see a roll of packing tape on the table next to me. I manage to grab it while still on top of him.

"No book is worth going to jail for!" He yells.

I hold his wrists together and wrap the tape. He has surprisingly little strength and his resistance is childlike. Despite his squirming I hogtie him easily like a young steer, wrists and ankles quickly bound. I take my weight off of him and stand up.

"Think about what you are doing, Ralph!"

"I will put a knife in your gut if you don't get me that book!"

"I don't think so. I don't think you'll do that."

Despite the anger coursing in me I know he is right. God knows I don't want Caleb visiting me on death row. I look around me, and then go to the shelf with the Steinbeck and Vonnegut first editions. I empty a box of lesser books that sits on the floor and pile all of the books from the shelf into the box.

"Jesus, be careful with the dust jackets," he implores.

I hold the box up tauntingly in front of HH. It's probably worth its weight in gold.

"I guess I'll be going," I say, regaining my composure with my upper hand.

"Okay. You can have your book, Ralph. If you want it so bad you can have it."

"Where is it?"

"Just let me go and I'll get it."

"Just tell me where it is."

He pauses for a few seconds and speaks.

"It's over there." He gestures to a bookcase across the room. I walk to where he points. He nods.

"Second shelf from the top. Far right."

The shelf is filled with classic Japanese manga books. On the end of a stack I see the book sitting inside a new plastic sleeve. Except for the protective sleeve it is exactly as I remember it. I remove it from the shelf and pull it out of its sleeve. Hemingway's picture on the back of the dust jacket is tinted blue as it should be in a first edition. I open it and turn to the publisher's page. I quickly find the identifying Scribners' seal and letter "A" on the Scribner's coliform to show it is a first printing.

"Nice book, huh?" says HH. His expression is worn and submissive.

I press the book close to me and urge myself to the door, hoping that there is no further surprise waiting for me, no other task to perform or secret to uncover.

"You want to untie me now? I apologize. I know I've caused you distress."

It flickers in my sizzling brain that untied he might be able to shoot me in the back with an M-16 or some other souvenir of his battle experience. I make it to the entry area as defined by a big, commercial rubber doormat on the floor, and I mean to say, "Goodbye." But instead I say, "Where were you wounded?"

"You mean where was I or where on my body?" he asks back.

I hesitate, my back to the door. "Both," I reply.

"You can't leave me here."

His bonds are not so tight that he shouldn't be able to wriggle out of them in ten minutes or so. I will be gone by then.

"You'll be okay."

"You know I tried to help you," he says.

"With what?"

"With what you want to know."

"What do I want to know?"

"Why is this happening to me? Am I right, Ralph?"

Of course he is right. He is crazy-perceptive enough to be totally, completely right.

"You think that's what I want to know?"

"Yes."

"But you say you can't help me, right?"

"That's right."

"Then why did we just play this fucking game? Why did you tell me it was for my own good and why did I have to play twenty questions for nothing to get my book back?"

"That's the thing about our condition. We have moments of clarity, where we think we understand it, but then it hazes over again. I thought I could help you, but I can't. I am in a haze."

"Our condition?"

"Our slide, Ralph. Our slide from grace."

My slide is not *his slide*. I resent the comparison.

"Why did you give me my book back?"

"Because I have love for you." He senses me recoiling. "Not faggoty love. Fraternal love."

I am only slightly relieved. "This isn't about Jesus, is it?" I ask, now concerned that I am about to be proselytized instead of butt-fucked.

"Jesus is another chapter."

"No offense, but antipsychotics and Jesus talk go together in a way that is off-putting to me."

"We don't have to talk about him."

"Then what should we talk about?"

I know what we have to talk about and that is what I am avoiding. It is what people always talk about. What I would prefer not to admit that we have to talk about—what we have in common.

But in the case of HH, I have long preferred to think that we have little in common. It is true that we are both bipeds who buy books on the street and sell them online. But I like to think that I am more than that, and frankly I like to think that he is less. At the moment, I am feeling uneasy about the equation.

"Were you in Desert Storm?" I ask. On a back channel I have been thinking about his "wound" and going through age, dates and wars and 1991's rescue of Kuwaiti oil is the only one that makes sense. It didn't come to mind before because the American casualty count was historically low. He nods assent.

"Yes, I was."

I pause. I notice a shiver or a tremor going through his body.

"I really am sorry."

"Okay."

"If you untie me I could fix you some eggs. I don't have much else around here now."

I hesitate a moment, then take some scissors and walk toward him. Perhaps he thinks I will stab him, but I doubt it. I free his bond.

"Eggs would be fine," I say, wondering if he might be crazy-clean or crazy-dirty in the preparation of food.

He leads me toward the loft-style kitchen area. It seems average clean. "I think my first instincts were right, Ralph. I think I can help you."

"With what?"

"To be a better bookseller."

Chapter 20

Reuters 4/11 Baltimore: Biogram Pharmaceutical Holdings (BGPH) reports that it has suspended stage three clinical trials for its artificial blood product Hemobiplastin after a research subject in Tucson died suddenly and unexpectedly after suffering a possible allergic reaction. Company spokesman Linda Seagrave noted that doctors were still trying to determine the exact cause of death but that Biogram was temporarily suspending its Hemobiplastin testing program. The stock was sharply down in morning trading.

Because I had signed up for a web service to follow the news on this stock I received this update as an email when I arrived at work the morning after I had written both my name and True's on a check for $105,000 to Roos and Selvin Investments. I checked the stock online and found that it had fallen from the $7 that I paid to $2⅛. Other news services confirmed this story and also reported that NASDAQ had halted all trading in Biogram. A chill went through me. I actually shivered and felt the blood fall into my stomach. I tried to assess what the news meant but my analytic faculties seemed to have drained to my abdomen with my blood.

I tried to formulate questions as I dialed Roos and Selvin. Foremost, I needed to know if my money was safe. I tried to think of it from a lawyer's perspective—my lawyer. It is true that I had contracted to buy the stock, fifteen thousand shares. On the other hand, if my check had not been tendered, and I was promised that it wouldn't be, then the stock must still technically belong to Roos and Selvin. The transaction is null and void. An oral contract (Chuck's clear promise not to cash the check) is a contract just as binding as if it had been written. Anyone knows that. I called Chuck and the receptionist picked up.

"Roos and Selvin"

"May I speak to Chuck Firestone please?"

"Who may I say is calling?"

"Mitchell Fourchette."

"Just a moment, please."

I had decided I would offer to pay the broker's commission and ask for them to please return the check. It's not as if they went out and bought it for me. That sounded like a fair compromise. It was stock they already owned in the company portfolio and if I hadn't been around yesterday they would certainly have had the loss. It was to no personal advantage to Chuck not to see the check returned. His warrants at ten would now be moot. Also, even though I know that Chuck's bottom line was self-interest, I felt that he and I nonetheless had a sort of a bond of trust and that he would look out for me and make the most favorable interpretation of the circumstances.

"Mr. Fourchette?"

"Yes?"

"Mr. Firestone isn't in. Shall I leave word for him?"

"Do you know when he'll be back?"

"I'm sorry, I don't."

"Yes please. Ask him to call me as soon as possible."

I tried to do some work while I waited for Chuck to call me back. Of course I couldn't. I checked the price of the stock and it hadn't moved from $2⅛. I decided that I would make sure that the money was in the bank and that the check hadn't been cashed. I couldn't access that account online, so I called Wells Fargo.

When I reached the automated Wells Fargo menu I was asked to key in my account number. I didn't know the number, but I had the checkbook in the car and I retrieved it and was about to call Wells Fargo again when my phone rang. I expected Chuck.

"Mr. Fourchette?"

I had no idea who this was.

"Speaking."

"This is Ashton LaVin in the accounts section of Seymour Schein on a recorded line. I'm calling because we have a deficit in your trading account here. It's for twelve thousand six hundred and fifty-nine dollars."

Shit.

"Yes, I know about it."

"Normally we expect those deficits to be paid in a forty-eight-hour period. Is that all right with you?"

"No problem."

"Then we can expect payment before close of business tomorrow?"

"Okay."

"If you like you can give me a bank account number and I can arrange transfer right away on the phone."

"No, that's okay. I'll take care of it tomorrow."

"How will you be doing that?"

"I'll stop by the office with a check."

"That's great, Mr. Fourchette. I'll note it on your account here."

"Okay. I have another call and I need to go."

"No problem. Have a good day."

I hung up and redialed Wells Fargo. At the prompt I entered the account number for the joint account and then my social security number. I was greeted with the voice of a woman who sounded like she was in Texas.

"Hello. May I have your account number please?"

"I just keyed it into the phone."

"I'm sorry. I'll need it anyway."

"Then why did I have to key it in?"

What did I care? Why was I wasting time with this? I've already spent more time than if I gave her the fucking number. She replied in a disarmingly folksy voice.

"You know, honey, people ask me that question all the time

and I never got a good answer myself."

I gave her the number and she laughed warmly when she asked me for my social. She was clearly good people. For a moment I felt like I had an ally and I wanted to believe that somehow she might be helpful in getting me through this.

"Where are you?"

"I'm in Beaumont, Texas."

"That's near Galveston, isn't it?"

"We like to say that Galveston is near Beaumont."

I forced a chuckle as I waited another second for her to pull up my account on her computer.

"Okay, darling. I show an account balance of four thousand three hundred and twenty-seven dollars and sixty-seven cents."

"What?"

The account was down $105,000. Obviously the check had been deposited immediately and cleared.

"Four thousand three hundred and twenty-seven dollars and sixty-seven cents. The last debit was for check number one hundred and five for one hundred thousand dollars even."

"When did you receive that check?"

"It shows it was paid yesterday. Is there anything else I can do for you, Mr. Fourchette?"

"No. You've done it." I hung up. I was oddly, disconnectedly, ethereally calm for a moment. Probably the same calm you feel an instant after a knife has plunged into you. And then when I picked up the phone my hand was shaking. I dialed Chuck's office again.

"This is Mitchell Fourchette. I'm calling again for Mr. Firestone."

I pressed my arm on the desk to stop the shaking. There was nothing I could do about the quaver in my voice.

"I have your message for him, Mr. Firestone."

"Did he pick it up?"

"I don't know."

"You don't know if he picked up his message?"

"I leave it for him on his computer. I don't know if he picked it up."

"Is he in his office?"

"I'm not sure."

"Can you go look? It's important."

"I'm sorry, I can't do that. But I did give him your message."

"Then he received it."

"I'm sorry. I have another call. I have to put you on hold."

Then I heard a dial tone. She had hung up on me. I called back.

"This is Mitchell Fourchette. We were disconnected."

"I'm sorry, Mr. Fourchette. I have left another message for Mr. Firestone."

"Would you tell him that if he doesn't call back within the hour that I'm going to have to go to my attorney."

"I will give him that message."

This time I hung up. I didn't really have an attorney. True and I hired a real estate attorney for two hours to go over the real estate contracts when we bought the house, but he was just a tired old guy in a sleepy office in a fading two-story building in Marina Del Rey.

I got in the Volvo and drove to Century City. I parked underground and traveled on the escalator to the elevator bank and then ascended to the twenty-fifth floor.

On the elevator I thought about True and what I would tell her. Should I portray myself as hapless and vulnerable—a victim of a professional scammer? That would make me weak in her eyes, but relieve me of some responsibility. I didn't want to appear weak to True. I knew that our bond was based partly on my strength.

I could just open up, tell her the whole truth, about how I misread the market and lost the money in JDSU and how I was humiliated and didn't want to tell her—so much so that I risked everything for a chance to set things straight. It was a foolish action driven by my desperation not to lose the things which were most dear to me. In the end it was only money that had been lost. The elevator doors opened on the twenty-fifth floor.

The waiting room was empty save the receptionist.

"Hi. I'm going to see Chuck Firestone."

She was surprised when I continued resolutely past the reception desk directly to the office hallway.

"I'm sorry, but you can't... Is he expecting you?"

I hadn't been to Chuck's office, but the suite wasn't that large and I could cover it in a minute or two. The receptionist followed me and although I tried to sublimate my anger, I think she could tell from the way I walked that it wouldn't be good to get in my way.

I saw a young ex-college football player type wearing khakis and a white shirt.

"Where's Chuck?" I inquired in a polite voice that may have been in conflict with my aggressive stride.

"I think he went into Nate's office." He pointed to a door down the hall, not really taking heed of me until he saw the receptionist in pursuit. I saw the door that read NATHAN ROOS on it. It was a quarter open. I opened it the rest of the way to find Chuck standing in front of the desk of a natty, silver-haired guy, presumably Nate Roos, a partner in the firm.

I planted myself inside the door. Chuck's jaw dropped. Nate looked to the receptionist who shrugged to indicate that she tried to keep me out.

"I tried to reach you, Chuck. You didn't answer my calls."

"Nate, this is Mitchell Fourchette. He's a client."

"I would have thought you would have called me," I said to Chuck.

"I'm sorry, I got backed up."

"You told me you wouldn't cash my check."

Chuck feigned surprise.

"I'm sorry?"

"You told me you'd hold my check and wouldn't cash it."

"There's a misunderstanding here, Mitchell."

"Biogram is down to two and a half points and I'm completely ruined. You said you wouldn't cash the check."

"Mitchell, we got you out. Not like Schein who are so fucking slow on the trigger that they closed out below your margin. You don't owe us anything."

"You mean it's all gone?"

Chuck turned to Nate to explain, taking on the air that the worst part of what was happening was that I was embarrassing him in front of his boss.

"Mitchell bought a position in Biogram from us." Nothing about holding the check. Nothing about his assurances. Then he turned to me. "Nobody saw this coming. We all got hurt, Mitchell. Believe me we're holding a lot more than you are."

"You said you were going to help me out! You lying, cheating motherfucker!!" I yelled and an instant later two broker/ex-USC linebacker types appeared behind me at the door.

Chuck turned to Nate. "I'm sorry about this, Nate."

Nate replied to him as if I wasn't there.

"The guy's just upset. I understand."

"Mitchell. I'm really sorry about what happened. But you can't come in here and act this way. Do you understand?"

Nate interjected addressing Chuck.

"Did you tell Mr. Fourchette that you were going to hold back a check for him?"

"No. Of course not." He pretended to be insulted.

"Nothing like that? Nothing that could be misinterpreted?"

"Nothing."

Nate spoke calmly to me in defense of the liar. "The firm isn't allowed by the SEC to hold checks. We try very hard to run this business by the book."

Chuck had the gall to look at me and nod his concurrence.

"You are a lying motherfucker, Firestone!" I screamed. This was too much. It would not stand.

I lunged for him and I was immediately grabbed by the two linebackers at the door. I squirmed, but it was a useless show. They pushed me against a wall and held me. The receptionist watched from the hallway.

"Do you want me to call building security?" she asked.

To my credit I saw the hopelessness of my situation and let my body go slack.

"I don't think that's necessary," Nate said.

"The check isn't legal. I signed my wife's name." I said after the guys eased their grip on me.

Nate looked to Chuck who averted his eyes in response.

"The check requires both our signatures. I signed hers. Chuck knew I did it."

There was a long pause while Nate considered what I had said.

"Apparently the bank seems to be satisfied. If you forged a signature I would say that is more a problem for you than anyone else, Mr. Fourchette."

He was right, of course. There was the problem with the law on this issue and moreover there was the problem with True. I would have to tell her. The fact that I had totally depleted her father's inheritance was not a secret I could keep forever.

But I didn't tell her that night. Not after we ate takeout Indian food from Hurry Curry down the street (Caleb is a young fan of samosas) and not after we all worked in the garden, planting tomato seedlings. It was light until eight o'clock and the sun bounced yellow into the garden off the side of our pale house and lit us all in a warm Kodachrome glow. True said that I seemed preoccupied but didn't ask me about how our investments were doing.

The next day on my way to work I avoided passing Chuck's house, partly because it was a painful reminder of recent events and partly I didn't trust myself not do something foolish. I didn't have a solution to my problem but even in my agitated state I knew it wasn't to be found by pounding on his door. Also his proximity to my house and to True made me want to keep a boundary between us. Alternate routes were easy on the square grid of our neighborhood.

On my way in to work I stopped at the bank and took a cash transfer check from my Wells Fargo MasterCard for twelve thousand dollars and then stopped by and paid Seymour Schein. For most of the day I thought about the ways I could replace the money. I looked at all my credit cards and they amounted to about $40,000 minus the $12,000 I had already borrowed. I could try to squirrel some money away from my paycheck, but that wouldn't amount to more than a thousand a month and I'd also have to pay back the credit card debt.

Any attempt to get money back from Roos and Selvin was fraught with problems. As far as I could tell, what happened was a matter for the civil courts or formal arbitration. I would never be able to pursue it without True finding out. Moreover, whatever chances I had of succeeding in court were subsumed by my forging of True's signature.

I could have just admitted that I forged the signature, take my lumps with True and then pursued a lawsuit. But it had to boil down to my word against Chuck's, and I didn't know how a jury would be able to ferret out the truth.

A simple solution would be to tell True, ask her to attest that the signature was really hers or was signed for her with her knowledge (I think there's a legal term for that) and then I could try my hand at suing them. As I said, however, I wasn't ready at that point to open up to True. Not that I didn't expect that ultimately she would vouchsafe the signature. She would have no other choice. And I trusted we could get past that in our relationship. I wasn't there yet.

I considered robbing a bank, more as an exercise in lateral

thinking than a real alternative. I considered it enough to find out that the FBI statistic for solved bank robberies is a tempting 18 percent. Also in the realm of out-of-the-box thinking I ran the suicide scenario. I have $100,000 in life insurance with True as beneficiary, but if the idea was to replenish the inheritance account without True knowing, this was less than half the amount required and without me around to supervise covering my tracks she would obviously find out what happened anyway. Anyway I felt cornered, and angry with myself, but not yet suicidal.

It occurred to me that if Chuck was an heir to the Firestone tire family, perhaps I could recover something from them. I could call Firestone *père* and tell him that his son was up to no good and that I would drag Chuck and the whole family and the good name of Firestone Tires in the mud unless he made good on my loss. Or instead of a threat I could appeal to his better nature and rely on his pity and sense of fair play to make me whole again.

I searched the Firestone genealogy from original tire maker Harvey Firestone on the internet but I couldn't find a Chuck or a Charles that was the right age and geography that fit a scion of the Firestone family tree. There were, however, innumerable Charles Firestones that didn't fit. When I tried to connect my Chuck Firestone with Roos and Selvin I found out that he was listed on their roster as Charles A. Firestone, but I couldn't glean anything else about him from their website, nor did I find anything revealing about what appeared to be a Charles A. Firestone (probably the same) who had appeared in a few wealth management seminars around town. I put him together in a search with both "St. Paul's Academy" and then with "Oyster Bay, New York" and got nothing. Like everything else about him, his provenance was in doubt.

I considered Vegas. I did have money left on the credit cards. I could borrow $10,000 and take a shot. Roulette seemed most likely as my card skills were nonexistent. In roulette I have a 47.5

percent chance of winning at each turn. If I could win at the first turn, which was definitely doable, I could put my $10,000 stake aside and play the rest with house money. Then at least there would be nothing lost. But although I tried to tell myself that my string of bad luck meant that things were about to turn around, I couldn't help but feel doomed before the start.

I wanted to contain this until I found a solution. True did not make a habit of reading financial statements and she left online access to our bank accounts to me. While I knew that I could not remain indefinitely on a path of nondisclosure, there was not much pressing me to tell True right away. There was too much at stake not to apply the best possible timing. I didn't want to get it wrong.

And so I waited. I think I turned inward during this period. I tried to be pleasant and participative. I had early on made peace with the clients at Turtle Wax by saying that my son had taken a fall and had to be taken to the emergency room but thankfully he was all right. (I don't like using Caleb for this purpose and have an eerie feeling that somehow saying these things invites karmic pushback.) I worked late hours and brought home flowers and little food treats. We took a drive north past Ojai in the Volvo to see the fresh wildflowers on the Carrizo Plain—Apricot globe mallows, Canterbury bells, fiddleneck, and acres of poppies. But these simple pleasures were barely an escape from the gnawing truth.

One night we left Caleb with a neighborhood sitter and went to the movies to see *Gladiator* with Russell Crowe. The film was a bit of a disappointment. Afterwards, we bought frozen yogurt and ate it in the car. True eats at half my speed, so I usually finish mine and drive home while she eats hers.

"The stock market went up today," she said between bites.

In fact, there had been a small rally after a series of disastrous days. But True never talked about the market. For a brief moment I feared she knew something and my stomach felt light.

"Really?"

"That's what the paper said. It said that stocks have been going down, but they went up today."

"They've been doing an up and down thing for a while."

"I was wondering how we were doing."

What did she know? Clearly this was the time to come clean if there ever was a time.

"So you're interested after all?"

I used driving as a reason not to look her in the eye.

"Of course I'm interested."

"We're doing okay."

"Are we making money or losing money? You can tell me."

She said it sweetly, signaling that if I chose the latter it would be okay. She couldn't know the real truth and maintain this calm.

In retrospect I think I should at least have let her know about the $50,000 that I had lost in JDSU. That would have at least been an entrée into more difficult matters. But I had recently been schooled to distrust my instincts and maybe that is why I chose not to tell her about our mutual problem.

"We're treading water."

"Oh well."

"Oh well?"

"I had hoped that we would somehow be magically rich."

"I'm sorry."

"It's all right. We're fine the way we are. We're very lucky."

I didn't say anything but I reached for the radio. She took my hand tenderly.

"Don't feel bad, Sweetie. Think of all the poor people out there who are probably losing their savings."

Caught in the discomfort of the moment I somehow found myself driving home by way of Chuck's house. No doubt Chuck was in the interior of my thoughts at the moment and perhaps that is what drew me there. In True's presence I tried not to show a special recognition, but I did note by turning my eyes and not my neck that the boat was no longer there and that the Jaguar was still under its cover on the edge of the front driveway.

"You know, I am not comfortable with the stock market. I know I said I was. But I'm not," she said as she turned down the Mozart on the radio.

"Not comfortable?"

"Just I don't like risk. You know how being near a blackjack table in Vegas makes me crazy and nauseous. And I think about my dad. Can you imagine what he would think if he knew we were playing his money in the stock market?"

"I don't know that 'playing' is the right term."

"He was very conservative about finances. You told me that you respected that about him."

"I did."

"Can we get out? Can we just sell what we have invested and get out? I mean it."

I hesitated a moment and swallowed.

"Sure. We'll get out." In a manner of speaking, we already were.

"You mean it?"

"Sure."

"You're not disappointed?"

"No. We'll get out."

"We could take a little vacation with some of it. What do you think?"

"Why not?"

"I'm glad. This high stakes gambling isn't for us. It isn't who we are."

I wondered what the fallout might have been for Chuck. I wondered what among the things that he told me might have been true. Did he indeed have four thousand shares of Biogram as he said? Did he suffer bigger losses than I did? I certainly hoped so. I would have enjoyed seeing a "for sale" sign on his lawn and a moving van parked in front.

Chapter 21

I really should depart chez Helmet Head. After HH's offer to teach me to be a better bookseller I find myself curiously hesitant to move on. Am I really considering accepting HH's offer of counsel? God knows I could improve. For some reason I seem to be drawn to him in his alternate persona.

"How could you help me?" I ask warily.

"You could start off by getting more comfortable in your own skin."

I nod, immediately regretting having given him the opening. He continues. "You think you're too good for the job."

"With all due respect, you don't know what I think."

"People sense it, Ralph. They sense that you think you're above them. I don't have that problem."

"You want me to follow your example?"

"Fuck no. But a little humility would enhance your business and your life."

He grins and pauses, feigns an "aha" moment. "Your wife dump you?" He continues on at my non-response. "Because of money?"

"In a manner of speaking."

"Could you perform sexually?"

"That is none of your business and yes. I thought you were going to tell me about Desert Storm."

He opens the refrigerator which is largely bare except for a large supply of cheeses and a box of eggs. He flips the lid on the egg box and there are only two eggs inside.

"Oops. Low egg alert. I have a nice Idiazabal here and I have a good Malbec-Cabernet from Sonoma that I've been saving."

"I'm guessing Idiazabal is cheese?"

"It's Basque. It's mildly aromatic and medium hard. I have some soda crackers. We could do that and you could eat when you get home. You're probably better off. I got stomach issues that make me fart big time when I eat eggs."

"Good. Where were you wounded?"

I have to wait for him to put the cheese on plates and pull out a bottle of wine from an impressive looking rack of wines over the counter.

"It's a 2005 from a little vineyard that only does a few hundred bottles a year. I got six bottles for a buck apiece in an estate sale in Hancock Park. Estate sale people haven't got a fucking clue about wine. It sells for about a hundred a bottle at Wine Merchant."

He opens it with one of those fancy openers that looks like a gynecologist's instrument and puts it on a butcher block counter off the kitchen area. He motions for me to sit on a bar stool as he finds a knife for the cheese. I am not totally comfortable, but pleased to see his knife is small and benignly rounded at the tip. He settles onto a stool, cuts several slices off the cheese and speaks.

"I was an E4 in the 37th Engineer Battalion and they flew me to Qatar in 1991. I never saw a living Iraqi soldier in combat. Plenty of dead ones after. After they buried half the Iraqi army alive in trenches and blew to shit the rest of them, my platoon was supposed to follow after and blow up their ammo dumps. You ever hear of a place called Khamisiyah?"

"Nope."

"Weapons storage facility in the middle of the fucking desert. Remember this is March already. We had a cease-fire in February and by the time the cease-fire comes, nobody's thinking chemical weapons anymore. The 82nd airborne has already done a security sweep of the area. If the Iraqis had them, they would have used them. We all had these MOPP suits but nobody was wearing them. We just carried our masks and we figured that if there was a problem the detectors would start buzzing and let us know. So we're basically in this place which is a bunker in the middle of fucking desert nowhere and there's ammo stored there. There's bullets, but there's mortars and explosive shells and rockets and grenades, too."

"Can I ask you something? What were you doing in the army? Did you just join up?"

"Hello? The draft's been over for thirty years."

"Was your father in the army or something?

"My dad was an art dealer on Melrose Avenue."

This wasn't the answer I was expecting but it could help explain the Ed Ruscha on the floor.

"Your mother was an ethnomusicologist and your father was an art dealer?"

"Yeah. And I dumpster dive for books. Is that what's bothering you, Ralph? The *incongruity* of it all? Maybe your great-grandfather was a slave."

"Actually it was my great-great-grandfather."

"Well, he'd probably be very disappointed in you if he could see you now, don't you think?"

"Why did you join the army?"

"Because I thought it would be better than jail. I was young and didn't know any better."

"You would have gone to jail if you didn't go in the army?"

"I got in some trouble. As I said, I was young and I might have been dealing a little meth to make ends meet."

"You were going to go to jail for dealing meth?"

"Let me say now that I think meth is a really bad thing and I would never be dealing it today."

That would explain a lot. Not enough, but a lot. He continues his story, however.

"Anyway, I sold a quarter ounce to some tasty little fox and I wound up taking part of it in trade if you get my drift. And it turned out she was fourteen. And she told her parents and they—well, you get the picture."

"So they let you go into the army instead of going to jail."

"It wasn't about me. It was about my 'poor parents.' Their friends in the DA's office couldn't let me put a black mark on their permanent parenting record."

"So they just let you off."

"There were some favors involved. My dad knew some people. It would have been bad for his business to have offspring in jail for meth."

"Were you in trouble before?"

"Of course I was in trouble before. I got suspended from Beverly Hills High School for selling a little pot to friends. But nothing like rape. That I didn't have before. I was still in school for Chrissake."

"Beverly High?"

"And University of Spoiled Children after."

This can't be. Deep inside I expected to find a Hector without a story. Someone who had sprung full blown out of a crack in the sidewalk and was destined from inception to tussle with old ladies over DVDs at church sales. But educated, upper-middle-class parents, University of Southern California? If he has a story of degradation and entropy, then anyone can have a story of degradation and entropy. Even I could. Part of me would like to end this conversation and part of me can't be stopped.

"I am on fucking Megan's list," he adds. "I thought you wanted to hear war stories."

"So what happened in Iraq?" I ask.

"It wasn't my job to be looking for chemical weapons. My guys were just support. Carry things and look out for trouble for the EOD guys."

"EOD?"

"Explosive Ordinance Disposal. Guys are fucking crazy. They do the roadside bombs and shit. Anyway the EODs were told that the Iraqis marked all of their chemical weapons with yellow bands. That's how they kept from poisoning themselves. And if there was any chemical stuff—and mostly we were expecting sarin and cyclosarin—they'd probably be in the 122mm rockets. And there's like a zillion 122mm rockets in cases there. So they go through half of them and none of the boxes they open have markings on the shells or on the boxes. Good to go, right? So they pack the bunkers with two hundred pounds of C4 and everybody in my platoon goes two clicks northwest which is upwind and we wait and there is the biggest fucking bunch of booms you ever heard and smoke and sand and pieces of ammo and boxes and everything goes up like a mile in the air. And we're thinking that's cool and then one of the M8A1's starts going berserk—"

"Who's an M8A1?"

"Not who. What. It's our chemical detector."

"So what did you do?"

"We're way the fuck away from things and we can see it's still blowing downwind, but the sergeant starts yelling to put on our MOPP suits, so we do, even though mine and most of the others are full of holes. So fine. And none of the other alarms go off and everybody says it was just a fluke."

"And did anyone get sick?"

"A couple of guys got nosebleeds the next day."

"And you?'

"I got the shits. But I had the shits half the time I was there."

"So what happened?"

"A week later I'm in a tent in the desert and I get up in the middle of the night and my skin is all burning and I can't breathe. I get sent to the hospital in Qatar and they say I have asthma. They don't know about my skin burning and it's stopped but I have like these red spots. I never had asthma in my life. And I can't eat anything. And my gums are bleeding. And I've still got the shits. And then I get this thing where I kind of twitch my shoulders. It's kind of subtle. I don't know if you notice it."

Subtle as a sledgehammer. But I give a kind of shrug to acknowledge without prejudice the existence of the twitch and he continues.

"And there's other guys there with a dozen different versions of what I've got and there's a buzz about chemical weapons. One guy says he was someplace where he got some kind of yellow powder all over him after an Iraqi rocket went off near the compound. But nobody wants to hear it and some lieutenant comes in to see me and says that it would be bad for the war or morale or something if rumors started about chemical weapons and that I should shut up and not jump to conclusions at least until somebody figures out what happened to me. And a doctor comes in and tells me that I've got PTSD. Fuck me. I've got Post Poisoned-With-Fucking-Chemicals Disorder is what I've got. But that's not even the completely weird part. You want to know what really freaks me out?"

"What?" I say, although maybe I don't really want to know.

"The medics decide to send me back to Qatar when I start coughing up blood and they put me in a Humvee with two lieutenants who were being reassigned and some shit-kicker kid from Mississippi driving the thing and he drives sixty miles an hour into a fucking ditch and the Humvee flips like seven times and then explodes. All three of them are totally wasted and dead. I get thrown out into a sand dune and outside of the fact that I'm poisoned by Saddam, there's nothing wrong with me besides a sprained shoulder. I mean what the fuck is that about? Is God preserving me so that he can torture me with Iraqi chemicals? Is that what this is about?"

"I don't know. You're the guy who goes to church."

"Anyway they ship me back to Walter Reed and I seem to have a bit of a problem with some of their cognition tests. I mean in some ways I'm still there, but in other ways you can see I've got wires crossed. The ones with all the squares and the triangles I always screw up. I didn't get stupid, but I have problems putting some things together. You ever go to Mexico and all the signs are in Spanish and everything seems the same but different. That's how I feel all the time. And I've got dreams about exploding puppies and falling in big vats of sulfuric acid. Before all this happened if I had a bad thought, I'd think of something pleasant or smoke some pot and everything would be cool. Now things are happening inside my head and I can swallow a pharmacy and they don't go away."

My phone rings. I look and it's True again. This gives me a chill. I haven't forgotten Caleb is sick. I also know True doesn't make a habit of calling, and calling twice never happens. I grab the phone out of my pocket and move a few steps away, turning from HH.

"True?"

"I'm taking Caleb to St. Mary's emergency room. I think he's having an allergic reaction to the Ceclor."

My stomach feels light.

"How do you know?"

"It started with a rash on his arms and then all of a sudden his face started puffing up. I called Dr. Levy and he said to give him Benadryl."

"Do you have Benadryl?"

"Yes! I gave it to him and it didn't help!"

I can hear the panic in her voice. It is a very unusual tone for her.

"He started turning blue and he's having trouble breathing!" Now I hear her speak to Caleb, "It's okay, baby, we're almost there. I'm talking to Daddy." Back to me. "Can you hear him wheezing?" I can't, but I can imagine it. "I called Dr. Levy back and he said to go to the emergency room and he'd meet me there."

"Where are you?" I ask.

"I'm two blocks away!"

"I'm coming over!"

"Where are you?"

"I'm in Hollywood. I'm leaving now." I am not sure why I am saying Hollywood instead of Crenshaw. It's a silly white lie for no good reason. HH senses I am about to leave.

"My kid is sick," I tell him.

"You know I was just fucking with you about the book. No hard feelings. Right?"

I kind of nod as I head for the door.

"You know, sometimes you should look past the publisher's page. Just a suggestion."

I take this as a small insult, as if I needed to be reminded that art is more important than lucre, but I let it go. I put the book under my arm. I am in a hurry.

Chapter 22

Weeks went by and I found myself unable to tell True the truth about my stock trading or to come up with a viable plan to restore the money. The NASDAQ had made a modest retrenchment from its April low, up 6 percent after losing more than a third. Mostly I chose not to read the financials because they only brought me back to the same unpleasant place, but when I did I found myself with a despicable case of schadenfreude applied to all investors, not just Chuck and his bosses. I am embarrassed to say that I cheered the market downward so that others might suffer as I have.

I had time to think, reason and research (going forward I will always begin with this process and not end with it) and I was able to come up with several plausible explanations of what happened to me. I probably will never know for sure, but here is the scenario that seems most plausible:

As Chuck had said, Roos and Selvin was a small investment brokerage that managed money and made trades mostly for its own clientele. They also traded for their own account and had sizeable positions in a number of stocks. Chuck was what was called a position trader and he had done quite well for the company, although in the late nineties it was hard to do badly. A fair amount of their portfolio was in biotech stocks and R/S became known as a market maker in the biotech area sometimes referred to as (the irony is not lost on me) "the smart money."

Roos and Selvin had taken a large position in Biogram, a relatively small biotech company, presumably because they had good information that it would succeed with Hemobiplastin. Now here is where I am still a bit confused—it is entirely possible that, suffering in the sudden new bear market, Roos and Selvin indeed had to come up with cash to satisfy the SEC as Chuck said. Frankly, I had no way of verifying that but it was a possible scenario.

It is alternately possible that Chuck and his company had inside knowledge that there was a problem in the trials and knew before I came along that the stock was going to tank. In that case, his ostensibly self-serving deal for warrants would have been part of the scam.

In either case they desperately needed to dump some Biogram. If a market maker like Roos and Selvin were to sell large quantities on the open market, buyers would recognize the source and immediately suspect that something was wrong because the "smart money" was getting out. Suddenly buyers would disappear and the stock would slide. Best for them to unload it quickly and privately, preferably not on their best customers who then would probably leave the brokerage in anger, but rather unload it on strangers. Enter good neighbor Mitchell Fourchette.

As I said, I don't know if Chuck had inside knowledge of the clinical trial problems. If he didn't, then what he did to me might have been a slightly less heinous equivalent to the moral difference between slaughtering elephants and slaughtering whales, for example.

Greater clarity did nothing to alleviate my problem, however. I consulted two lawyers, one a callow and sweet young man in a shared office in Culver City who gave me a free consult and the other a bearish Century City heavyweight who charged me $400 for the session that yielded the same result. Both told me that no lawyer would take this as a case on a contingency basis and that pursuing it would cost tens of thousands and I was undoubtedly wasting my money to hire anyone. As I didn't have the money for lawyers, pursuing it wasn't an issue anyway. Although I lied and told them that True knew I was signing her name, I was still warned of my vulnerability to forgery charges if a motivated litigator worked the other side of the table and chose to use that as a lever against me.

Life went on. I continued with the secret knowledge that True and I had nothing in the bank. True continued on the false assumption that we had $200,000 in reserve. In fact, it really didn't make that much difference in how we conducted our everyday lives. We had friends to dinner, took little daytrips into the mountains and watched *The Sopranos* on television. We took turns reading bedtime stories to Caleb. We argued about whether or not it was safe to drink raw milk, if I would inevitably get a ticket for rolling through stop signs and whether we should put down natural stones or cement pavers in the muddy area in the side yard by the trash cans. True, who had used a sabbatical to nurse Caleb after he was born, took on teaching an extra class. Things picked up for me at the agency. I helped pitch and we won Red Bull malt liquor as a client. I think the agency thought that it helped that I was somewhat black. I didn't mind.

True and I made love about three times a week, but not on a schedule. On a Tuesday night in June as we lay in bed I felt True's hand on the lower part of my stomach—one of her signals. Her timing seemed good. I reached over for her and she snuggled into me. As I gathered her in she spoke softly.

"Don't you think that maybe we should have another?"

I blanched slightly and not for any reason that she might have intuited.

"We could, you know," she continued. "Now is a good time for Caleb. Two or three years is a good spread for siblings."

She was right, of course. Under ordinary circumstances this would be a good time to be planning another child. How could I respond? Certainly not with the truth. Not now. Not here. One does not add to one's pack when traveling up a steep trail.

"Not that I don't agree, but could we talk about this some other time?"

That was certainly lame. It was officious and off-putting in response to words that reflected consummate intimacy. I could feel the hurt run through True, although she didn't say anything. I pulled her to me and she didn't resist, but I could feel the stiffness of her resentment.

"We will," I said to ameliorate. But those words were vague. We will talk about it? Or we will have another child? True chose not to parse them. There would, however, be no lovemaking tonight.

"I promise," I added, just to button it. I then looked up thoughtfully at the ceiling. I don't know what she thought my reasoning was for not wanting to talk then. Perhaps she assumed my mind was too caught up in something at work, or I had a headache or I was too horny to want to have a serious conversation.

For my part I didn't like to talk about things that incorporated the future. Having drawn a blank on how to replace the missing funds, I preferred not to think about what might happen. Like a wretch in a dungeon I waited passively for a knock on my door and the saying of my name that would bring my doom. Mixed with my dread was the innate desire of all condemned men to be relieved in any way from their transitory state, even by a gallows march.

My name was announced while I was on the white beach of Cancun, sipping bubbly water in Video Village which is what film crews call the area under a portable blue canvas canopy where the production companies purposely distance clients and agency people from the working crew. Video monitors were strategically placed so that we could sit in folding chairs to chat, eat and imbibe as far as possible from the action. I was there, overdressed in white slacks, along with the client, our agency art director and a few others as we watched on a shaded monitor a slender young model in a bikini walk out of the water and approach a bottle of Red Bull in the foreground. For the twentieth time. The first five were ruined when the art director realized that you could see red bumps on the juncture of her upper thighs, presumably the displeasing after-effect of her bikini waxing. The makeup person was held to task and managed to construct from bottles and jars of brown goop a neatly porcelained crotch.

My cell phone rang. I saw it was True and at the moment there was some delay having to do with the speed of the camera or the lens or some other such thing that makes what should take five minutes take all day. I answered it as I got up and walked into the sunshine and onto the hot sand. Probably it was to share a Caleb moment—perhaps something cute he said. She knew if I was busy that I'd let it go to voice mail, so she was free about calling.

"Hey, sweetness."

There was a bit of a pause on the other end of the line. The connection wasn't terrific.

"Did you change bank accounts or something?"

Uh-oh. If you can believe it, I hadn't really planned for this moment and I found myself vamping helplessly.

"What are you talking about?"

"Our Wells Fargo statement came in the mail this morning and I happened to look at it. I thought it was for our checking account, but it was the money market account. It only has two hundred dollars in it. Did you transfer the money?"

Think fast, Mitchell.

"Yeah. I put it in a brokerage account."

"At the bank?"

"No. At the broker."

"Why would you do that?"

I was beginning to have a feeling for the lie. My voice calmed a bit.

"I got a better rate."

"Don't I have to sign for you to transfer the money?"

"All I did was transfer it."

"But still I should have had to sign. I mean I'm not faulting you, but didn't the bank make a mistake?"

"Not if it went into an account that had both our names on it."

This was plain dumb. True isn't that interested in money, but she has a PhD in education and she's not stupid and she understands the fine points.

"So it's in a new account?"

"Yes."

"Where is it?"

"What do you mean?"

"If it's in a new account where is that account?"

"At Seymour Schein. It's a brokerage account at Seymour Schein."

"Then who is Roos and Selvin?"

This was bad. This was my name being called for the gallows.

"Who?"

"Roos and Selvin." The bank says that we wrote a check to them for a hundred thousand dollars. It has both of our signatures on it. I asked them to send it to me so that I could look at it."

"How could that be?"

"That's why I'm calling you. I'm asking you how that could be. Do you think somebody forged both of our names?"

"Do you think somebody forged both of our names?"

"I don't know."

"I thought you said you transferred the money to Seymour Schein. There is a check to Seymour Schein for fifty thousand dollars. That's the one that you told me about. I don't understand what this other check is."

"Well, neither do I."

"You see what I'm saying, Mitchell. If you transferred the money to Schein like you said you did, there would be a check or a transfer for that. But there isn't. Do you have any idea why?"

"I'm trying to figure it out."

"So am I. Is that all you have to say?"

"We'll talk about it when I get back. I'm sure there's a good explanation. They're calling me on the set now. I've got to go."

"Well what should I do now? Should I call the police?"

"No, don't call the police. I'll deal with it tomorrow when I get back. They need me on the set. I've got to go."

"You know I trusted you with everything."

"I know."

"Everything, Mitchell."

"I know."

"Was I wrong?"

"No. You weren't wrong. They need me on the set. I have to go. I'll call you back."

I closed the phone. Of course they didn't need me on the set. The director would rather I was back in Los Angeles so that he could use more backlight and flare out the model's silhouette. I was feeling suddenly queasy. I was a dead man walking.

It occurred to me that maybe being in Mexico was an omen. I had three changes of clothes in my suitcase. I had my credit cards. I could just stay here. Maybe I could find a job in Mexico City. They have advertising agencies there. They could probably use my gringo expertise. I could learn to speak Spanish.

Sitting alone that night in my courtyard-view room of the Marriot Casa Magna Cancun Resort I tried to think of something that would assuage my anxiety. Not hookers. Not booze from the minibar. The television had *CSI* and old episodes of *Seinfeld*, neither of which could ever hold my attention on an angst-neutral day. A good self-inflicted hammer blow to the head sounded appealing. It could give form to the anger I felt toward myself and it could help me to sleep.

As I lay on my bed, still in my white slacks, it came to me what I had to do. This required more than a phone call. That would wait. I would go home on schedule and tell everything. I knew True and she was a forgiving and empathic person. Part of our strength together is that she always saw the best in me. I decided I would lay out the whole story, being as honest and unsparing on myself as I could be. I would offer a plan to recoup the money. A conservative plan that would include enforced savings and perhaps life insurance or an annuity. People have suffered financial disasters before and come through stronger. We could have just as easily lost everything in a flood or an earthquake. We would rebuild. We could do it together. It would, in fact, be an opportunity. I knew True. She couldn't resist a challenge. She had every right to be upset or angry at first, but she would come around.

I didn't call True the next day. It seemed best to allow a small interval for her to burn off some of her justifiable anger. This combined with what would be for her a cold and empty bed one more night might redound to my benefit. As my plane flew on approach over the large circuit board that is Los Angeles I was full of hope for our tested, renewed and stronger relationship. Of course I couldn't wait to hug Caleb. Although he was too young to understand I would apologize to him for jeopardizing his college fund and remind him that we had plenty of time to refurbish it.

I had a brief vision that perhaps they would meet me at the airport in a tearful reunion. There was no plan to pick me up, but True had my flight information and it was not unusual if she didn't have class for her to show up at the gate with Caleb in tow. I got off the plane and scanned the lounge and there was no sign of them. There was, however, a familiar face. It was True's brother, Adam.

"Mitchell?"

I was surprised to see him. Perhaps he had a plane to catch in the same terminal. His law practice was in Denver but it is possible he had business in Los Angeles. His look was severe. He spoke something to a man standing next to him who looked about forty and was dressed in a sport jacket and no tie. The pair approached me. The man opened a wallet in front of me and there was a badge pinned to it.

"I'm Detective Garcia with the Los Angeles Police Department.

Are you Mitchell Fourchette?"

This couldn't be happening.

"Yes."

"I'm investigating a forgery and fraud case involving Wells Fargo Bank. Would you mind coming with me to the West Los Angeles station so that we can ask you some questions?"

"What is going on, Adam?" Adam looked past me, not answering.

"Am I under arrest?" I asked the cop.

"No, sir. If you don't choose to come I can place you under arrest, though."

"Where is True?" I asked Adam.

"I can't believe you did this to her."

"I want to see her."

"She doesn't want to see you."

"I don't believe it."

"She is very angry, Mitchell."

"Tell her I am sorry."

"You know, none of us wanted this marriage."

"What I don't need now, Adam, is racist bullshit."

"You think this is about race?"

"What else is there, Adam?"

"How about that you are a lying, cheating motherfucker?"

I still don't have a good comeback to that one.

It took some getting used to that what I had done was written indelibly in India ink. There would be no going back. As True saw it this was not about money. It was an irreparable breakdown of trust in the relationship. It was not about the one lie. It was about the series of lies.

I was taken aback by the depth of her fury. For True this was not a matter for marriage counselors or twelve-step programs and she was not desirous of any intervention. Adam engineered it so that the fraud charges would disappear if I dropped out of True's life.

True for the most part refused to speak to me for almost a year. I helplessly acquiesced to all of her demands made through her attorney save her insistence on sole custody for Caleb with prescribed visitation for me.

There was a buzz about it in our circle and our friends naturally chose to gather by True. The fraud charge and the possibility of me going to jail lingered for a while and advertising is a small if generally tolerant world that tends to look on peccadilloes as a byproduct of creativity. Stealing a wife's inheritance seemed to transgress those boundaries and subsequently I found myself in a spiral that culminated with being sacked from Sather and Knowlton.

What followed was a cascade of events leading to me living in my small apartment. I found myself broke and with almost no possessions except the clothes and some books that True had thrown into boxes and placed on the back steps for me to pick up while she wasn't there. In an effort to survive I found that a few had some value and I thought to advertise them on Amazon. I knew something about books. I went to Goodwill looking for a coffee pot and noticed there were several books on the shelf for a dollar that could be sold for more. One thing led to another.

Chapter 23

The Volvo and I lurch into the hospital parking lot. Two ambulances in the driveway in front serve as sentinels to the emergency room entrance. St. Mary's is a good hospital by reputation, burnished by its luxury-suite, platinum-card treatment of a number of past Hollywood luminaries.

I hurry inside and look around the small lobby; it is not obvious who is in charge. It was no doubt easier in the days before corporate hospital takeovers when nuns ran things and you could just look for a woman dressed in a habit. A security guard catches my frazzled affect.

"You need some help?"

"My son and his mother are supposed to be in here somewhere."

"The duty nurse is over there."

He points to a uniformed nurse who bends solicitously over a frightened middle-aged man on a gurney looking quite pink and exposed on the white sheet. I interrupt her.

"Excuse me. My son's supposed to be here," I say breathlessly.

"What's your name?"

"Fourchette. His name is Caleb."

She nods in recognition.

"He's with his mom in bay four. You can go in through that door." She hesitates a beat and then smiles reassuringly. "He's okay. They just had a scare, that's all."

I exhale a big breath. Sometimes things get out of control and you suspect that your spell of immunity is broken and anything bad can happen. But we don't live in a remote village under the stars at the mercy of the whims of nature. We live in Westside Los Angeles, where we have three of the top hospitals in the country with the best doctors and the best equipment. We are strong. Eleven million people live in a hundred-square-mile clump so that we can cover each other's backs and so that we will not suffer the misfortunes of the weak. We fight fire and flood, vermin and disease. We have pillowtop mattresses and air conditioning and fresh and fragrant vegetables. We should not forget that we are blessed because we are indeed blessed. Although I no longer believe in my mother's Roman Catholic conception of God and son, I understand why people look up and give thanks. At this moment, with the knowledge that my boy is safe, I am struck by that very impulse.

The swinging glass doors open automatically as I rush to bay four. Inside I see a lineup of monitors and sundry wheeled medical equipment outside the entryway to a large room divided into curtained areas.

I notice a familiar purse on the floor at the base of a curtain. True always has the big, floppy leather ones that have room for several books and she likes bright colors. This one is aqua. I approach past the semi-closed curtain and find True standing at the foot of a gurney. She's in jeans and a loose blouse, not put together, but still attractive. On the gurney is Caleb, his trunk upright on the propped-up backrest. He looks much like himself, his face barely puffed beyond normal. He is dressed in a boyish striped jersey and shorts, like the breakfast table urchin in a cereal commercial. Dr. Levy is at the head of the gurney, peering into Caleb's eyes with an ophthalmoscope.

True sees me and turns. I don't know what to expect. We have been talking through lawyers. She is full of emotion, but seems happy.

"He's all right. They gave him a shot of epinephrine and in five minutes the swelling went down and he's breathing okay."

We stand awkwardly for a moment. I want to reach out to her, but I don't want to underestimate the depth of her anger at me. I try to speak reassuringly and without too much inflection.

"I'm glad you got him here quickly."

"I must have driven a hundred miles an hour. I could have

crashed and killed us both." She is looking to me for validation.

"You did good."

An awkward pause. I take a chance and raise my arms and she approaches. I fold them around her. She begins to cry.

"It's all right," I say and I run my hand over the top of her head. I look over her shoulder at Caleb. Dr. Levy has a blood pressure cuff on Caleb's arm and seems lost in the procedure. Caleb looks to me, smiles. It clearly pleases him to see his mom in my arms.

"You okay, kiddo?" I ask Caleb.

"I'm okay now."

"Scary, huh?"

He nods. Dr. Levy sighs audibly and straightens up. He catches my eye briefly as he moves to walk away. I disengage from True. He knows about our divorce and enmity and True and I are both uneasy after our display of affection.

"Thanks," I say. I am grateful to everyone here, including every clerk and orderly for saving my son. I would like to hand each a box of chocolate.

"That's all right," he says as he exits quickly. I am surprised he doesn't dally. Perhaps he has to get back to a dinner engagement. I see him walk quickly down the middle of the room, looking into each curtained bay as if trying to find someone.

I watch as he finds a thirtyish woman dressed in a white doctor's coat who has the appearance of a bright young resident. They talk for a moment as she looks at a chart in her hand. At first she seems slightly combative in the exchange, then stricken. The two of them leave the room as if in search of another as True speaks, "What's going on?"

"I don't know," I reply. Something is wrong.

"That's the resident. I thought she was really good. She went to Berkeley."

There is an awkward pause. I turn to Caleb to fill the space and smile comfortingly. "You gave everybody a big scare."

True steps over to the head of the gurney, grabs his little hand tightly.

"Maybe it's Halloween," he grins and chuckles. "This is my costume. A big head." He finds this irresistibly funny and starts to giggle. "I've got a big head for Halloween! I've got a big pumpkin head for Halloween!"

"Maybe that's your new name—Pumpkinhead."

He is in paroxysms of giggles. A man across the way who is prone on a gurney strapped up with a heart monitor and oxygen tube looks sadly across at us.

"Down a notch," says True. "We are in a hospital."

But Caleb can't be stopped. He stretches his mouth jack-o-lantern style and cries out. "I'm a Pumpkinhead!"

"Sssshhh," says True.

An orderly arrives and presents himself at the foot of the gurney, addresses Caleb.

"Caleb? I'm going to move you to another room now, okay?"

Caleb looks helplessly to his mother. She looks to me in surprise. I say to the orderly. "I thought he'd just be released."

The orderly looks at the chart on the foot of the bed, replies, "Caleb Fourchette? I have an order to take him up to the ICU."

I am stunned. True speaks first.

"Why are you doing that?"

"Did your doctor speak to you?"

"Nobody spoke to us," says True firmly.

Dr. Levy appears at the edge of the curtained area. He's a small, cherubic man in his forties in a rumpled suit. He has bad breath. Has no one ever told him? He is mild mannered and smart and I respect him for that and for his lack of pretense including the halitosis.

He looks to Caleb with a doctor's smile.

"Caleb, do you mind if I talk to your folks for a minute."

The orderly looks to Levy. "What about ICU?"

There is something grave in his response. "We can wait just a minute on that. Okay?"

Dr. Levy guides us to an empty curtained area and then speaks in a low voice so that we have to strain forward to hear.

"I noticed that Caleb's heartbeat was unusually fast when I examined him."

"Isn't that normal if they give him epinephrine?" I say. I already know that epinephrine is a form of adrenaline and adrenaline makes your heart pound faster.

"It was a little high considering. I looked at his chart and checked the resident's medication order. It was for an injection of 10cc of a .001 solution of epinephrine." His voice lowers again and he looks pained. "It should have been a .0001 solution. It seems there may have been an error in the order."

True gasps. "What are you saying?!"

"The resident made a decimal point error when she wrote it down. Caleb received ten times the recommended dose."

It lands like a rifle bullet. I don't know what it portends, but I know on the face of it that it isn't good and Dr. Levy's somber expression confirms it. He continues.

"I've seen it happen that somebody puts a decimal point in the wrong place, but the pharmacy or the nurse always catches it. Somehow they both missed it. She's a really good resident and she's not careless. I talked to her and she feels terrible. She wanted to talk to you and apologize, but the hospital administrators have a rule on this and won't let her."

I blanch but True lashes out.

"Won't let her?! What do you mean they won't let her?!" says True.

I am thinking it's not about the resident, True. I don't care about the resident. It's about Caleb. What about Caleb?!

"It's a policy thing," Levy replies, noting my annoyance at True's outburst. "She's a good doc and she feels bad. I've asked to move Caleb to a room upstairs so that we can keep him overnight. We'll put in an IV and monitor him."

"Monitor him for what?" I ask.

"The epinephrine elevates his heart rate and blood pressure. We need to be looking at it."

"And what if it goes up?"

"It is elevated right now. The question is, where will it go next?"

"And what do we do if it goes up?"

"I'm about to talk to the cardiology resident here and there's a senior pediatric vascular guy at UCLA I'm going to try to get a hold of. I do want to get your boy on the monitor ASAP and I want to set up an IV in case we have to medicate him."

"With what?" asks True, ending the phrase with her jaw agape.

"That's what I need to talk to the cardiologist about."

A woman dressed like an office worker wearing a hospital badge approaches us with a clipboard and holds it forward with a pen in her other hand.

"Mr. and Mrs. Fourchette? I have some things here for one of you to sign," she says.

I look at True whose excellent State of California employee insurance policy covers Caleb and say, "Maybe you should sign. It's your insurance."

"I don't want to sign unless I know what I'm signing."

Levy interrupts, "I'd like to get Caleb going. I'm going to have him moved up now."

"Can we do this upstairs?" I ask.

"I'm sorry. I need a signature."

"I want to go up with Caleb," says True.

"Can I sign?" I ask, trying to nip this fight for primacy in the bud.

"I need the signature of the main insured," she replies. I shrug and True simmers.

I see movement out of the corner of my eye. Caleb is being wheeled out to the hall. I start for it. She grabs the clipboard and the pen, scans the papers angrily.

"What room?" she asks.

The hospital lady answers, "I'll find out and let you know."

I follow the gurney without True through a hallway maze into an elevator. Levy follows, talking on his cell phone. I look at my watch. It's quarter after ten.

The doors on the elevator close. It's me, Levy and Caleb.

"Where are we going?" Caleb asks.

"The doctors need to keep an eye on you because you got some strong medicine." It's the truth, but I can't help but feel a little dodgy for hiding my concern. He extends his hand off the gurney palm up and I grab it and hold it tightly. Too tightly. I fear I am transferring my anxiety.

I try to listen to Levy on the phone, wondering if his cell signal will fade on the elevator, wondering if that means he will miss a crucial piece of information he needs to help my son. At the moment, however, he is just leaving messages, asking for them to call back.

"Would you see if you can page him and have him call back? It's Dr. Jonas Levy."

The doors open and we proceed into a room that looks part Catholic hospital (crucifix on the wall) and part NASA control (stacked computer screens). To my surprise we are to be the only occupants, and the nursing staff who greets us is clearly on a higher level of the profession than what I am used to. That simultaneously cheers and worries me.

"Hey there, handsome," says a take-charge redheaded nurse with a name tag identifying her as Beverly O'Neill. She points out the stacks of electronics. "This is where we train all the astronauts." Caleb, unnerved, manages a meek smile. "You *are* one of the astronauts going to the moon, aren't you?" He gravitates to Beverly's confidence and smile.

She and an orderly in green scrubs whisk Caleb off the gurney and put him on a bed/table near the middle of the room. Levy remains on the phone in the hallway. I take a moment and find him, wait for him to get off the line. Just then True arrives off the elevator.

"Where is he? Is he in there?" I nod. "What is happening?"

"They're hooking him up to the monitor," I reply.

"Do we know anything?" I look up to Dr. Levy who is impassive.

"Nothing more I don't think."

She goes into the room to see Caleb where they are pasting the electrodes for the monitors on his chest. I stay with Dr. Levy.

"What now?" I ask.

"I'm trying to talk to a pediatric cardiologist, but I haven't gotten a hold of one yet."

"Why a cardiologist?"

"The concern with the epinephrine is about his blood pressure and what the effects might be on his circulatory system. It's 160 over 110 now which is elevated, but not dangerous for a young person. The thing is we don't know how high it's going to go and what the effects of that might be. His pressure could spike suddenly."

"What effects?" I wonder and am steeling myself to ask, but Dr. Levy intuits what would be a slippery conversational slope and cuts me off.

"I really want to answer your questions, Mr. Fourchette, but I need to get going on this cardio guy," he says, placing a sympathetic hand on my shoulder. The funereal hand-on-shoulder has the opposite effect from easing my apprehension. Levy moves off and I return to mission control where I find True standing over Caleb, holding his hand, smiling false cheer.

"At least you aren't having your appendix out. I had my appendix out when I was nine and that was no fun."

"What's an appendix?"

"It's this thing in your stomach that you don't really need, but it's in there anyway and sometimes food gets stuck in there and it really hurts and they have to open you up and take it out."

"The food?"

"No. The appendix, silly."

"I know. Your food comes out when you poop." He starts to giggle. She encourages him.

"Who poops?"

"You poop!"

"I do not. Mom's never poop."

It's a sweet exchange but I suspect she's also playing the part. You want people around you to know you are a communicative parent. It's all right, True. I do it, too. Yes. I sometimes make a show of amusing conversations with Caleb in supermarket lines so that everyone can see what a good dad I am.

Meanwhile I can see Beverly in a corner, removing an IV catheter from its wrappings, her eye on Caleb. Seeing the panic in Caleb's eyes, she speaks to me.

"Doctor said to put in an IV in case he wants to administer something quickly."

"Is that a needle?!" Caleb yells out. "I already had a needle!!"

"It'll be over in a second," says True, with one of life's least persuasive arguments.

"I don't want it!" he screams.

"He's really phobic about needles," True explains to a quasi-sympathetic Beverly. True is right. Once, when he needed a flu shot at Dr. Levy's office he just jumped off the examining table and ran out. We had to chase him into the hall, drag him back with tears streaming and threaten and cajole him to take the injection.

She turns to Caleb. "You were so good downstairs, before."

"You said it wouldn't hurt and it hurt!"

I suppose he's right. These are the inevitable effects of being lied to. The nurse approaches him with the needle in hand and his eyes widen.

"No! Please!!!" begs Caleb.

"It'll be over in a second!" True says, obviously starved for a better rejoinder. She looks to me for support, a look I have missed over the past year and despite the circumstances, it feels good.

Beverly addresses Caleb. "What if I rub something on your arm so you won't feel the needle as much?"

Caleb is ahead of her. He knows lidocaine from previous visits to the doctor and the dentist.

"That doesn't work!"

"What doesn't work?" asks Beverly.

"The stuff you put on that's supposed to make it not hurt."

Beverly tries to grab Caleb's arm, but he pulls it away and sits on his hand. She looks at me with exasperation. It's my turn.

"This is going to happen, Caleb. Okay? There's nothing you can do about it. It's for your own good and you can give your arm to the nurse now or I can make you do it. You hear me?"

Caleb is taken aback by my sternness. It even surprises me a little. He hesitates. Tears are in his eyes.

"I'm afraid!"

I move toward him. The nurse follows my lead, IV in hand.

"Don't force him!" says True.

At least I'm not lying to him.

"Give the nurse your arm! Now!"

Helplessly he offers up his little wrist. Beverly grabs it and I grab his shoulders to make sure he doesn't move. Beverly swabs him quickly with alcohol and senses that the best gambit is an assault now and skips the lidocaine swab. I put a firm hand on his arm in support of Beverly. She jabs in the catheter. Caleb winces and cries out. She tapes down the tube. It's over.

I look to True and try to intuit her reaction. I think she is glad that I stepped in but she won't give me the satisfaction of approval. She looks away from me to Caleb.

"It's over, baby. You did good."

Dr. Levy steps in. He looks quickly at the monitors, puts a

stethoscope to Caleb's chest. I wonder what the stethoscope tells him that all the electronics don't.

The transparency of Levy's distress is getting to me. I look at him questioningly and he motions with his hand to follow him to the hall. True is torn between staying with Caleb and following him, but when I move, she follows. In the hallway Levy speaks in a quiet tone.

"I wanted to bring you up to date. My sense is that everything is going to be okay and Caleb's going to slowly come down, but there's not a lot of clarity. There's plenty in the literature about normal pediatric epinephrine dosage and side effects, but there's not much on overdose. You can see the problem, which is they can't just go out and overdose children in clinical trials so all we have are a few anecdotal accounts from previous accidents. I've talked to three cardiologists and they all agree that we're doing the right thing, which is to monitor his heart rate and his blood pressure closely and have a catheter installed in case he spikes so we can give him something immediately to slow his heart rate."

"Why can't you just give him a small dose now?" True asks.

"It's tricky."

"Tricky how?"

"The cardiologist I talked to said that benzodiazepine would be the drug of choice for an adult but it can sometimes have a paradoxical effect on young kids. His heart rate could actually go up if we administer it. He thought we should probably watch him and give him IV nitroprusside that is effective at bringing down the heart rate. The pluses are that it's got a short half-life so if he gets too much it won't last that long, but it's hard to figure out a dosage and you really don't want to overdose because then he can become hypertensive."

"What happens then?" I ask.

"Then we worry about organ damage, especially the liver. That's why we don't want to create new problems, but just watch him and be ready. We're going to admit him overnight and keep a monitor on him."

Levy seems nervous and I feel like he's talking too much.

"He's going to be all right, Mr. Fourchette. It's going to be a long night, but I'm pretty sure he'll be fine."

It is a small but rare satisfaction to know that you have a doctor's sole attention. Levy is there for us. What I don't know and I'm afraid to ask is what the odds are for something to go badly wrong. Or I should say badly wrong again.

"No!!" I hear from inside the room. I enter to see Caleb squirming petulantly and Beverly with a grip on his arm, trying to keep him from flailing as True exhorts him to calm down.

"It hurts!" he cries as he tries to dislodge the IV.

"Just a little bit, Sweetie," says True impatiently to no discernible effect. She looks at me pleadingly, the failed good cop. It's clear that Beverly also has exhausted her bag of tricks and they need a bad cop.

"Caleb," I address him in an unyielding tone. He pointedly looks away from me.

"Caleb," I reiterate, even more seriously. This time he looks up. "I need you to calm down."

As I look at Beverly I sense that Caleb's behavior with the IV is taking on new meaning. Will his wriggling become a displacement of the hospital's guilt and responsibility for overdosing him? *We did our best, but the kid wriggled too much. Too bad his dad couldn't keep him still.*

"It's pinching me!" Caleb protests.

"How bad is it?" I ask, trying to sound both unyielding and concerned.

"It's really bad."

"What if you try to think about something else, Caleb? Will that help?"

"No."

"Well, what will?"

At least he's distracted for the moment while he considers. Beverly eases her grip. I may be wrong, but True now seems grateful for my presence.

Beverly clucks impatience. "I'm going to have to restrain him." True frowns.

"Would ice cream help?" I ask Caleb. A bribe is brazen and bespeaks bad parenting, but we are past the niceties. Beverly reacts disapprovingly, catching my eye and shaking her head to the idea. Apparently ice cream is not allowed. My bad for inviting the possible interaction of pistachio (his favorite) and the hospital's massive drug overdoses. While Caleb considers the scotched ice cream barter, I try to divert him with another option.

"What if we play a game?"

"It still hurts."

"I can't make it not hurt, but if we play a game maybe you won't think about your arm so much." I am surprised at my own candor. Why didn't I think of that before? Even a six-year-old can respond well to not being bullshitted.

"It won't help."

"What if you try?"

"What game?"

"What in the room starts with 'A'?"

He tries to resist what is a favorite car game, but I can see that he can't. His eyes dart around the room full of stainless steel machines and electronic screens. He's challenged and a little bit stumped. True encourages him.

"I see an A-word." she says.

"Aspirin!" Caleb blurts out.

"Do you see aspirin?" I say. There's none in sight. He's vamping and I'm calling him on it. That's good because it's engagement.

"There's aspirin in the room," he replies.

"You've got to see it. That's the rules," I reply. I have him now.

"What if I can find some aspirin?"

"You can't find any aspirin because you can't get up. If you could get up we wouldn't even have to be talking about aspirin."

He smiles appreciation. I love that he gets the complexity of the joke. At around his age they are capable of some fairly convoluted thinking.

"I see a astronaut!" He laughs. "I see a anteater!" "I see a art!"

"A art?" No need now to nitpick about "a art" versus "an art."

"A art painting! I see a airplane!"

"All right. What about 'B'?" He's wound-up excited and a bit manic and I let it slide that there are no paintings or airplanes in the room. It's the drug talking.

"I see a apple! It's a big apple!" He makes exaggerated chewing movements. "Ummm! It's so good."

He keeps on with his chewing pantomime. He's totally in an agitated mode. I sneak a glance at the heart monitor that's reading 170 beats per minute. I think of a washing machine spiked with electricity, spinning out of control, banging and beating on the floor. I want to dial him back to a comfortable normal cycle. *Swish-swish, swish-swish.*

"There is no apple," I challenge him.

"There is! I am eating it! Can't you see it?!! It's red!!"

He opens his mouth even wider to take an imaginary bite. This mania is starting to freak me out. We're only at "A." True intercedes in an effort to restore sanity to both of us.

"I see something," she says calmly and sweetly.

"A apple?!!" he giggles mischievously.

It could be that we are caught in an irretrievable apple feedback loop, stuck forever in apple-land. Perhaps that is what Caleb is trying to tell us. He doesn't want to advance, because advancing brings the unknown. It is better to remain in the uninformed present. I completely understand. If you were to offer me a trade for an uncertain tomorrow or the unresolved and uncomfortable present, I wouldn't know how to decide.

"I see something else. I see another 'A'. Do you want a hint?" says True.

"I don't want a hint," he says. "It's a apple!"

"It's not. But I can give you a hint. We all have one."

"A penis!" he shouts out with glee. Clearly his ability to censor himself is one of the casualties of the overdose.

"I don't have a penis," True reassures him evenhandedly.

"Yes you do!"

"I do not and anyway it doesn't start with 'A'. What starts with 'A'?" She's measured and calm. Caleb could not help but be soothed by her steadiness. I admire her. As she leans over Caleb I see the smoothness of the back of her neck and I think of how it feels to touch. Perhaps all of this is an unexpected way to bring us all together again. Perhaps we will look back at this someday as a fated, mysterious intervention designed to reunite us.

"What is between your shoulder and your hand?" she persists. I am sure that Caleb will just give another wise guy answer. But he answers seriously.

"It can't be something on me. It has to be something I see."

"You can see my arm," True replies. But Caleb is right. It is a car game and the rules are that we can name things that we see only out the window. Transposing it to a room would naturally exclude parts of your own body. Yielding to our young logician, True looks around the room for an 'A' word. Caleb interrupts her process, however.

"Air-conditioner!" he shouts, pointing to the air-conditioning console that sits at the base of the window. Perhaps his amped-up circulation stimulates his brain. I am impressed, and not only because he is mine.

"That's right. That's really good," she smiles with approval. "Now what about a 'B' word? Do you see a 'B' word?"

Caleb squirms again, suddenly not interested in the possible 'B' word.

A fortyish man in a Nike jogging suit and nicely coiffed salt-and-pepper hair appears in the doorway. Despite his outfit, he radiates gravitas.

"Mr. and Mrs. Fourchette? I'm Harry Sanford. I'm cardiology chair here at Saint Mary's. Excuse the get-up. I was out taking my evening run and got paged. Is this Caleb?"

He steps in, addresses Caleb as he looks appraisingly at the monitors.

"How are you doing, champ?"

"Belt," says Caleb pointing to the intruder's midsection. "I see a belt."

"We're playing an alphabet game," True explains. "We're just starting on the B's."

"That's good. I'm looking at the oxygen and BP on the monitor here. It's high but it seems like Caleb's still in an acceptable range. I just wanted to check in with you. I wanted to let you know that we're all up to speed on what's happening and the hospital is totally behind you on this. You're in good hands."

We can't help but be impressed with his seriousness. He studies the monitor again, flips a switch to change the range, and speaks to Beverly.

"Look. BP's trending down."

"Yes. It's down another five from ten minutes ago."

"Borrow your stethoscope?"

She offers it up and he puts it on and places the diaphragm on Caleb's chest.

"Levy talked to Rheinhardt?" he continues.

Beverly nods.

"I really can't see we're going to need to administer the nitroprusside. It was the right call to intubate him, though."

He turns to us. We are pulsating with relief at his upbeat assessment.

"His vitals are fine and his numbers seem to be going down for the moment and I think we're out of the woods. It's still going to be a long night, though."

"We've got a lot of alphabet to go," I say.

"I don't want to do the alphabet thing anymore," says Caleb. Sanford rolls his eyes to us.

"Good luck. My family is expecting me, but I still have my pager on."

He leaves. I look to True.

"Do you want to take a break?"

"I'm fine. You go."

I don't want to be the one to leave first, but she offers me cover.

"Maybe you have to go to the bathroom."

"Where's my Gameboy?" says Caleb.

"How are you feeling, baby?" True asks.

"I'm okay. Is my Gameboy in the car, Dad?"

I nod, look at True. We could both use the break the Gameboy will bring us.

"I'll spell you. You can get something to eat if you like," True offers.

"I'm not hungry. I can bring you back something."

"You can bring me a Coke if you can find one."

I remember times when a simple, uncolored request from True was ordinary. Now it seems peculiar but pleasing.

As I exit, I reassure Caleb, "I'll be back soon."

The elevator opens soon after I press the button. Inside is a dark-skinned couple, presumably visitors. The woman has tears running down her cheeks. They converse animatedly in what I take to be Farsi. There is also an old man in a wheelchair accompanied by an orderly. The old man wears a gray gown and has a short growth of white beard. An oxygen tank is attached to the wheelchair and a tube runs up and around his head to a nosepiece. His breath comes in short gasps. His teeth are yellow and his head falls toward his left shoulder. The orderly looks pointedly away from him. The old man seems calm and unconcerned as if in acknowledgment that the hospital is an accustomed habitat. That Caleb currently resides in the same ecosystem seems to me a brief and evanescent anomaly.

I escape the elevator and hurry for the exit through the main lobby. I am relieved not to have to pass through the emergency room again. It is nearly midnight and the lobby is still. The information desk is eerily unmanned. I step through the automatic door to find the parking lot.

Even though it is late, there are rows of cars in the parking lot. I find the Volvo and see that the door lock buttons are raised. In my haste I forgot to lock it. I open the door and reach inside to open the glove box. I go for the Gameboy and suddenly remember my book. I pull out the Gameboy, and reach to the floor under the passenger seat where I had hidden my copy of *The Old Man and the Sea*. Of course no thief save one would recognize it for what it is and I could have left it with impunity on top of the dashboard. I hold it gingerly, contemplating its value and what I endured to retake it. I think I will bring it along, too. It seems right. Something extravagant. Something special. I will be like a great, proud hunter from an African tribe who has slain a lion to lay before the bed of an ailing son in the belief that the power of the gift will bring strength to his progeny.

And then I will read from it. Shall I start from the beginning? I haven't read this book since I was in high school. I remember that it is about a simple fisherman who hooks a very large fish after a long run of bad luck. He perseveres and lands the big fish. This is most of what I remember. It is a story of hope and redemption.

I am interrupted by a bright flash of light that streaks across the dashboard. I turn to find a flashlight in my face. I squint and the light moves down to my hand and the Gameboy. "Sir?"

Now that the light is out of my eyes I can see that it is coming from the flashlight of a uniformed security officer. He is a black man. I don't know what he wants or why he is shining the light.

"Sir...?"

Perhaps it is due to my state of mind, but the light in my eyes is the switch on my kettle.

"Can I ask what you're doing?" he continues, the light now shining on the Gameboy.

"I don't know. Can you?" is my terse reply.

"Is this your car?"

"I don't have time for this right now." I pick up the book and the Gameboy and I turn and brush past him, harder than I anticipated, and I bump his shoulder. He stiffens. I back-pedal a bit.

"I've got a sick kid upstairs. I've got to go."

"May I see your ID?"

"Really. I have to go."

"May I see your ID, please?"

I see he has a gun in a holster on his side.

"Shoot me if you want. Okay? Shoot me for pulling a Gameboy out of my car for my kid that your hospital just nearly killed. Okay? But I'm leaving now."

I start to walk away. He picks up his walkie-talkie, holds it close to his mouth and speaks into it.

"This is James. I've got a possible 504 in the parking lot and I'm going to need SMPD to send an officer please." Someone replies into an earphone and I don't hear it.

I continue to walk. He follows and calls after me.

"Please stop, sir. If you don't I'm going to have to arrest you."

I reach into my pocket and his immediate reaction is to unholster his gun and point it at me. I retrieve my keyring as he unsteadily points the gun at me. I press on the Volvo key fob and there is a chirp from behind him. I do it again and he turns to look and sees the lights on the Volvo flash and hears another chirp.

"You see. It is my car. These are my keys. I want to go to my son."

He hesitates a moment. I look at him kindly and speak softly. "I am sorry."

"We had a bunch of car break-ins last month."

"Call the cops off. Let me go to my son,"

He lowers the gun. I walk back to the hospital under the pale light of the vapor lamps overhead.

Inside, I make my way to the elevators, press the button. I have the Gameboy in my pocket and the book in my hand. The lobby is empty except for a janitor who polishes the floor behind me.

I am feeling relieved and optimistic about Caleb. The walk and the mission and even my encounter with the security guard have relieved me of some of my panic. We are through the worst of it. It was fortunate that True recognized the emergency and brought him here quickly. Among my many disparate feelings about True, I will remain grateful for that. And I will be grateful for the perseverant good care of Dr. Levy and Nurse Beverly. I know I have been racing for a long time, but in this moment I feel I can pause. I take a brief moment to examine the book.

Hemingway's iconic whiskered (and appropriately first-edition, blue-tinted) face stares at me from the back cover. The original three-dollar price beckons from the left fold-over of the dust jacket that has only a few small scuffs and no significant tears on the edges. The book is also remarkably clean and crisp for its 1952 publishing date. Once again I confirm that the first edition Scribner's seal and coliform "A" are exactly where they are supposed to be. Across from the publisher's page is a printed dedication page thanking Charles Scribner and Max Perkins, publisher and editor respectively.

I turn to the title page and notice what appear to be ink stains—no it is a bleed-through from the opposing side. I turn the page over. Oh my God! Holy Jesus! On the reverse side of the title page are an inscription and a signature.

"Hello to my good friend Ernesto. Thanks for all of your good advice

even if I don't always follow it. Ernest Hemingway"

This book is signed and inscribed! The price of this book just tripled! This lowly picker who has always been thrilled to find a hundred-dollar coffee table book owns a signed Hemingway first edition!

Wait. All right. But how do I know it is authentic? Maybe HH signed it in a fit of even deeper perversity. I examine the signature, but I don't know what a genuine Hemingway signature is supposed to look like. I look at the ink, holding the page up to the light. It was clearly written with a fountain pen. The ink lacks gloss and appears to have aged. I suppose there are ways to confirm it. I would have to find out who Ernesto is. I would have to take it to an expert. If I take it to Sotheby's I am sure they could authenticate that it was Hemingway who signed. But what if they say it is a fake? Maybe I am better off to put it on the market unauthenticated with a disclaimer. No. That would be a mistake.

Who can I tell? This is too good not to share. Shall I call Nick? It's too late. I can't tell True. To her it would be evidence of assets yet to be recouped by her legal team. I won't say anything. I will bring it up like it is an ordinary old copy and I will read it to Caleb.

I retrace my steps to the elevator and press the call button.

True's Coke. I almost forgot. I go off in search of a Coke. A janitor tells me that there is a machine near a back entrance. His directions are imperfect and it takes me a few minutes to find the machine. I trust Coke still means Diet Coke to True and I fumble for a dollar and buy one.

I make my way back to the elevator carrying the Gameboy, the Coke and the book. It ascends quickly, the doors open and I take a right at the hall to the monitored care room.

As I approach I feel a chill. I realize that for a moment I have been displacing my fears about Caleb with my excitement about the book. Now that I am here I feel a cold wave of dread pass through me. It will only pass when I enter the room and see that he is all right and that True is entertaining him. Perhaps I have made a mistake in bringing the book. Perhaps Hemingway is not the right choice for a kindergartner. What a fool I am.

I turn to enter the room but I see that it is empty except for one orderly. There is no Caleb, no True and no doctors. There is an untidy array of equipment and monitors with wires and tubes hanging to the floor. I look around to make sure I am in the right room as I ask the orderly.

"My son was in here…"

I don't like the look of distress on the orderly's face. He is very uncomfortable hearing who I am.

"They just moved him over to critical care ICU."

"Critical?"

"Third floor south wing."

"Caleb Fourchette?"

"Sorry. I don't know the name."

He walks to the door to show me where to go. I walk quickly. He points down the hall to the left.

"Left in that corridor and then the first door on the right."

"What happened?"

"You need to go to the nurse's station at critical care. Tell them who you are."

Of course I'll tell them who I am. All right. The room is empty. Caleb has been moved. I will follow this through and go to critical care. Why did they move him? Is there a development? Maybe it's only a precaution. Maybe they need some kind of a monitor in the critical ICU that isn't available here. I try to ignore the feeling that emanates from the pit of my stomach that something might have gone terribly wrong. I fast-walk out the door and turn toward critical care.

There is a circular nurse's station under a sign that says *Critical Intensive Care Unit*. I see a nurse at the station. She looks up to see me coming. My communication is simple.

"Caleb Fourchette?"

"Are you the dad?"

"Yes."

"They were looking for you. Right there. Room 411." She points. I try to read her affect, but I can't. I see the half-open door and a nurse walks quickly out. I don't catch her eye, but she is clearly upset. If I don't go in there will that make it not be so? Can my denial stop time? Will my perception of whatever is behind that door be the link to its reality? If so I should plant myself where I am and not move. I hesitate long enough for True to exit the room, tears dripping down from her cheeks, gasping and heaving in anguish. I don't know what to do with the book in my hand.

Chapter 24

Nothing in my experience and nothing that I know can inform my reaction and my behavior. I simply don't know what to do. Should I lie down on the floor and kick and scream? Should I be philosophical or religious? Should I attack someone? Should I attack myself? True will know. She is better grounded than I am. She has a knack for knowing what is appropriate. In the past her guidance has helped me gather feelings when I am unable to collect them myself. Now that her anger at me has subsided she will help. But for this moment she won't allow her eyes to meet mine. It makes no sense because we both know that we need each other. It isn't helpful to her or to me.

The hospital has herded True and me into some sort of meeting room. It has a nondescript commercial couch and a large laminate table with six chairs. We have already waved off a solicitous Methodist minister, further evidence of the waning influence of the original Catholic Sisters. A callow young social worker named Jessica offers condolences and an offer of help dealing with the "arrangements." A hospital middle management guy who has clearly been dragged out of bed tries to assure us that the hospital will absolutely positively live up to its responsibility to determine the cause of what happened and gives a non-legal, non-binding non-apology apology. It is, to use his terms, an "unfortunate and tragic incident." To him we are a fire to be put out. I can see that True is not reacting well to him, but still holding her counsel. As for me, there is a part of me that would like to see the resident who prescribed, the pharmacist that filled and the nurse who administered the outrageous overdose dragged in chains into an Afghan soccer stadium to kneel before me as I brandish a long scimitar and administer swift and public justice. As it is, however, True and I share an enervation that cannot be touched by finger pointing and rage. We are too sad and too angry with even ourselves.

It appears that Caleb suffered a severe hemorrhagic stroke a few moments after I left the room. He had a full-blown grand mal seizure, peeing and shitting and biting his tongue. True screamed for the nurse who called a code blue as she put a bite stick in his mouth. Doctors and staff flew into the room, moved him to ICU, forcing air into him by squeezing a plastic bag. He went very quickly as a result of massive bleeding in his brain. The complete details won't be clear for another day or so after there is an autopsy. The hospital guy can't resist mentioning along with his put-on empathy that Caleb's blood pressure never peaked past 170, a level that would not normally have a catastrophic effect on someone whose arteries are young and elastic. There had to be an anomaly. The anomaly for me was that we took him to St. Mary's but that seems of small importance now.

The social worker asks if we need someone to drive us home, wrongly assuming that it would be the same domicile for both. It is a natural mistake. True and I thank her and refuse. We are eager to be free of their alien solicitude although I am tempted to demand a white Rolls-Royce with a uniformed driver just to test the boundaries of their eagerness to please.

As a burgeoning sunless gray dawn creeps acidly over us, we walk side by side out of the hospital toward the parking lot. I don't think it is lost on either of us that six years ago we entered here as two and left as three, but this time the process has reversed itself. I flash that we should be walking backward, muzzle myself rather than say the unspeakably inappropriate to True.

"Where are you parked?" I ask.

"I don't know. I jumped out in front and the attendant took it," she replies. We look around and don't see an attendant.

"I can drive you home,"

"I'm sure he's around," she says, stretching her neck but the place seems empty.

"I think I should."

"Then I'll be without a car."

"You can take a cab later and pick it up." The mundane quality of the conversation jars both of us. Shouldn't this be about God and angels and the soul? Shouldn't this be mournful looks and solemn appraisals? Why are we talking about jockeying cars now? How can we stop being routine? It is a sacrilege and an insult to Caleb's memory. His memory? Has Caleb become a memory? Yes.

True doesn't respond, but follows me listlessly toward the Volvo. I open the door for her. I have the Hemingway book in my hand and I toss it sloppily in the back seat. I don't want its value to sully the moment. Should I have left it at the hospital as proof of my distress? True enters and sits. I walk around to the driver's side, get in. Suddenly she starts to wail. It is loud, heaving and uncontrolled. It is also how I feel, but she has preempted me. I lean back in my seat, unable to put key to ignition switch as I suffer the sounds of her agony over the silence of mine.

I find the transitions difficult. To do nothing except to passively let the grief wash over me seems most right. To be caught in any other pursuit seems sacrilege. To be as active as to move from one irrelevant activity to another is an outrage. What I want the most is to lie passively underneath a stinging waterfall of remorse, longing and recrimination, uninterrupted by the quotidian exigencies of starting cars and opening doors.

True still makes loud, gasping sounds. I allow myself to move an arm to place a hand on her shoulder. She accepts it, but her gasping and wailing are unabated. I move the other arm and pull her toward me. Again she dolorously accepts and I can feel the paroxysms of her breathing against my chest. I smell her perfume and her tears and the staleness of her breath. I feel the sharp edge of her clavicle against my arm. To my senses she seems a delicate package of skin draped over bone. Nobody is built to last.

I hear a light thumping on the window of the car and look up to see a swarthy middle-aged man dressed in a windbreaker leaning toward me as he taps on the window. When our eyes meet he shouts through the glass, "Are you guys okay?"

I nod, still holding True.

"Do you want me to call someone?" he asks.

"We're okay. Thanks," I say trying to dismiss him. He sees the despair, probably not for the first time, waves his hand lightly, moves off.

His intrusion has the effect of quieting True. She pulls away from me, gathers herself together, smoothing her slacks. She reaches into her purse and pulls out some Kleenex, daubs her cheeks. I sit there for a moment, and then turn the key in the ignition. A small circuit is completed and as a result an electric current surges from the battery to the starter motor. In a watershed instant the Volvo stirs to life. Caleb stops. The Volvo starts. It is an odd continuum.

I put the car in gear. True searches for the buckle on her seat belt as I pull out of the parking space and into the aisle. She fidgets and fusses with the belt as I approach the parking shack. I don't know what I did with my parking ticket. I look around the car. True manages to click her belt into the receptacle as I search for the ticket.

"The ticket," I say to True. She nods, makes a small effort to look about for it. I pull to a stop in front of the swarthy man who stands patiently. I put the gear lever in Park.

"Maybe I'm sitting on it," says True. She undoes the buckle that was so hard won, lifts her ass and roots around on the seat but the ticket isn't there. I reach into my pants but it isn't in any of my pockets.

"It's okay. Go ahead," says the parking man as he opens the gate for me. His expression is compassionate. He is probably a family man and he knows we must have lost a child. I still hesitate.

"It's all right. Just go," he says. I put the car in gear, pull forward through the gate and onto Santa Monica Boulevard. I turn right, deciding to take the longer route that passes along the ocean front. True doesn't question the route, but sits impassively with her eyes trained forward, conspicuously missing the ocean. But of course the ocean is nothing we have in common. She is from South Dakota, a farm person, a person who finds solace in dark soil. I am the one that feels communion with the ocean and am comforted by its blue-green expanse. Its unacknowledged presence on the right side of the Volvo, her side, serves only as further evidence today for why we doubtless do not belong together.

A red traffic light looms overhead at the foot of Ocean Park Boulevard. Must I stop? Am I not exempted today? If I were to be brought before a judge and told him I had just lost my only son, would he fine me for such a piddling offense? I start to submit to the light and apply the brakes, but I feel in honor of the moment I must transcend this useless mundanity. I will go through the light in tribute to Caleb, or as we now say "Caleb's memory." I slow a bit and then keep going.

"What are you doing?" asks True.

"It's six in the morning. Nobody is on the road." I prefer not to explain my true thoughts. I look at her reaction and I realize that my small act of defiance in homage to our lost son has only served to remind her of my latent criminality. On this day it is impossible to do anything right. It is only possible to fuck up.

Fortunately there are no more red lights between here and the house on Colonial. I pull into the narrow driveway. The lawn is brown and scraggly where it meets the cement tracks of the driveway. I turn off the engine and wait for True to move, but she just sits there, silent, staring straight ahead. After a few stretched minutes she speaks.

"It's my fault. I looked at the nurse and I thought that's an awful lot of stuff in that syringe. I should have known."

"How could you have known?"

"I could have asked. If I had just asked…"

"It's not your fault."

"Why didn't I say something?"

"It's not your fault."

I mean it. How could she know what was the appropriate volume of solution to inject? On the other hand, there is a small part of me that is glad that I wasn't the one there with an opportunity to stop that nurse and failed to act. I don't know if True would be so kind to me.

She reaches for the door handle. I realize I don't want her to go. I don't want to be alone. We look at each other. Clearly neither does she. I reach for my door handle and we exit together and I follow her up the walk to the front door. I let True reach into her purse and pull out the key, open the door.

"I can make coffee," she says.

"You probably want to go to bed."

"I have to find someone to take my two o'clock Urban Ed class and it's too early to call."

"You could let them fend for themselves."

"I can't do that."

She goes to the kitchen. I look around the living room. Not much has changed. There is a comforter folded on our old sofa that I don't recognize and a bookcase has been moved over a few feet and a chair placed in the space. Nonetheless I can't help but perceive even these small changes as a subtle rejection of our former life together.

"You probably want to go home and sleep," she calls out from the kitchen.

"I don't know what I want to do."

She appears at the doorway to the kitchen.

"I can't believe this is real. I can't believe this is happening." I walk toward her. I know that she wants to be held. "It's like a dream," she continues.

I approach her, open my arms and she reaches for me, is about to pull me to her, then says, "I think I'm going to be sick." She disengages, quick-steps to the bathroom. I hear her retch into the toilet bowl. I press my back against the wall in the hallway, slide down until I am seated on the floor. I wait there until she reemerges from the bathroom.

"I'm going to go to bed," she announces.

"I'll go."

"You can stay."

"I'll go."

"Stay."

She turns and walks toward the bedroom.

"What about your class?"

"Fuck them."

As I sit on the floor she gives me a last look before disappearing through the bedroom door. There is no regimen for what to do next. I hear the springs of the mattress compress as she flops on it. I remain sitting as the events of the past few hours race through my head.

I think of what Caleb might have been. I try to imagine him as a teenager and as an adult. I can imagine the natural deepness of his brow commanding a soulful and masculine visage. There was never a question about his intelligence. Mrs. Samson, his kindergarten teacher, said he was one of the brightest. His boundaries were limitless.

Then I think about Helmet Head. Did not his parents have similar aspirations for him? Certainly he would have been one of the brightest in his kindergarten class as well. I try to imagine him whimsically but carefully dressed in Scandinavian cotton prints for school by his art dealer father and his musicologist mother. He probably had cleaner, softer lighter hair and likely a cute little ponytail.

It is a mistake to make assumptions. That is where I always go wrong. It leaves me vulnerable. It is not that I am unable to deal with adversity. In fact I think I am remarkably flexible and adept at adjusting to the unpleasant surprises that come in life. What I am not good at is anticipating them. I am too often blindsided.

I am not sure how long I sit here. Perhaps a half-hour. I hear a trash truck outside. After it passes, the house is quiet. True is probably asleep. It is probably time to leave. I get up, go to the bedroom door to find True. She lies on the bed, eyes open. She wears her simple blouse and tan cotton slacks. Her shoes, reddish loafers, are still on her feet. I speak from the doorway.

"I think I'll go."

I know this creates another transition problem. It places the event further in the past. It embosses the loss with finality and therefore I am not totally surprised by True's request to postpone.

"Stay."

I raise my eyebrow in question. She nods. She pats the space on the bed next to her with a single motion. I walk to the side of the bed, and sit. She slithers left, leaving me room. There is a pillow for me. I set down on my back next to her, resting my head on the pillow. Our hands are at our sides as we lie there. I move mine to cover hers. She responds by intertwining her fingers over mine.

I can speak only for me, but I suspect it is mutual that we are electrified by the delicate movement of finger over finger. For simple old friends, the ritual can be deep and comforting. For mere lovers it is full of sexual anticipation. For longtime partners, a former husband and wife for example, it is a unique and elegant expression of both. I don't mean to make too much of it, but under the circumstances it is probably impossible to make too little.

We maintain this for a while in an odd rhythm, being still and then rubbing and intertwining fingers. I am drifting. I feel a disconnection of the senses, no doubt a dissociative reaction to the stress. The touch of her fingers now seems inordinately large and rough. Her fine index finger feels like a clumsy wide thumb against mine. Or no, perhaps it is just that I haven't slept since yesterday. I am drifting. I am drifting off to sleep... Thank God. May I never wake up.

I don't know how long it has been. I feel a pressure against my neck. It is cool and wet. It is a kiss. True is snuggled up against my body, nuzzling my neck and cheek. It feels odd and familiar—a reprise of old feelings. But it is impossible to react simply like I might have done in the past. The sense memory says this is my wife waking me up to initiate lovemaking. The current situation, however, is layered with ironies and complexities that I cannot resolve.

Her touch feels familiar but strange. The extended continuity of our former lovemaking has for better or worse been interrupted by new couplings with other people. What we do now has to be informed by that even if we try to ignore it. Angela's skin is smoother and moister. Her smell is a little duskier. Her hair is finer. I would prefer not to think of Angela. As a total package Angela is really not even in the range of acceptable, but I can't just release the touch of her from my mind. On the other hand, the comparative roughness of True's skin has long ago burrowed a niche into my memory and I find it comforting. It is less an "other" and more a part of me. It is a friend. I feel her hand on my chest, then her fingers slide into my shirt. This is not exploration. This is intention.

Is this the next transition? Is this how we next ease ourselves from our current crater where we know we cannot remain? We commence our journey with slow, languorous moves. It would not be correct to describe it as tentative in any way. It is really a retracing of old steps. If you were to reenter you childhood home, you would do it slowly, pausing at the entry, and then stop in each room, in order, as the shock of recognition emerges from deep neural repositories and into your awareness.

A light fingernail touch above the navel, tickling the dark hair on my stomach and tracing downward, pauses a tantalizing instant at my midsection. My pilot light is on, my switch is switched and my mechanism is engaged. I feel the insistent torque of my motor pushing me forward. I draw her toward me and we kiss. Brushing softness of lips, a light touch of tongues, and then my insistence and I press my lips to hers. She eases back and I follow her so that her head is deep in the pillow. I reach down and feel the familiar curve of her hip. It's not unlike finding an old friend in a crowded room. I follow it with my hand, first up into the small of her back, and then down onto the flank of her ass.

She kicks off her shoes. I hear one of them fall while the other presumably remains somewhere on the bed. I unbutton her slacks at the front and slide down the zipper. She wriggles out of them. She wears cotton bikini panties and I strip them away as she lifts her legs in the air. She tugs at my belt, manages to loosen it and I wriggle out of my pants and boxer shorts. We touch and fondle in familiar ways. We still know each other's buttons.

I am hard and ready for her. I feel buck proud of my hardness for an instant, and then an image of Caleb appears somewhere in my head. He is on his bicycle in the park. I struggle to banish him and to switch the whole of my perception to the naked flesh in front of me. A failure now would be…one more failure. I must break the string. I am desperate for a success of any sort as a positive sign. I look down at True as she gazes back at me. Her look is beyond description, a complex stew of passion and sorrow, love and anger, strength and frailty.

True and I believe that Caleb was conceived at the Posada del Sol hotel in Guaymas, Mexico. The hotel was pleasantly upscale but small and not ostentatious, sited on a white, sandy beach. We had a spacious room with a balcony overlooking the Sea of

Cortez. There were stucco walls, tile floors and artful hangings of local fabric. We went there on a long weekend splurge. True had been making hints about having a child for over a year. The idea terrified me and when the subject came up I would put it off. I was working hard, but felt that my job wasn't secure. It would be a financial strain for True to stop working and if she did we knew we would have to hire someone to help at the house. We were living in a two-bedroom duplex in Brentwood, but there really wasn't enough room for us and a child and a nanny. I knew that most families had more children with fewer resources, but the commitment freaked me out.

The Posada del Sol had given us narrow twin beds. This virtual bundling-board gave us each a not-unpleasant feeling of autonomy as we opened up newspapers, stretched and ate crackers unfettered by the equal and opposite reactions that we were used to in our queen bed at home. After an afternoon in the warm waters of the Sea of Cortez, a dinner of fresh prawns and snapper, followed by hot showers in our oversize ceramic tile bathroom and then fresh linen on the beds, we found ourselves in our underwear, refreshed and irresistible to each other. I moved over to her bed. There was no room for us to be side-by-side, so I quickly found myself poised over her.

"I didn't take my Ortho-Cept," she told me.

"Why not?" I asked although I knew the answer.

She smiled and shrugged. As I was poised over her, I had a feeling that I don't think I had ever had before. It was somewhat electric, deep inside my brain, and had an aura like being touched by the hand of God. Instinctively I knew it to be a signal to procreate. I smiled and shrugged and continued. It is indeed possible that Caleb's little egg was fertilized a few days later on the Posturepedic in Los Angeles, but after we found out about True's pregnancy, we told each other that it was at the Posada del Sol to reinforce our tacitly agreed myth. It would not do that such an extraordinary and blessed child was the result of a local and mundane coupling.

As I kneel in front of True I know that the same issues are being replayed. I have no idea if she is taking birth control. If not, what would be the possible consequences of True becoming pregnant? Do either of us have it in our power at this moment to rationalize what we are doing? Of course we don't.

But the force that commands us seems to be stronger. Is it elemental and Darwinian? Is it driving us to produce new offspring to protect and feed us in our dotage and perpetuate our precious lineage? Or are True and I merely suffusing our mutual pain in the distraction of lovemaking? Is this a once-in-a-lifetime transcendental experience or is this desperate sex? Are we gaining clarity or piling on confusion? There is no more time to parse my feelings as she grabs my flanks and pulls me to her. I enter her.

Chapter 25

After several lessons with a singing coach and earnest practice with a cassette recorder, my singing voice is still imperfect but not unpleasant. I find it hard to believe in Jesus, and the words to the hymns seem to mock my personal experience, but during the past year or so I have found comfort in the choir loft of the Ray of Light Missionary Baptist Church and the presence of the Reverend Doctor Lightfoot.

Why should I feel discouraged
Why should the shadows come
Why should my heart be lonely
And long for heavenly home
When Jesus is my portion?
My constant friend is He
His eye is on the sparrow
And I know he watches me
His eye is on the sparrow
And I know He watches me.

I should say that I am in the third string choir—Ray of Hope has three choirs and I am there with the oldsters and the preternaturally out-of-key. I am content with my status as I am not here because of ambition. Without making too much of the anthropological aspect of this, I find it comforting and a welcome change to be among black people.

Two years have passed. The news is full of Hurricane Katrina devastating New Orleans and I have thoughts of my great-grandfather toiling in the sun in the nearby fields. He had an indisputably hard life, but he saw his son go to college and graduate.

We didn't have a funeral for Caleb. It was too painful and

the idea of being present in a hailstorm of pity was anathema to both of us. We got some spiritual satisfaction donating Caleb's organs. Several weeks after the "event" (I don't really know what to call it and this term is the least painful) True arranged a small memorial ceremony at the Mar Vista Lutheran Church. Some parents of Caleb's school friends and a number of coworkers from True's college attended. True sat next to me, I don't know if it was for comfort or for show. We were numb and listless and gave no hint of our desperate coupling that day in Mar Vista. If there is a benevolent God, he must have prevented that egg and sperm from meeting. There was to be no new offspring.

At Sotheby's, *The Old Man and the Sea* first edition, first printing, signed, was appraised at eleven thousand and it sold a week later for a serendipitous thirteen-five less commission to an unnamed collector in Minneapolis. I paid off some credit card debt and bought new brakes for the Volvo. I reread the volume before passing it along. As I remembered the story, it was about Santiago, a fisherman who hooked a great and elusive fish and landed it through sacrifice and perseverance. What had slipped my mind was that after Santiago caught and killed the giant fish and lashed it to his small sailing skiff, sharks attacked the giant fish, nearly destroying the small boat in the process. By the time Santiago made it back to his little harbor and village the carcass of the fish had been picked clean and there was nothing but a few bones for anyone to see. But despite his great loss and humiliation, Santiago, undeterred, resolved to fish again soon. Although the story might have been a bit sophisticated for Caleb's young mind, I think there are elements he might have absorbed.

Caleb was my tie to True and with him gone, all that remained was the lawsuit against the hospital. We agreed on a lawyer based on the recommendation of one of True's acquaintances. There was no more chance of dialectic between us. We were past that.

We were deposed by defendant's council and forced to relive our greatest pain in excruciating detail. When our attorney informed us that it was a tactic by the hospital's insurance company to wear us down so that we would settle, I think True and I individually resolved not to settle.

The autopsy found that Caleb had an arteriovenous malformation deep in his brain that was the site of the bleed. AVMs are congenital and usually not discovered until they cause problems, which may present as subtle and chronic or as suddenly critical. It was sudden here and catastrophic. The hospital would have argued in court that the hemorrhage was inevitable. We would have said that the hospital brought it on by needlessly elevating his blood pressure. I never had contact again with the doctor who wrote the prescription. If she had persisted in her effort to apologize I might have offered her my forgiveness as Reverend Lightfoot would advise me to do.

I learned that because a small child is not yet an earner and his potential is unresolved, a large financial settlement was unlikely. We were awarded $250,000, diminished to $180,000 after the attorney was paid. I signed it over to True, and the irony of paying some of my debt to her with this blood money reverberates in my head to this day. Clearly with escape in mind, True took a position at the University of New Mexico at Albuquerque. Before she left I think I felt forgiveness from her, although our dealings were limited and circumspect. It may be that she had just been drained of her anger. Occasionally I go to the university website, look up the faculty roster and stare at her photograph. The internet was made for voyeurs like me.

After word of Caleb's death got out, my standing in the ad business changed from disreputable to "tragic." Worse than garnering sympathy, it made me untouchable, as if my misfortune were a virus to be caught.

If it were not for the fact that Jerry, my former benefactor at Sather and Knowlton, got into a serious tiff with the other partners, bolted the agency to strike out on his own, and offered me a job in his fledgling agency, I might still be dodging Helmet Head at the Council Thrift Shop. Well, that's not entirely true. At dinner at Nick's and Doreen's (I still visit with them regularly) I learned that the LAPD narcotics squad raided HH's warehouse on an anonymous tip and found six ounces of cocaine on the premises. With six ounces it seems likely that he was a dealer of some sort, and that might help explain HH's expensive art and furniture. He protested that it had been planted there by a local street gang because they resented his presence in the neighborhood. Six ounces seems like a very expensive amount to plant, but perhaps the credibility of planting more and not less was important to the gang. Although HH's high-priced lawyer managed to get him a suspended sentence and probation with a nolo contendere plea, HH now has two strikes in a three-strike state (contrary to rumor, he had but one strike before this bust) and although I see him occasionally on his motorbike or at weekend yard sales, his behavior is less aggressive as would befit a man in his precarious position. I wish him well.

Unfortunately, The Reverend Dr. Lightfoot evicted him from the premises and he is no longer a member of the choir. In fact, Dr. Lightfoot subsequently offered the warehouse space to me, but I was then transitioning to my new job and this was a much bigger space than I could use. Also there was clearly not going to be a discount related to my singing abilities. I took solace from participating in the choir and the services at the Ray of Light church but it was not my intention or my destiny to follow HH's footsteps.

Although I find the music comforting and Doctor Lightfoot's cadent sermons inspiring, I can't say that my experience has made me a religious person, or even a believer in God. I sing that "Jesus has his eye on the sparrow," but I do not believe it to be true. I do believe in science and in metaphor. I know that if you remove a hydra (a small sea creature) from its home and toss it into a blender, then pour it through a strainer and place the scrambled cells in a container, in the space of a few weeks it will reform as a complete, functioning and intact hydra.

What I also know is that this hydra could have no way of anticipating that a much more complex creature would someday scoop him up and place him in a tall glass bowl seated over a chrome base with a powerful electric motor beneath it. The hydra's power is not in its prescience, but in its ability to withstand injury and reorganize. Perhaps it is a part of the divine that as living organisms we all seek the homeostatic condition—which is to say self-sustaining, circular and complete. It is inevitable at times that we all will be blindsided and injured. We can try to take precautions but we cannot predict and we cannot escape. Our continuing existence depends more on our ability to repair ourselves than anything else.

I still scout for books. After that last night with True I scouted books the next morning. It was a welcome ritual then as it is now. But these days I have scaled it back to an avocation and I stock only a few hundred books on the shelves of my apartment. I tour garage sales on Saturday mornings and I pack and ship a few books to customers before going to work each day. It brings in a small amount of money that I hold separate from my other, more substantial check. I still relish the search for treasure and find calm in the ritual of packing the books, preparing the address labels and driving to the post office.

Acknowledgments

A few years ago, I didn't know I had a novel in me. I would like to thank those friends who encouraged me to push through. I would also like to thank the network TV producer who said unkindly, when I resisted her ham-fisted notes on a teleplay I had been hired to write, that I should really be writing novels instead.

My wife, Shelley Wiseman, who has been a writer and editor for most of her career, was of immense help. She cheered me on through the process, read the drafts and gave terrific notes. Thank you also to my longtime good friend and accomplished book editor, Alison Chaplin, for her time invested, her encouragement and her excellent and bracingly clear suggestions for improvement. Thanks to Dr. Dennis Green for being my source on medical matters. I would also like to thank Chuck Spear for his help bringing the financial aspects of the story to life and for regaling me with great stories from the tech bubble.

Roundfire

FICTION

Put simply, we publish great stories. Whether it's literary or popular, a gentle tale or a pulsating thriller, the connecting theme in all Roundfire fiction titles is that once you pick them up you won't want to put them down.
If you have enjoyed this book, why not tell other readers by posting a review on your preferred book site.
Recent bestsellers from Roundfire are:

The Bookseller's Sonnets
Andi Rosenthal
The Bookseller's Sonnets intertwines three love stories with a tale of religious identity and mystery spanning five hundred years and three countries.
Paperback: 978-1-84694-342-3 ebook: 978-184694-626-4

Birds of the Nile
An Egyptian Adventure
N.E. David
Ex-diplomat Michael Blake wanted a quiet birding trip up the Nile – he wasn't expecting a revolution.
Paperback: 978-1-78279-158-4 ebook: 978-1-78279-157-7

Blood Profit$

The Lithium Conspiracy

J. Victor Tomaszek, James N. Patrick, Sr.

The blood of the many for the profits of the few... *Blood Profit$* will take you into the cigar-smoke-filled room where American policy and laws are really made.

Paperback: 978-1-78279-483-7 ebook: 978-1-78279-277-2

The Burden

A Family Saga

N.E. David

Frank will do anything to keep his mother and father apart. But he's carrying baggage – and it might just weigh him down ...

Paperback: 978-1-78279-936-8 ebook: 978-1-78279-937-5

The Cause

Roderick Vincent

The second American Revolution will be a fire lit from an internal spark.

Paperback: 978-1-78279-763-0 ebook: 978-1-78279-762-3

Don't Drink and Fly

The Story of Bernice O'Hanlon: Part One

Cathie Devitt

Bernice is a witch living in Glasgow. She loses her way in her life and wanders off the beaten track looking for the garden of enlightenment.

Paperback: 978-1-78279-016-7 ebook: 978-1-78279-015-0

Gag

Melissa Unger

One rainy afternoon in a Brooklyn diner, Peter Howland punctures an egg with his fork. Repulsed, Peter pushes the plate away and never eats again.

Paperback: 978-1-78279-564-3 ebook: 978-1-78279-563-6

The Master Yeshua
The Undiscovered Gospel of Joseph
Joyce Luck
Jesus is not who you think he is. The year is 75 CE. Joseph ben Jude
is frail and ailing, but he has a prophecy to fulfil ...
Paperback: 978-1-78279-974-0 ebook: 978-1-78279-975-7

On the Far Side, There's a Boy
Paula Coston
Martine Haslett, a thirty-something 1980s woman, plays hard on
the fringes of the London drag club scene until one night which
prompts her to sign up to a charity. She writes to a young Sri Lan-
kan boy, with consequences far and long.
Paperback: 978-1-78279-574-2 ebook: 978-1-78279-573-5

Tuareg
Alberto Vazquez-Figueroa
With over 5 million copies sold worldwide, Tuareg is a
classic adventure story from best-selling author Alberto Vazquez-
Figueroa, about honour, revenge and a clash of cultures.
Paperback: 978-1-84694-192-4

Readers of ebooks can buy or view any of these bestsellers by
clicking on the live link in the title. Most titles are published in
paperback and as an ebook. Paperbacks are available in traditional
bookshops. Both print and ebook formats are available online.

Find more titles and sign up to our readers' newsletter at
http://www.johnhuntpublishing.com/fiction

Follow us on Facebook at https://www.facebook.com/JHPfiction
and Twitter at https://twitter.com/JHPFiction